ORPHANED

ORPHANED

John E Keegan

ISBN: 978-1-63901-465-1   (Paperback Edition)
ISBN: 978-1-63901-466-8   (Hardcover Edition)
ISBN: 978-1-63901-464-4   (E-book Edition)

Some characters and events in this book are fictitious. Any similarity to real persons, living or dead, is coincidental and not intended by the author.

Book Ordering Information

Phone Number: 315 288-7939 ext. 1000 or 347-901-4920
Email: info@globalsummithouse.com
Global Summit House
www.globalsummithouse.com

Printed in the United States of America

Take most people, they're crazy about cars . . . I'd rather have a horse. A horse is at least human.

—Holden Caulfield
from *Catcher in the Rye*

Victory has a hundred fathers and defeat is an orphan.

—John F. Kennedy

Dedicated to Joseph Gottstein who lost his heart to the Sport of Kings when he was given his first thoroughbred horse at the age of eight. He later founded and built the Longacres racetrack in Renton, Washington, which opened on August 3, 1933 and became one of the premier tracks in the United States. Joseph's son-in-law Morris Alhadeff and his sons Michael and Kenny later managed and enhanced the facility until it was sold to the Boeing Company and closed to racing on September 21, 1992. The "Gottstein Futurity," a stakes race for the best two-year olds at the track, was inaugurated in 1940 and continues today.

Dedicated also to the generations of people who lived on the Longacres *backside*, the world of stables and barns where trainers, grooms, valets, exercise riders and jockeys, many of them horse savvy Mexican Americans, woke each morning before God to exercise and train these beautiful athletes.

And dedicated finally to the handicappers, horse lovers and spectators with $2 or more in his or her pocket looking for a longshot, who gathered to watch these magnificent creatures run their hearts out at Longacres on Green River sandy loam in full view of Mount Rainier, the highest peak in the Continental United States.

Thoroughbred horse racing never died in the Green River Valley. The Washington Thoroughbred Breeders and Owners Association, established in 1940, wouldn't let it happen. On June 20, 1996, horse racing resumed at a new racetrack, Emerald Downs, in the City of Auburn, a few miles south of Renton, spearheaded by Ron Crocket and today continuing under the ownership and management of the Muckleshoot Tribe. Still with a full view of Mount Rainier.

The Auction

1

Dean Hostler raised his hand as the auctioneer started the bidding and a trickle of sweat ran from his armpit to his belt. Beer always made him sweat. That was one reason he preferred hard liquor. The auctioneer nodded and Dean was in for four hundred, something he knew he could cover with his paycheck from the body shop, especially with the extra hundred bucks his boss had given him for finishing the Pomeroy Lincoln early.

The filly who was in the sale arena tugged to free herself of the shank in the grip of a black man in a pool table green blazer. Bouquets of steam shot from her nostrils and disappeared into the rafters. A pretty girl with creamy cheeks and a blonde ponytail had shown him this same filly on the grounds before the auction. When he saw her kiss this horse on the lips, he couldn't help but follow them to their stall and gawk. The man in the blazer circled the horse around the roped-off arena and the spotlights lit her up like she'd been buffed with Turtle wax. Then she let out a melancholy whinny that echoed through the barn. For reasons that he already knew would be difficult to explain to his wife Lorraine, Dean had already bonded with this animal, connecting him to something ancient and incorruptible. This horse, he felt, had the power to change his life. He was already inside this petrified creature looking out.

The auctioneer prowled the arena with his microphone looking into the stands for takers. "Who gonna bid, who gonna bid, who gonna bid . . ."

Dean had noticed in the bidding for the previous horses that nobody shouted back numbers or waved money at the auctioneer. They just flicked their wrist or nodded their head at the price being offered. It was easier than buying a six-pack.

"Who gimme more, who gimme more . . ." There was an urgency in the auctioneer's voice that energized the room and agitated Dean. For him, it was a cry for help.

A man in the front row bid, and Dean raised him. The auctioneer peered over the top of his glasses at the man in front, who raised the bid again. That man and Dean were the only two people bidding. Dean stood up and squinted, trying to see who his competitor was, but all he could see was the back of his head and the tan sport jacket. It was becoming difficult to understand the auctioneer. His microphone cut in and out as he rattled off strings of words without recognizable beginnings or endings. The crowd buzzed and shuffled. Spotters moved up and down the aisles looking for more bidders. The spotter with a moustache that buried his upper lip squatted in the aisle and flung his thumb in the air when Dean upped the bid to "eight." Dean didn't know that much about horses but he knew when he was on the outs with Lorraine. He'd buy this one for their boy, Ricky, and get back in her good graces again.

Dean had taken a seat in the back row, a carryover from high school where he thought it improved his odds of never being called on. His beer was beginning to taste like the wax on the paper cup, so he crushed the cup in his fist and dropped it through the bleachers. The filly he was bidding for was listed as "Hip 113" in the sale book, a coincidence Dean had recognized while doodling hearts and stars on the page in the sale book. Lorraine's birthday was January thirteenth. Dean Hostler believed in the prophetic quality of coincidence. That's how he'd found Lorraine at the Liberty Park pool the day he was supposed to help his dad bury a wire to the telephone pole in front of their house so they could turn the streetlight off at night and watch for satellites. The white stripe with freckles down the face of this horse also reminded him of Lorraine; hers were the pin holes into her soul.

Each time the guy in front raised the bid, Dean threw his right hand in the air, the hand with the middle finger shortened to the first knuckle by a table saw accident, a disfigurement that inspired no end of jokes at work. The back benchers and fish balls in the seats around Dean who didn't have the wherewithal to bid were shouting *atta-boys* and *go-gettums* each time he went for it. The woman in front of him was stealing nips from a chrome flask in her purse. Dean tried to imagine their astonishment that this guy with the putty spots on his coveralls could stay in the bidding. In truth, he was bidding for them too.

Dean's mind drifted. He thought of what the country girl on the backside had said about the power of this horse. She'd raised her from a foal and just talking about the sale had started her blinking back tears. *Lungs like a locomotive*, that's what she'd said. But it was the filly's eyes that had sucked Dean in. Dark and deep, Dean could see his future in those eyes. It would be a clean start with Lorraine. Dean could already feel her hand slipping between the buttons of his shirt when he told her his surprise.

Dean raised his hand at "sixteen" and the adrenaline rushed through him like his veins were fire hoses snaking out of control. *I can make sixteen hundred bucks doing overtime*, he thought.

They'd conceived Ricky before the wedding. He weighed only four pounds and change at birth and Lorraine's parents told their friends he was a preemie to deflect suspicion of pre-marital conception, but he was full term all right. Lorraine had counted the days. Ricky was slow to walk and toilet train, and they held him back a year from kindergarten, mainly because of his size. When he couldn't keep up with the other kids in primary school, they held him back another year. The school said he had an "attention deficit disorder," something Dean had never heard of. Lorraine cried for a week. If Ricky was wounded, she was wounded. That's just the way she was. She'd lost interest in sex and Dean was sure that she blamed him for Ricky's condition. The Hostler genes.

The bidding stalled, with Dean's still the last bid on the floor. One of the spotters stood over the man in the front row, and the auctioneer's gavel was poised to strike. Dean would have sworn that the filly's eyes were already locked on his. He cursed the back of the sport jacket in the front row. *Don't even think of it!*

"Going once, going twice, sold to the gentleman in the back row!"

The backbenchers slapped Dean and high-fived him. The woman in front squeezed his cheeks between her hands and planted a wet kiss on his lips. Dean recognized the taste. *Southern Comfort*, something he loved but had sworn off in favor of an occasional beer. The man with the walrus moustache rushed over to hand him a clipboard with a pen dangling from a string. "Go to the cashier's office out back!" he yelled. Dean scribbled his signature on the form and headed toward the aisle. On the way out, he stopped at the portable bar in the hallway and noticed they had a bottle of *Stolichnaya*. This called for a celebration. Lorraine had always wanted a pal for Ricky. If they let him pay by installment, he figured there would still be something left over to pay the bills with. That's the last thing Lorraine had said to him when he left for the body shop that morning, the same thing she said every payday. "Don't forget the bills, Dean!"

While Dean was stirring his drink with a plastic swizzle stick, Gifford Pomeroy came by, someone Dean knew from high school who he'd seen earlier that day when he dropped his car off at the body shop, the car Dean had worked on. Dean had overheard him telling his boss that he was going to the Longacres horse sale. Gifford was stocky, about five-foot nine, and Dean guessed he was wearing a Johnny Carson leisure jacket to make himself look more fit. But the boutonniere in his lapel looked like bunched Kleenex dabbed with lipstick. Gifford was at the horse sale with some of the high school buddies who'd ended up working for him and driving company cars with the *Pomeroy Realty* name and the white lightning bolt logo on the door. The logo had a John Travolta disco feel that made Dean shiver. He preferred folk and country.

"Lorraine know you're here?" Gifford said.

Dean resented the fact he'd even mentioned his wife. She was no longer any of his business and hadn't been since Dean won her away from him in their senior year. "I'd say that comes under the category of my business, not yours."

He chuckled. "Well, you beat me out again, Dean."

"That was *you* bidding?"

"Just wanted to make sure you were serious."

Dean turned away to avoid the smirks on the faces of Gifford's chumps. It bothered him that he and Lorraine viewed Gifford so differently. "He's a great businessman," she'd always said, "and he helped you get on at the body shop." Gifford hadn't helped, Dean remembered, he'd just used his name.

The portable trailer that served as the cashier's office was set up on blocks at the edge of the parking lot out behind the auction barn. As Dean made his way towards the trailer, he could feel a pull from deep inside as he watched the grooms leading more horses to the auction. He missed his boyhood in the Palouse, that period in his life before his dad gave up dry land wheat farming and moved the family to Renton. They never had horses or livestock, but a herd of mule deer grazed on their farm every winter, probably because the Hostlers had no fences and his dad's sloppy harvesting left a lot of wheat standing. Forty or fifty of them gathered every winter out of the wind in the draw that cut across the far side of their acreage, the snow so deep that it covered the stubble. Dean's dad said it was nature's way of thinning the herd. Dean couldn't sleep at night thinking of the mule deer standing in the Hostler draw, starving to death. So after school one day he hitched up the flatbed to their John Deere, threw on a bale of the timothy hay they'd stored for the cows, and pulled it out to the herd. The deer scattered at the sight of the wheel tractor, but next day the hay was gone and he took out more. When his dad caught him, he exploded. "It sounds cruel, son," he said, "but deprivation of food in the winter is part of their life cycle!" So, when the snow melted, there were carcasses in the draw every spring that had been picked clean by the coyotes. Maybe the mule deer were why he'd bid for the horse.

The cashier's trailer rocked from side to side as an ample woman with a *Longacres* emblem on her baseball cap walked to a desk at the back to retrieve the papers for his deal. The rig he was standing in was about sixteen feet long, four feet shorter than the used Nashua Dean's dad had given him and Lorraine as a wedding present, and still the only home they'd ever owned. Lorraine wasn't thrilled at the prospect of living in a trailer, but she'd fixed it up cuter than a Swiss dollhouse. When the heavyset woman came back to the counter, she shoved the papers in front of Dean.

"I need sixteen thousand dollars," she said.

Dean rose up on the balls of his feet and glared at her. "That's wrong, Ma'am! It's sixteen *hundred!*"

"You signed the sheet."

"I know what I bid for and that's not it!" He started sweating again as his eyes went back and forth across the numbers at the bottom of the page, fumbling in his memory for something to support his case. He was never good at arithmetic, but he certainly knew the difference between hundreds and thousands. Why hadn't the bid spotter said something? It should have been obvious a guy like him couldn't afford sixteen thousand dollars. "I could hardly understand the man. Why didn't he make himself clear?"

"He sells horses all over the United States . . ."

"Not to me, he doesn't."

The buxom woman went to the back again and sent up a tall man in a string tie and a cowboy hat with sweat stains around the band. Dean assumed this was her boss. He had a more savvy look than the woman and Dean thought surely he'd understand the situation. But there was no mercy in this guy's face, and he looked tired of talking even before he opened his mouth. "What's the trouble here?"

"I must have misunderstood, sir. My hearing . . . I've had a lot of industrial jobs."

"Can you put up collateral?"

Dean cupped his hand to his ear. "Some what?"

"Stocks, bonds, a second on your house?"

Dean's armpits were dripping, and he looked around for help. Through the dirty window on the door panel, he could see Gifford Pomeroy heading toward the cashier's trailer. Pomeroy was the last person Dean wanted to witness this little dispute. So Dean quickly flipped through the plastic holder in his wallet -- past a picture of Lorraine on the Oregon Coast in a one-piece bathing suit the summer he drove for Mayflower, past the credit cards he'd maxed out, past his driver's license with the organ donor notation -- until he found the title for the Nashua trailer. They'd put the Nashua up for his dad's bail once. That's one thing his dad had taught him, always know where your bail is. Dean assumed they'd hold the title until he could come up with the dough, the way the bowling alley held onto your driver's license until you returned their shoes. He heard the screen door to the cashier trailer bounce shut, and he knew who it was.

"Here," Dean said, handing the man the title.

The man studied the front of the title, then the back. "You've got to sign it over! We'll hold it till you pay the sixteen thou. No ands, ifs or buts."

Dean glanced behind him, "You don't need to shout." Gifford was coming toward the counter.

"Just wanted to make sure you heard right this time."

Dean took the long way home, heading south on SR 167 so he could get his speed up and feel the wind rushing through the cab of the pickup. A *Beach Boys* song was playing and he turned the volume up so he could hear it over the wind. Lorraine wasn't always so good with surprises and he needed time to think of the best way to break the news. There had never really been anyone else for Dean but Lorraine, not anyone serious. They were twelve years old when she first walked past him in her blue polka dot swimsuit at Liberty Park. She was in Catholic parochial school then and he was in public, so their paths had never formally crossed. Dean was standing on the deck, feeling the cement indentations in the bottom of his feet, his arms wrapped around his skinny ribs like the sleeves of a straitjacket. The elastic in his bathing suit had worn out so, using one of his mom's crochet needles, he'd strung a piece of heavy twine through it to keep it up. He would have sworn she winked at him that day, but she told him later it must have been the *first day* chlorine in her eyes because she didn't remember it.

Whatever Lorraine said about his buying the horse, he hoped she wouldn't say it was like something Dean's dad would have done. He hated when she said things like that. Lorraine's father had prejudiced her against regular people. He was a King County Superior Court judge, a big shot in Renton, who called the Hostlers *scattergoods* and his dad a *reprobate*. Dean didn't know exactly what he meant by all that but he knew her father would have felt differently if he'd ever seen the Hostler garage, which was full of contraptions his dad had invented with his wits and a slide rule. His dad was an artist with a pair of tin snips, crafting rain gutters that swirled like corkscrews and a reflector oven with a lazy Susan that rotated muffins while he listened to Bing Crosby on the radio. When Dean's mother made his dad sleep in the garage, Dean snuck him cheese from the refrigerator and they sliced it onto Ritz crackers and melted the cheese with the heat of a 40-watt bulb. The garage was the family fallout shelter, stuffed with cans of Campbell's soup and Starkist tuna that his dad bought by the case. There was also a distillery in the garage, with pipes and condensers that resembled a ship's engine room. The stuff that came out could take grass stains off the knees of a pair of jeans.

It was late when Dean finally got home and he picked a bunch of flowers from the bed at the entry way to the trailer park, along with some greenery to make it look professional. Although Lorraine sold flowers every day from her portable stand on wheels, she never tired of them. This whole thing wouldn't have been so bad if he hadn't just missed coming home on time a couple of nights ago, after a card game with some guys from the body shop. Against his promise, he'd had a drink that night so thought best to sleep it off on somebody else's hide-a-bed. Lorraine didn't like to have him around Ricky when he had liquor on his breath. As he added things up in his head, standing outside the Nashua, he thought about turning around and finding somebody's hide-a-bed again. This whole business would be easier to explain in the daylight when everyone had a good night's sleep and Ricky was up. She'd be enthused for Ricky's sake.

He closed the door softly so he wouldn't wake her, but Lorraine emerged from the back of the trailer in her robe and deerskin slippers, heading directly towards him. He stood up as straight as a royal butler and extended his makeshift bouquet in her general direction. The book she'd been reading hung open from one hand. Lorraine read books on how to do things like some people prayed. She thought they could make you a better parent, a smarter customer, healthier, richer. Dean knew she didn't need one to make her more beautiful. She glared at him, her freckles now as dark as ink spots.

"I hope you didn't go drinking on payday!"

Not exactly the note he wanted to start on, but Dean charged ahead with his story, trying to recreate the excitement of the auction, glossing over the actual price, and avoiding any mention of the collateral he'd posted. He watched Lorraine's body language for some sign of support, even amusement, but she stiffened as he talked and said nothing when he paused to take a breath. "I guess it was one of those things you had to be there to appreciate," Dean said meekly, fingering the stems of his bouquet. Then he remembered the most important thing. "We can give the horse to Ricky for his birthday!"

Lorraine's eyes grew as large as brown shooter marbles, and her fists were clenched at her side. "You missed his birthday party, Dean! Remember? That was tonight. You were supposed to get him a wallet at Pay Less and stick some money in it."

"Oh, shit."

"What kind of dim signal was going through your brain? Ricky was crushed when you didn't show up."

"But remember, this *is* for Ricky."

"Ricky's not going near that horse! And you're not going near Ricky!"

She yelled some more stuff that Dean had heard before, a litany of other memory lapses and late arrivals. Her face was getting red and she seemed to be inching taller with each accusation. Then she started pushing him toward the door, hammering against his chest. "Get out! I've had it with you, Dean! Just had it!" This was worse than their other fights, he thought. It was usually just words. She'd never hit him, Lorraine wasn't a hitter. He was trying to tell her he'd make it up to her, but she wasn't listening. He put his hand on the door jamb to keep the door from closing, and she threw her shoulder against it, crushing his knuckles. When she drew the door back, he pulled his hand free and tossed in his bouquet before her next lunge slammed the door shut. The cheap lock assembly engaged, and he realized he'd been kicked out of his own home.

Dean stumbled back to his Dodge Sweptline pickup, trying to think of what he should have said. He hadn't even gotten to the part about needing to save face with Gifford, and he consoled himself with the thought that she'd feel differently once she'd seen the horse. That was Lorraine's only shortcoming. She didn't believe in the power of dreams.

He slept in his pickup that night, in the corner of the Longacres parking lot closest to the barns. Stretched out on the front seat, with his head next to the steering wheel, he could reach over and fire up the engine when he got cold, run the heater full blast until it was so hot he had to open a window, then shut it off and fall back to sleep again. He could see the silhouette of his twenty-two rifle on the rack over the seat, the gun his dad had given him, the gun he'd shot targets with but never used on an animal. Dean figured by him owning it there was one less hunter in the woods. Lorraine hated guns, didn't even want one in the house, made him separate the bolt from the rifle, and forbade him to let Ricky touch it.

As he peered out the windshield of his pickup, he wondered how he'd gotten so far off course. He knew he'd never be an inventor like his dad, but for some reason he always thought he'd be famous. He'd envied the jugglers on TV who could suspend a dozen bowling pins in the air like clothes pins on a lasso. If he could have just gotten on some show like *Let's Make a Deal*, things would have been different.

2

Lorraine picked up the blue violas and weeds that Dean had tossed through the door at her, rearranged them into a milk glass that she filled with water, and placed them on the kitchen table next to the funeral arrangement of Canterbury Bells and Bachelor's Buttons that someone had canceled on at the last minute at her flower stand and she'd brought home for Ricky's birthday party. In order to supplement their income, Lorraine had started her own business, a flower cart on wheels that she dragged over to the front of the Renton Courthouse. Her plan was to use her flower income to hire a private tutor for Ricky, refusing to follow the advice of the doomsday counselors who advised her to lower her expectations. She shamelessly exploited her father's reputation as a King County Judge, calling her stand "Culhane's Floral." Dean protested the fact she'd used her maiden name until she put her foot down. "I'd show cleavage if I thought it would sell more flowers," she told him.

She'd closed the stand early that night so she could fix Ricky chicken burritos and bake an orange cake with chocolate frosting, from scratch. It was going to be just the three of them, the way Ricky wanted it. "Yore really my only friends," he'd said.

She didn't worry that much when Dean was late. She figured he'd probably driven over to the mall and gotten caught in traffic. When he wasn't home by seven she called the body shop but nobody answered. Then she took the burritos out of the oven so they wouldn't dry out and made Ricky study his math.

"Maybe Dad's gettin' me a motorcycle," he said.

When Dean wasn't there by eight, Lorraine reheated the burritos and started dinner over Ricky's objections. Lorraine wanted to cry, but she knew she couldn't in front of Ricky, so instead she just gritted her teeth like she always did, trying to make up for Dean's elusiveness by being the rock. They were supposed to be a team, but Dean had always glossed over Ricky's problem, saying he'd grow out of it. She was the one who helped with his homework and taught him how to fix a flat tire on his bike and pound out the dent in the wheel rim if he hit a curb. She was the disciplinarian, the one who paid the family bills, and prepared the tax returns. Dean was the one who made up bedtime stories for Ricky when he was younger and they would trade nights, so that Ricky could tell Dean his stories.

It was when Ricky's attention deficit disorder became more of an issue with his teachers that Dean seemed to turn away. He felt it was his fault. He didn't know how to support Lorraine. He became unpredictable. And Dean couldn't stand the idea that his son had any *mental problems*, as he called them. Dean gradually wore her down, and it became harder and harder to excuse his erratic behavior. It started to feel purposeful. Just when she had Ricky up and running on all cylinders, Dean would pull something stupid and Ricky would take a nosedive that even his pills couldn't overcome.

That's what had happened to Ricky's seventeenth birthday party dinner. Lorraine had planned it for weeks, what to get him, whether to surprise him with school friends, what to fix. They couldn't afford much. Dean's employment had been irregular. Every time he found a place with promise he'd quarrel with the boss and quit or get fired. "Life's too short to put up with that kind of crap," he'd say. Then he'd mope around the house for a month until he steeled himself for a try at another job. Bogle's Body Shop was a perfect fit. He'd come home at night enthused about his work. "I just pretend the fenders I'm sanding are your buns," he'd say.

Lorraine plunged a dollop of liquid soap from the dispenser onto the wash rag and scrubbed the kitchen table and sink counter for the umpteenth time, trying to settle the trembling that had erupted in her when she saw Dean walk through the door with that sorry fistful of flowers he'd ripped out of someone's yard in the trailer court. She was taking anti-depressants, and each time the potency of one brand faded her doctor prescribed another. She had a stack of pharmaceutical brochures that she kept in her lingerie drawer. Not only was she worried that she'd become immune to the pills, she thought she might become addicted as well. However, it wasn't her own health she was concerned with; this was about Ricky, and Dean buying that horse was the tipping point. She was out of forgiveness.

She went to their bedroom at the far end of the trailer and sat down on her side of the bed, her arms braced at her sides for balance. She kept a framed 8-by-10 family picture next to her bed, but all she could see that night was her dad, with his penetrating judicial glare and no hint of a smile beneath his tidy salt and pepper moustache. He was the closest thing she could imagine to God on Last Judgment Day. Her father still served with distinction on the King County Superior Court, which required a commute into downtown Seattle, the big city, something he also loved. He was justice personified in her household and preferred to be addressed as *Judge* the way military fathers liked to be called *Sir*. Growing up, they argued in the kitchen on subjects he cherished like *search and seizure* and the *right to bear arms*. The Judge barely accepted the idea of suffrage for women and worried that a bunch of *women's libbers* were going to rewrite a document that was as sacred to him as the New Testament.

"The gentlemen who strung our Constitution together were the smartest SOB's this country's ever seen," he'd told her.

"Think how much better it would have been if there'd been a girl on the committee," she said.

"Government's like marriage, women are the helpmates."

Lorraine was the oldest of three sisters, which meant Judge Culhane leaned on her the hardest. And his standards were high, something she was reminded of every time she walked by the trophy case at Renton High, where it seemed he'd been captain of every team and president of every club. One of her teachers who'd played football and partnered with him in Lincoln-Douglas told her how everyone thought he'd end up being President of the United States or at least Governor.

She thought her younger sisters had turned out prettier than her. They always had a wide circle of friends, and boys whistled at them when they walked by. None of them were pale or cursed with freckles that she imagined spreading like the measles every summer. "I'd die to have legs like yours," her sisters said, "and slim hips. Big breasts just droop after you have babies."

Lorraine was petite with thin eyebrows and thin lips, and she wanted to be full-bodied and fleshy. Her mom always told her she looked like

Audrey Hepburn in *Breakfast at Tiffany's*, which was her mom's favorite movie. "Nothing's more attractive than the truth," she said.

It was no accident, she guessed, that she'd wandered into the bedroom to sort out the aftermath of her encounter with Dean that evening. This was where she conducted her daily examination of conscience, where she could hear her father's voice, who'd been opposed to Dean Hostler from the beginning. He always referred to him as that *Hostler guy.* The Judge had never inhabited a world where people accumulated grease under their fingernails and neglected to say grace before meals. What could he find in common with a family who failed to arrange early greetings from the Notre Dame Registrar at birth for their newborns and who didn't open safe-deposit boxes for their graduating eighth-graders, as the Judge had done for his daughters?

Dean Hostler was a poor kid from one of the tract housing projects that sprang up in Renton at the end of World War II, a mediocre student with a fertile imagination. She honestly couldn't remember meeting him at the swimming lessons her parents made her take at Liberty Park, but he could have been any one of the boys who swam underwater and tugged on her bathing suit. After they married, she sometimes pretended she'd remembered seeing him at the pool just to see the charge it gave him. They officially met in high school, when he picked up a prayer card that had slipped out of her social studies notebook one day and handed it to her. In the years that followed she could feel his eyes on her whenever they passed in the halls. Eventually he started slipping notes through the louvers in her locker with things like, "My favorite color is the color of your eyes." In all, she counted one hundred and eighty-four of these notes that she still kept in the drawer of her nightstand, most unanswered. That didn't mean she didn't read them in the privacy of her bedroom. Who wouldn't? Passion is flattering. Still, Dean made her nervous. Everyone in town knew how daffy his dad was.

Lorraine could remember with absolute clarity the day she finally decided to answer Dean's parade of solicitations. She'd ended up walking side-by-side between classes with Dean on the way toward the cafeteria. Lorraine always bought a Coca-Cola from the vending machine before her study period; it kept her alert, and in those days, she still wasn't drinking coffee. Dean put a quarter into the dispenser and retrieved the can from the pocket in the middle of the machine.

"Do you like it dry?" he said.

"Dry?"

The way Dean locked onto her eyes made it seem as if he was seeing things he shouldn't be seeing. "I mean on the outside. There's always moisture on the outside. My mother always said you should dry off the cans so they wouldn't slip out of your hand."

She laughed. "Well, one has never slipped out of *my* hand!"

He extended the Coke to her at eye level. "You have good hands then." When she took it from him, she could see the print where his thumb used to be.

Lorraine was drawn to light and ecstatic that winter was almost over. She always took desks in the row closest to the windows. She kept Windex in her bedroom at home so that she could maximize the light that shone through the glass. In spring, she took her books outdoors for study period and sat on the bench in the middle of the flower garden behind the school. The garden was circular, with paths like spokes that met at the bench in the center. It was how she imagined a villa in Italy. The garden was the hobby of the school custodian, a sweet Japanese man she'd gotten to know during her study period escapes. She was an *A* student and could always get a pass to go outdoors. The garden is where she led Dean, out the back door of the school on a fractured concrete walk that passed a compost pit full of clipped grass and weeds baking in the sun.

"Smell that?" she asked.

He looked around. "Odor's not my strong sense."

"It's like brown sugar on oatmeal."

She'd never really talked to Dean, probably because she was afraid it would encourage him and she'd lose her fortification. She'd been afraid of boys, especially ones she perceived as indifferent to learning who would drag her down. She'd never been with someone as transparent as Dean Hostler though and his transparency made her realize how pretentious she was.

They sat on the concrete pedestal bench, she with the sun warming her neck and he straddling it so that he could look at her straight on. He reached down and pinched off a salmon-colored flower with his fingers and handed it to her. "Maybe we could do something some time . . . just go somewhere by ourselves." She studied the saw-toothed edges of the flower petals that looked like they'd been cut with pinking shears. Coming from a Catholic background where all the students wore uniforms, the boys with salt and pepper cords and beige shirts, she was attracted to Dean's mussed hair and the wispy growth of hair on his chin that wasn't worth shaving. Most of all she loved the idea that he was totally, unalterably nuts about her.

Lorraine pushed herself off the bed and went to that cramped little closet that served as the Nashua's bathroom. Still shaky from her fight with Dean, she squeezed a row of mint toothpaste across the bristles of her brush and scrubbed her teeth. She hadn't eaten any dinner, but still flossed then rinsed her mouth with Listerine to rid herself of the taste of the argument with Dean. Then she cracked Ricky's door wide enough to make sure he was covered. His transistor radio was next to his pillow, still on, and that's probably how he'd gotten to sleep.

She went into his room and knelt beside the bed. Ricky was a beautiful kid. Sure, he was rambunctious and never a star at school, but that was true of lots of kids his age. Until his school raised the possibility that he had a learning disability, she would have sworn that he was *normal.*

Lorraine wasn't sure how much she slept that first night after kicking Dean out of the trailer. She found a talk radio station to go to sleep by. She needed voices other than her own and Judge Culhane's. Approving voices.

She hurried Ricky through a bowl of Cheerios at breakfast and fibbed when he asked where his dad was, telling him he had to leave early. She made Ricky's lunch, gave him his Ritalin, put another pill in a baggie to take at school and ushered him toward the door as soon as he was finished eating.

A folded piece of paper fell onto the mat when she opened the door, and she scooped it up before Ricky could and slipped it into the pocket of her robe. She waited until she was sure Ricky was on his way before opening what turned out to be a note from Dean that he must have left the night before.

> *Remember the time I took you in the hot air balloon and you said how small everything looked . . . that's how I feel now, Lorraine . . . smaller than a rat turd.*

She wadded it up and stuck it in the garbage can under the sink, to make sure Ricky didn't come across it. Sure, she remembered the hot air balloon. It was that first summer they were married, before Ricky was born. They were in the Sammamish Valley and she was scared to death something was going to happen to her baby. Now it had. How prophetic, she thought.

She dressed in a hurry, just jeans and the same blouse she'd worn the day before. Normally, she had her cart ready for the morning rush into the courthouse. Not this morning. Her customers would have to wait until she'd told Mercy Kirk about her fight with Dean. She rushed her makeup as she thought about what Mercy would say. Mercy was a cousin of Dean's on his father's side, but Lorraine's friendship with her had been forged in their years at St. Anthony's grade school together, long before she'd met Dean. Mercy was one of those naughty girls who tied her blouse so her midriff showed and painted her nails, even in grade school, until the nuns told her to dress like a lady. In public high school, Mercy and Lorraine became a sorority of two. They ate lunch together and wore matching outfits -- black pants and pink blouses one day, white miniskirts and tight sweaters another. Lorraine prayed that some of Mercy's sex appeal would rub off on her.

Lorraine waited in a booth at the Ram, watching Mercy balance breakfast plates on her forearms, dash back for a forgotten order of toast, and make the rounds for coffee refills. Mercy took the time to flirt with everyone, even the women. She had big eyes, big lips, and a body that squirmed when she was excited.

But things hadn't panned out that well for Mercy. Men took advantage of her. She'd made it out of Renton, her childhood dream, but eventually circled back, which was good news for Lorraine. The Ram was across the street from the courthouse, and close to Lorraine's flower stand. Sometimes Lorraine took her sack lunch into the Ram and sat in a booth by the window so she could watch the stand while she ate. If it wasn't busy, Mercy would join her. Mercy was the only girl in their class who'd gotten pregnant before Lorraine. She was a single parent to a boy and girl who bracketed Ricky's age. Cory's father was an athletic, good looking guy who Mercy had boasted was *well hung* and Lorraine remembered thinking at their wedding what beautiful children they'd make. The trouble was he wanted to make babies with everyone. Mercy kept taking him back, trying to reform him until, finally, he took his act out of town and disappeared. The only thing she still had of his was his son.

"Hallelujah," Mercy said, when Loraine finally had the chance to tell her what she'd done to Dean. "He's walked over you so many times I can smell the shoe leather."

"We'd been living on the cheap so we could build up equity for a house. I don't even know where he slept last night."

Mercy winked and smacked her Spearmint. "Same place other tomcats sleep."

"You think he's seeing somebody?"

"Do little boys eat green apples? Trust me, he didn't sleep in a church pew." Mercy still wore both of her wedding rings, as a reminder of past mistakes and to discourage customers from hitting on her. "Oh, I'm not saying he's in love with someone else. They're afraid of love. How'd Ricky take it?"

"I haven't told him yet."

"Stop pretending his dad is Jesus, Lorraine! Tell him a decent man gets haircuts more often than he changes jobs."

After leaving the Ram Lorraine kicked herself for not telling Mercy sooner what she was afraid to tell anyone else. The secret that stained her soul. And because Mercy was Dean's cousin, she didn't know whose side Mercy would be on. Or who she might tell.

3

Dad always told me stories at night when I could'n sleep. Like when he told me Mom was a saint, and I asked him what a saint was, and he said, "Like Joan of Arc."

"Who's Joan of Arc?"

"Someone they set on fire in the Dark Ages."

He didn't tell me who *they* were but the fire part seemed true. Mom made sparks. Like when the guy who pumped gas at the Conoco put the wrong oil in and she made him give us a free car wash and lube job while we sat on a bench drinkin' Squirts. When they were done polishin' the car with their rags, she paid him anyway.

"It's the principle," she said, and at first I thought she meant Mr. Toner at school 'cause she was always mad at him for somethin' they wern't doin' for me at school 'bout my concentration. When I told Dad what Mom made the Conoco man do, he laughed. "That's how wars start," he said.

Mom was a'ways askin' me what's happ'n at school and I'd tell her somethin' a teacher said and she'd want details that didn' matter, like what was the look on the teacher's face?

"Just hangin' there with nothin' on it," I told her.

Mom thought I was allergic to peanuts for a while and sent notes to school tell'n em not to give me peanut butter or Cracker Jacks. She thought peanuts might be the reason for me bein' stupid. She didn' call it that. Instead she beat 'round the bush, calling it 'distracta bility' or 'inpul sivity'. She typed up a "No Peanuts" card to carry in my shirt pocket that I was s'posed to show in the cafeteria line, which I never did 'cause she mostly packed my lunches. Anyways, it was the coin machines that had the Baby Ruths and M 'n M's and I never had any money for them. Dad said to just keep the card in my pocket like Mom wanted, which was a good idea because it finally ran through the wash and turned into a spit wad. Then she thought it was the sugar, and I told her the smartest kids in school won Hershey bars in the spellin' bees. Then it was salt and I couldn' eat potato chips. If I'd been a lube job, she'd have probably asked for a do over.

Mom would tell me things I didn' even want to know, like why your nipples got hard when it was cold. And she was always talkin' 'bout my *condition*. When I ovr'heard her talking to Dad about it, she called it *A-D-D*, which I remembered stood for *A Dumb Dodo*. "I'm gonna be your coach," she said. "We can work you up to first team." Mom didn' even like sports.

She told me the man who invented light bulbs had what I had. So did Win'son Churchill. She gave me pills, yellow ones I'd take in the mornin' on school days with orange juice and again at noon hour. For my dopa mime, whatever tha' was.

"They're like eye glasses," she said. "You'll see better with 'em."

Except for Dwayne Cotter I was the shortest boy in my class. Cotter had steel braces and one leg shorter than the other so it looked like he was going to fall over when he walked. Kids took magnets outta the science room and stuck 'em on his braces when he wasn't look'n to see how far he'd go before he noticed. Every summer Dad said I'd have a growth spurt the way he did and showed me how to stretch myself out by hang'n from the tops of doors with my fingers.

Dad also taught me how to shoot his twenty-two out at the river. We set up beer bottles on top of a log, and he showed how to hold my breath an' squeeze the trigger when the bead lined up with the label on the bottle an' cradled into the notch like a baby. It was too many things to think about at once.

"It kicks," I said.

Dad put up a full one thinkin' I wouldn' hit it and I fired off a whole clip before it exploded. The beer hung in the air like God had stopped the rain'n. Then Dad got bored and started throw'n bottles in the river and I shot at 'em as they bobbed by. I couldn' hit the broadside of a barn. Dad could hit 'em while he was runnin' along the bank, hurdlin' bushes, firing from his hip.

"Just like Army," I told him.

"I don't do wars an' don't you ever run with a gun unless the safety's on."

Mom picked me up at school the day after my birthday, and right away I knew somethin' was funny. She asked me if I'd like to eat out, so I said, "Jus' you an' me . . . what about Dad?" So I was a'ready suspicious. We hardly ever went out. I told her I was good with takeout. Jus' burgers, fries an' a root beer shake. None of the reg'lar fast food places did root beer so I knew that meant we'd go somewhere new. She was bustin' to tell me somethin' about Dad. Tha' was pretty obvious. Duh. He missed my birthday. I'm not stupid. So we sat down at our kitchen table and she told me, "This ain' workin', Ricky." Then she said, "Yore dad won' be livin' with us for a while," and my head got all blurry, and I felt like cry'n right there. Or even better, runnin' somewhere with the safety off.

4

When Dean woke the next morning, he had to look around before he realized he was in the Longacres parking lot. He got out of his pickup, pulled a comb through his hair, and peed the mud off the back tire. The clouds were as bright as buffed hubcaps and he had to squint, a result of his light sensitivity and over-dilated pupils, which were the reasons he tended towards the nocturnal. He could visualize his baseball cap scrunched up in the bureau no more than ten feet from where Lorraine was sleeping. He also pictured her turning over that morning and regretting that his side of the bed was empty. He missed her already like he missed his own childhood. So much of his aspirations were wrapped up in Lorraine. He could barely remember who he was before seeing her at the Liberty Park pool that day. Nor could he have recalled what he was looking for before he found her. She had pushed every other possibility off the board.

He headed for the barns determined to find the owner of the horse he'd bought, explain what had happened with Lorraine and ask them to take their horse back. He could smell the horses still on the grounds as he crossed the parking lot and he wondered if they knew they'd been sold. He remembered the lady in the cashier's office saying the track took care of the sold horses for twenty-four hours while the buyers made arrangements for transportation. He was looking for the stall where he'd first seen his horse the day before and tried to retrace his steps. He remembered the card table and chair in front of the stall where the pretty girl had sat, with the pop-up "Griffin Place" sign on the table and the handouts with the filly's lineage diagramed on it. Dean hadn't bothered with the handout. Why read about it when the horse was standing right there?

As he entered the barn, he sucked in the pasta aroma of hay stacked in bales in the aisles and the tang of leather saddles hanging in the equipment rooms. Peering into each of the stalls as he passed reminded him of visits to the sanatorium when his dad was drying out, where the lucky rooms were the empty ones. He watched a group of men in cowboy hats pushing against the rear end of a big gray horse, urging him into a nifty trailer with an aluminum canopy and side windows.

The stall with the *Hip 113* sign tacked to it was empty, and Dean's dry-mouth swallow caught in his Adam's apple. Even though Lorraine's reaction had frightened him, the thought of abandoning that horse produced the same feeling of dread he used to experience each spring when he discovered the mule deer carcasses in the draw.

Then the stable girl in the ponytail, wearing the same blue flannel shirt, jeans and cowboy boots she'd worn the day before, turned into his aisle, leading a brown horse he thought seemed noticeably smaller than the one he'd purchased. "I was walking your filly . . . and kinda wondering if you'd come back," she said. Her eye teeth were being crowded out of the upper row and she seemed thicker in the hips than yesterday.

"They said I had twenty-four hours."

"No problem. I had my sleeping bag."

"You slept here?"

She pointed into the stall. Her other arm was wrapped around the underside of the horse's neck in a way that was almost sexual. "She's my girl! Bred her, birthed her and raised her!"

"Look, we've gotta talk." Dean reached out to rub the horse's muzzle, and she nipped at his little finger. "Shit! What was that for?"

"She doesn't trust you yet. But she knows something's up." The girl was looking at the horse and getting teary-eyed as she spoke. "You gotta go slow. She's leery of new people. Her mother died foaling her and we had to find another mare to nurse her. I followed the new momma around with a bucket till her water broke and then doused our foal with it so the momma would think it was hers."

For Dean, seeing a pretty girl cry was right up there with someone slapping his child or whipping his dog. "Maybe we should just cancel this whole auction thing."

She snapped her head sideways and wiped her eyes with the back of her sleeve. "No! No . . . we can't! We hafta sell her so Mom can fix our truck. Without the truck, we're out of business."

"You're selling her so you can fix your truck?"

"She'll warm up to you, just mother her a little. And, please, don't shrink her."

"What do you mean?"

"Train the spirit out of her. She's got lots of life and loves to run. She's a horse with her *ears up*."

"Her ears up?"

"She pays attention to everything. Her eyes go where her ears go."

Dean was weakening. She was the wrong one to talk to about this. She loved this horse and he was already thinking of other options. "What's her name?"

She looked down at her scuffed boots. "That's the privilege of the new owner."

She was making Dean teary now. Not many people in his life had stepped aside and given him the chance to do something they could do better themselves. He didn't want to let her down. "What's your name, young lady?"

The girl hoed the ground with the heel of her boot, still holding the horse's lead. "Annalina. We're Swedish."

"That's a pretty name."

"Mom says it means graceful light."

Dean moved over to the horse and stroked her cautiously on the neck. She held her head up this time and rotated her ears toward Dean as if waiting for him to say something smart. He was right next to those whale eyes, and he could see his face in them. "Well that's it, then, girl. We're gonna call you Orphan Annalina!"

"Oh, you don't have to do that, sir."

"I want you to get your truck."

Annalina agreed to keep the horse one more day while Dean explored his options. He couldn't bear to tell her he was homeless. He wanted to leave her with the impression that he'd be a good father to her horse.

Dean walked over to the portable cashier's office again, praying they hadn't closed down the operation. The door was locked and he peered through the windows at the desk and file cabinets inside. There was a vase of wilted roses standing on the laminated counter.

His hope was that the people who ran the sale would put him on to someone who would buy the horse from him. All that money, all that bidding, Dean thought, there had to be a frustrated bidder out there still wanting a good filly. At about five to nine, a tall man in a leather jacket with a fleece collar showed up with a crowded ring of keys. It was the same man who'd taken his title for the Nashua.

Dean followed him into the trailer and watched him turn the lights on and set his papers down on the desk before saying anything. While the man emptied the grounds from the coffee pot, rinsed out the basket, and scooped fresh coffee into the filter, Dean explained his situation. When he'd finished, the man plugged in the coffee pot and looked at him.

"A horse sale is like a movie," he said. "Once you've seen it, you don't pay to go back. The people with money have gone home."

"But I paid sixteen thousand dollars!"

He reached for a packet of stapled papers and flipped through them to the last page. "See. It's instant deflation. Our average sale price was forty-three hundred bucks a horse. You're definitely on the high end of that." Dean was sweating again, his mouth parched. "Someone must have been bidding against you to go that high." He paused and studied Dean. "You know who it was, don't you?"

Dean looked again at the swelling across his knuckles where Lorraine had slammed the door on him. "Yeah, Gifford Pomeroy."

The man went back through the pages again, running his finger down the last column. "Looks like your man Pomeroy bought a couple of horses that day, including the sale topper. I'd give Mr. Pomeroy a call if I were you."

"I can't do that, sir . . ."

"By the way, which one did you say is yours?"

"Hip 113."

The man grabbed a sale book off the counter and split it open. Dean watched his eyes work their way down the page. "Uh-huh, you got the first foal out of this mare, and the sire's unproven. To be honest, you ain't going to resell her on the basis of breeding."

Dean asked to borrow the man's phone and he called the body shop to tell them he'd be late. "A family problem," he told the receptionist.

After leaving the sales trailer, Dean drove the freeway again trying to decide what to do. He did his best thinking behind the wheel of his pickup. Somehow the motion of the pistons stimulated his brain, so did the sound of the radio turned up loud and the roar of the wind coming through the half open window. He punched open the glove box, unscrewed the cap on a pint of Old Grand Dad, swished it around his mouth to maximize the exposure to his taste buds, and swallowed. He started to screw the cap back on, then unscrewed it and took another swig, this time straight down the rain gutter.

The first time Dean had a conversation with Gifford Pomeroy he was sitting on an apple crate in front of the Renton Post Office with merchandise spread out on a pea green blanket. Although he was only twelve years old at the time, Gifford was wearing a man's dress hat with a pinched crown and a vest with a gold chain that disappeared into the pocket.

"It's a Bulova," he said, pulling the watch out of his pocket. "Fifteen bucks, it's yours."

"You're selling it?"

Gifford waved his hand over the china, silverware, and ceramic figurines spread out on the blanket. "The whole world's for sale."

Dean had always assumed that Gifford was rich until the first time they went to his house. The front steps had rotted away and there was a ramp consisting of an old door with the knob still in it that swayed when you walked across it. The roller shades inside were darkened and frayed at the edges, and there was a pathway from the front hallway to the kitchen where the carpet had worn through to the pad and, in some places, to the bare wood. The basement had a monstrous furnace in the middle of it with air ducts you had to duck under to get by. Gifford's bed had a scratched-up headboard and shelves that held his radio and pocket stuff. His clothes were draped over a couple of mannequins standing guard at the foot of the bed. On the far wall, there were a series of wooden crates turned on their sides with planks stretched between them, each plank loaded with merchandise.

"This is my warehouse," he said.

"Where'd you get all this stuff?"

"The dump, garbage cans, things people throw away."

He lived with his aunt and his aunt's boyfriends. Gifford's parents were deceased. His dad killed his mom because he thought she was being unfaithful to him. At least that's what Gifford said he heard him yelling when he gunned her down in their bedroom. Gifford chased his dad out of the house and, next day, his dad drove his car into a bridge abutment. "The dumb bastard was hiding something," Gifford said. The day Gifford told him about his parents was the same day he gave Dean the Bulova.

"I can't take it, Giff, it says fifteen bucks!"

"I found it," he said. For Gifford, *found* meant stolen out of garages and off the backs of delivery trucks. Twice he'd been caught and talked his way out of it, the second time at knife point when he was caught with a glass clock in some guy's toolshed. Gifford specialized in time pieces. "It didn't even work," Gifford said.

They told Gifford the next time he was caught he'd do time, probably miss a year of school. That would have been a major waste, Dean thought, because Gifford Pomeroy was one of the smartest kids in school and always had an answer when the teacher called on him. School was Gifford's opportunity to make money playing marbles and gin rummy at recess in the boiler room or the janitor's storage room. Dean still remembered the day they were playing penny poker and, on the last draw, Gifford pulled out a clean $100 bill and laid it across the change in the pot. "I raise you!" he said. There was paralyzed silence – none of us had ever seen a $100 bill before. Everyone folded, Dean too, even though he had three kings.

The first time Dean hitchhiked with Gifford, they caught a ride up Rainier Avenue so that Gifford could sell a man a watch. Pretty soon, hitchhiking wasn't enough. Gifford wanted to have his own car. When they were sophomores, Gifford was peeved because he'd gotten a bad grade in trigonometry and wanted to hide his teacher's Mustang. To teach him a lesson. Dean knew it was a stupid idea, but once Gifford made his mind up, he was immoveable. Dean had learned from his dad how to hot-wire a car and he showed Gifford where to put the screwdriver to arc the spark, while at the same time trying to talk him out of it.

"You do it," Gifford said.

"In the big picture, who cares you got a *C* in trigonometry? And, by the way, I can smell whiskey on your breath."

"Nipped it from a bottle my aunt's boyfriend left at the house. Come on, I'm getting nervous."

Dean took the screwdriver Gifford found in the glove box, stuck his head under the dashboard and placed the screwdriver so it crossed the solenoid and the battery terminal at the same time. The engine coughed then hummed. "Bingo! She's all yours!"

Gifford drove. The original plan was to just take it around the block and park it in a new spot as a joke, but when he got behind the wheel Gifford decided to take it on a spin. He handled the car the same way he handled his business in front of the Post Office, like he'd been doing it all his life. They drove into the City Hall parking lot and back out again, then headed south on Lind to the city limits. Gifford was biting his lip and looking around for landmarks. When they came to the Burlington Northern railroad tracks, he signaled with his arm and jerked the car left onto the tracks. They straddled one of the rails, with the wheels socking the ties and the car bouncing up and down. Gifford stuck his head out and screamed something that sounded like, *Just come and get me, you bastard!* I thought he was yelling at his trig teacher, but maybe he was yelling at his old man.

When somebody started toward them in a truck on the maintenance road next to the track, Gifford didn't slow down, but Dean could tell he was feeling trapped. Finally, he slammed on the brakes and the car fishtailed back and forth, the insides of the tires bouncing against the rails. He put it in reverse, but they were caught between the railroad ties and the back wheels just spun. Two men in coveralls were running at them from about a hundred yards away. Gifford pushed open the door, "I'm outta here!" If taking the car was stupid, Dean knew that running was probably pea brained, but at that time in their lives their fates were intertwined. If one of them took a fall, they both took a fall. Gifford was a friend to die for. They outran the first set of guys, who turned out to be billboard paper hangers. The problem was the second set, who were Renton police officers coming at them from the other direction with their guns drawn. "Don't worry," Gifford whispered as the officers closed in on them, "I'll take the rap."

"No way. We go down together!"

The police took them away in separate squad cars and they were interrogated separately back at the station. They read Dean his rights, told him he could have an attorney, but Dean told them he didn't need an attorney. What could an attorney do? To take the heat off Gifford, Dean told them, "We took turns driving,"

It worked almost the way Dean had imagined it. They charged Dean with driving without a license and he pled guilty. Gifford asked for an attorney and they let him off with a warning. When Dean asked the prosecutor why the different treatment, he found out that Gifford had told them Dean did all the driving, that Dean said he had permission to borrow the car. Dean was bitter. He'd learned how you could only really hate someone you'd once loved.

Dean knew where Gifford's real estate office was -- he cringed every time he drove by that obnoxious neon lightning bolt on the face of the building -- but he'd never set foot inside the place. Gifford's Lincoln Town Car was parked in the Reserved space next to the main entrance, the same car he'd puttied the creases out of and painted the day of the horse sale, the damage from a mistaken lane change. Dean's job was *make-overs* and he took pride in his work. He was one of Bogle's best. Even his boss said he had great hands.

Praying for good karma, Dean closed his eyes and fingered the letters on the Pomeroy Realty plaque before opening the main door. There were glossy photos of houses under glass in the frames mounted on the walls of the lobby. A girl at the reception desk with frizzed hair and looping silver lariat earrings asked Dean if he had an appointment. "Mr. Pomeroy's very busy."

Dean rubbed his chin stubble. "He knows who I am."

While she called into her boss, Dean cupped his hand over his mouth and nose and exhaled to check the quality of his breath. About *C minus*. He'd have to keep his distance. The receptionist glared at Dean while she listened to what were apparently the instructions coming to her through the receiver, then she set the phone down and ushered Dean through a huge mahogany door with Gifford Pomeroy's name on it. More brass and the aroma of brandy pipe tobacco. Gifford was already on the phone again, while Dean studied the collection of framed certificates and commendations on the wall behind a desk that was wide enough to host the Last Supper. There were several Renton Rotary Club plaques with bronze gavels melted onto them. Square in the middle of the wall behind Gifford's high-backed judge's chair there was a framed $1,000 dollar bill with something written underneath it. Gifford had never married, so there were none of the usual photos of the wife and kids on his desk. When Gifford finished his call, they shook hands, something Dean had vowed on the way over *not* to do, but what choice did he have? This was business and he was the beggar. It was the first time he'd touched Gifford since scrambling out of the car on the railroad tracks. Gifford broke their shake with a practiced smile through clenched teeth and waved his hand in the general direction of nothing, "Have a seat."

Dean didn't know whether he meant one of the antique armchairs next to his desk or the stuffed club chairs surrounding the glass coffee table on the other side of the room. Dean took one of the armchairs, which kept Gifford behind his desk. This was Gifford's *deal room*, where he'd undoubtably made deals much bigger than the one he was about to propose. Dean had never bought or sold a house, never even made a mortgage payment.

"You look a little under the weather, Dean."

"Say, I'm kind of in a hurry, Giff. Let me just ask you something."

"If this is about a job, I told you I could find something here anytime you want it."

Dean didn't want to lose control of this meeting and he searched his brain for the lines he'd crafted on the way over. No matter what, he couldn't tell him what had happened between him and Lorraine. He had to deal from strength. He looked Gifford straight in the eye, "You know that good looking filly I bought at the sale . . . how'd you like another chance at her?"

Gifford erupted in laughter, the back of his head socking into the leather pillow hanging over the top of the chair. "What's the matter, buyer's remorse?" He leaned forward and put his forearms on the desk. "I was just trying to have a little fun with you, Dean. See how high you'd go. That horse toes in. Her breeding's practically non-existent. I'll make you a loan but I don't want your filly."

Dean stopped at a pay phone at the service station and called the body shop again to tell the receptionist that he might not make it in at all that day. "Something has come up," he said. She put him on hold, and when a voice came back on the line it was Harold Bogle, Dean's boss.

"Dammit, you've already used up your sick leave, Dean!"

"I know, I know . . . but can I borrow the scrap trailer for the day?"

Harold slammed the phone down, "No, and hell no!"

That's one of the things Dean hated about work. Someone paid you for forty hours of work and the next thing you knew they wanted to control your whole life, as if everything you did belonged to the company. Dean liked the jobs that didn't touch him, the ones he could drop at the end of the day and do whatever he pleased at night.

Watch the tube, make love with Lorraine, take Ricky to a ball game. When your employer started getting grabby, it was time to reestablish yourself.

Dean went back to the track and begged Annalina to let him borrow her horse trailer. She said okay and helped him hitch it to his pickup. They tried to load Orphan, but she smelled a rat and they had to slap her on the butt and lean their shoulders into her to get her to move. Annalina gave her horse a prolonged goodbye hug, kissed her all over the neck and face, and then fled from the trailer in tears.

It's you and me now, Orphan.

Dean thought the Cedar River valley offered the best chance for a place to board the horse. It still felt like country, with its large fenced off hobby farms, some strewn with abandoned cars and galvanized covered chicken coops in the yards. Besides, the Cedar River flowed through downtown Renton and it was on the banks of the Cedar where he and Lorraine had one splendid evening consummated their love.

The first two places Dean drove into had fenced pastures but no barns. He couldn't imagine Orphan just standing outside all winter. The next place had a good pasture that belonged to a crusty know-it-all German with a limp who said he'd do it if he could rent out the horse for riding by the hour. The barn at the next place was full of white chickens and green guano, and Dean had trouble getting the horse trailer turned around in the cramped driveway. Each time he came back to his pickup, he stuck his head in the side window of the trailer, patted Orphan and promised her they'd find a place if he had to look all night. She just stood there like someone being shipped to boot camp.

The next place looked promising, with a freshly painted fence, cattle in the pasture on one side of the driveway and a few horses on the other. He spoke with a blonde woman through a screen that had been spray-painted black. She probably thought he was a solicitor. When Dean explained his business, she introduced herself and invited him in for coffee on a vinyl and chrome kitchen table. Jill Sprague was in her early forties, with muscular forearms and a slight paunch that pushed out the waist of her jeans. Her husband worked different shifts at Boeing, which she called the *Lazy B.*

"I run the farm. Chuck hates shoveling shit and worrying about cracked udders."

"Is Chuck going to go for this?"

"He's not around much, but tough squat. It's not like I'm taking *you* in."

Her speech had a bite to it, and Dean wondered if he was making a mistake. He preferred a little more give in a woman. On the other hand, he couldn't imagine her ever kicking him out over a horse. She was probably the one on top when she made love with her Chuck. "I'd be no trouble, Ma'am. I'd just slide in and out of here to feed the horse. I could even help out around the place if you needed a hand."

"How far's the commute?"

"The commute?"

"Where do you live?"

He probably should have explained the situation more thoroughly to begin with, although in the face of this hard-nosed rancher, he wasn't sure how impressed she'd be with the truth. And, again, he didn't want to mix business with his personal affairs. He should have at least mentioned Lorraine, but maybe the reason she was going along with this was her fascination with the idea that he was a lonesome cowboy with a hankering for large animals. Dean knew from experience that it was possible to over-communicate. If people really knew each other from the *get go*, how many relationships would ever take root?

Jill stepped into the back of the trailer and lifted Orphan's tail, felt her legs, ran her fingers over her gums, pushing her from one side of the trailer to the other to give herself room to work. Dean didn't know what this was about; he hadn't asked for a checkup. He expected Orphan to nip her, but she didn't seem to mind being manhandled by this woman. Instead, she lowered her head and rolled her lips, as if they'd met before.

"Where'd you get her?"

"Long story, I guess."

"She's long-barreled. About sixteen hands, I'd guess." She pointed to the box in the corner of the trailer. "What's that?"

"My records." He was going to explain that they were the vinyl kind, mostly Willy Nelson, Bob Dylan and Waylon Jennings, but she was already on to something else. Without bothering to ask, she pulled the ramp out from under the end of the trailer and dropped it to the ground with a thud.

"Yeah, I'll board her! But you're responsible. I've got my own to take care of."

"Wouldn't have it any other way, Ma'am."

They put Orphan in the barn and went back up to the house for a cup of coffee. Dean talked about his work at the body shop and found himself trying to make it sound more technical than it really was, how he had to calibrate the sanders, worry about the density of the putty, and electronically mix the paint colors. "My work's probably a lot like your husband's," he said.

"Chuck's an electrical engineer."

"Oh."

"I'm the one who fixes the machinery around here. Frankly, I'd rather work a machine than screw around with people."

Dean was taken aback, but something about this woman fascinated him. "Your dad must have farmed."

"I didn't have a dad." She was tapping the table with her fingers in a rapid pattern. "Look, Dean. I'd like to settle up at the end of every month. That's when I do the books."

"Sure, Ma'am."

"I'm not your cleaning lady. Call me Jill."

5

A man from a collection agency called later that day to tell Lorraine they'd be coming for the Nashua. Aghast at how quickly things were moving, she called the Department of Licensing to see if Dean could legally sell the Nashua without her signature. They told her it was registered in the name of "Dean Hostler" so all he had to do was sign the back of the registration to pass title to someone else.

She and Ricky stopped by the liquor store and carted off about twenty Jim Beam and Smirnoff cartons to pack their things into. It wasn't exactly the image she wanted, but the boxes were reinforced and had lids.

Lorraine and Ricky met Mercy after work one night with her station wagon. By the end of the ten o'clock television news they'd made five trips, including dropping off Dean's things at the back door of the body shop, and crammed everything else from the Nashua into Mercy's apartment storage locker. Mercy was Dean's cousin, and Lorraine had always treasured the idea that Ricky was therefore a cousin to Mercy's two kids. So she treated this as a sort of family reunion.

When they were finished, Mercy gave Lorraine a big hug. "You're part of the disenfranchised now, dear."

Lorraine wanted their move to Mercy's place to feel like a choice, an upgrade, and in some respects it was. They wouldn't have to take down the kitchen table at night to make up Ricky's bed. Lorraine would have her own mirror, she wouldn't have to brush her hair and do eye shadow in the bathroom while Ricky showered, a practice that Dean had objected to. "He's going to turn out queer you keep doing that," he said. Lorraine knew that what Dean really meant was Ricky would develop an Oedipus complex and want to marry his mother.

That's one of the things Lorraine had missed out on growing up with Judge Culhane, who was so distant. "Fathers don't raise daughters," her mother had explained, summarizing a whole culture in a single breath. From her reading, Lorraine had become convinced that her father's aloofness contributed to her own sexual insecurities, and there was no way she was going to let Ricky drag that kind of baggage through his life. What was wrong with a glimpse of skin while you transitioned from the shower to a towel? That wasn't sex, it was honesty.

Ricky begged his mother to watch them haul away the Nashua, but Lorraine was convinced that wouldn't be a nourishing memory for him. "We don't know when they'll come for it, honey."

"Three days you said."

"It'll just be a big bummer."

"I want to see Dad!"

Lorraine wasn't one to leave things to chance. She called back the man who'd notified her of the transfer. His name and number were in the miniature tablet she kept under her pillow, on the same page as the note she'd made to herself about finding a second job. She explained to the man how she'd lived in that trailer for over fifteen years, and the least they could do was tell her when the darn thing was going to be pulled away.

"We don't make appointments for repossessions," he said.

"This isn't a repossession. My husband sold it!"

"That's one way to look at it, Ma'am."

Lorraine felt invaded. Everyone in Renton must have heard what Dean had done. It was almost enough to make her move to Seattle and take an apartment in Ballard where nobody would know her. She could take evening classes at the community college and learn to do something she'd dreamed of doing before Dean. She'd once wanted to become a nun. She liked the nuns in grade school, they'd been decent teachers, but they were pawns in the Church's larger scheme. Of course, celibacy was also part of the appeal for her then.

Lorraine had expected that a truck would just back up to the hitch on the kitchen-end of the Nashua and pull it out of the trailer park. Five minutes tops. They'd be in and out of there before they had to talk to anyone. She finally acquiesced to Ricky's wishes on the theory that the whole repossession experience was an educational opportunity, like farm kids learning about the life cycle by watching their pigs get butchered.

A tow truck was already parked in the lane with its red light flashing when they arrived at the trailer park in Mercy's station wagon. Someone had put strips of gray duct tape in 'X's over the windows of the Nashua. A heavyset man in a denim jacket was squatting next to one of the wheel cavities, jacking up the trailer. A huddle of trailer park residents gawked at the goings on.

"Why don't we just watch the show from the car?" Lorraine said.

"I want out," Ricky said.

Lorraine wanted to be with him, to help him process this, but she didn't want to have to talk to the old widow who used to come by and nag her to take better care of the flowers in the border around the Nashua or run into the lecherous carpet layer who always wanted her and Dean to come over and play pinochle and boat with him to Alaska in his Bayliner. As soon as Ricky disentangled himself from the seat belt straps, he ran for the Nashua, heading straight for the guy in the wheel cavity.

"They always go for the men, don't they?" Mercy said.

Ricky picked up the cross-shaped lug wrench, and Lorraine assumed it was just boyish curiosity, until he lifted the wrench over his head.

Lorraine flew out the door. "Ricky!"

The man seized Ricky's wrist in mid-swing and the lug wrench fell harmlessly to the ground. Then he grabbed a fistful of Ricky's sweatshirt and lifted him off the ground until they were eye to eye. "You little pissant!"

Lorraine crashed into the man and bounced off him like she'd hit a tree trunk. "Put him down! I'm his mother!"

He glared down at her, with one still eyeball and one that quivered. "So?"

"Put him down, I said!" Lorraine's whole body trembled.

The man's meaty fist under Ricky's chin had twisted his sweatshirt into a noose that made his head tilt back. Lorraine expected Ricky to be crying, but his teeth were clenched and his arms taut at his sides. She'd seen that same look when she told him his dad wouldn't be moving with them to Mercy's. The man mumbled under his breath as he lowered Ricky, then dropped him, causing Ricky to stumble over the portable wicket fence that Lorraine had put around her flower bed to keep the dogs out. "Better chain him up, lady!"

As she tugged on Ricky's arms to drag him out of the man's reach, she expected her old neighbors to rush up and help her, but nobody moved. Neither were there any goodbyes or sorry to see you goes. The stares maddened her. *It wasn't as if your marriages all worked,* she wanted to yell. Park residents had stood on this very spot and filled Lorraine's ears with stories of trailer park infidelities. *If these little trailers had tongues,* she mumbled to herself. Of course, they had tongues. That's what the crew was hooking up to for the pullout. Their home was portable, a vehicle under the law, with axles and wheels.

"Why wasn' Dad here?" Ricky said, as Lorraine stuffed him back into Mercy's station wagon. "He could'a stopped this."

Mercy put a hand on his knee. "You ever heard of Harvey, kid?"

Ricky mumbled "No."

"He's a big rabbit everybody loves, but he always disappears. That's what dads are."

Lorraine motioned to get out of there. Mercy dropped the wagon into first gear and gave everyone the finger as they drove past.

With Mercy's help, Lorraine was hired on at the Ram to wait tables in the evening and help with food preparation for the next day. There wasn't that much restaurant business that time of day unless a jury was still deliberating. The Ram offered a discount package for District Court juries that included a choice of three entrees and a non-alcoholic beverage. Serving up chicken fried steak to the jurors made her feel like part of the judicial system. Her father used to say that he was never so proud of what he did as when he could step aside and let the jury decide a case. Jurors didn't have to tip -- the package with the county included a gratuity -- and they seldom engaged her in conversation the way other customers did. When she'd finished peeling the potatoes and cutting up the vegetables for the next day, she'd sometimes sit with a customer if there was one, keeping one leg under the table and one out, ready to spring to the cash register or refill a coffee. She learned quickly that the more she visited the fatter the tips would be. At first that made her feel dirty, but then she remembered she was doing it for Ricky.

Mercy worked days, fixed dinner and stayed with the kids in the evening. It was built-in day care, but Ricky resented the arrangement.

He'd become moody since his dad left and seemed out of gas in the evenings. He'd started sneaking junk food and griping about school. He wouldn't show her his homework, and he was getting in arguments with other students. He had trouble falling asleep at night, then she couldn't wake him up in the morning. He was acting bossy for no reason. He didn't listen to her. He'd blow up over trivial things. Worse than his outbursts were his silences when she had to coax the words out of him. She thought of increasing his medication, as well as her own.

"I don' like Cory and Sam that much," he said. Cory and Samantha were Mercy's kids from two different fathers, who were also miffed because their mom had made them bunk up in the same bed so that Ricky could have his own.

"It's not permanent," Lorraine said, rubbing the rounded corners of Ricky's shoulders. "That's why I'm working nights, so we can have our own place again."

Sometimes, if the kids had finished their homework or even if they hadn't, Mercy dropped them off at a show and stopped by the Ram for a cup of coffee with Lorraine. "I don't know why on earth you'd come down here on your time off," Lorraine said. "Why don't you get a baby-sitter and go on a date? We could split the cost."

Mercy laughed with her eyes shut. "You slay me, Lorraine."

"You can't just hide out."

Mercy leaned her head across the table, a lock of hair falling across one eye, and puckered her lips. "I've forgotten how to date, honey, although I wouldn't mind a little bouncy-bouncy. Without all the claptrap."

"The claptrap?"

"High hopes."

They laughed. "You've just had bad luck," Lorraine said.

"And Dean was a good catch?"

A disheveled man with a knapsack and a reddish beard entered the restaurant and stood at the cash register. Lorraine slid out of the booth, straightened her skirt, and patted her hair. The waitresses were under strict instructions to shoo vagrants out. The owner didn't want the place to become a soup kitchen. Lorraine grabbed a menu off the counter and tried to usher him towards a booth and out of sight, but the man held his ground at the cash register, glancing around nervously. She poured him a cup of Styrofoam coffee and stuck a handful of sugar bags in his jacket pocket. When he turned for the door, however, Lorraine tugged on his sleeve to stop him. She reached into the pie rack and slid a piece of day-old lemon meringue onto a sheet of aluminum foil. With the extra foil, she fanned one end into a peacock's tail, molded a neck and head at the other end, and handed the package to the man.

"Big sale, huh?" Mercy said as Lorraine slid back into the booth.

"Don't you just feel for those guys?"

"I worry about you, Lorraine. For all your brains, you don't have such good sense. Maybe that's why you fell for a Hostler. I keep waiting for you to find *me* out."

"Oh, stop it. You're brimming over with class."

Mercy took Lorraine's hand and fingered her wedding ring. "Why don't you put this back in the jewelry box? Maybe I'm out of place and all, but I think you should take back your maiden name too. Lorraine Culhane. It's beautiful. No wonder Dean fell in love with you."

"I can't do that. It's not Ricky's."

"Oh, honey, that notion went out with sanitary napkin belts."

"It's not even been a month yet!"

"Wrong, sweetie. It's been seventeen years!"

The next day a Renton police car pulled up to Lorraine's flower stand, with Ricky in the backseat glaring at her through a layer of steam on his window. It was his lunch hour at school and she assumed he'd gotten into a fight. She locked her money box, shoved it under the green tissues and twine, and walked over to the patrol car.

"We caught him shoplifting at the Fred Meyer," the officer said.

Her insides seized. "How could he? He was at school."

"Two Baby Ruths and a pack of Rum Crook cigars."

"Cigars?" she gasped, looking back at Ricky through the wire mesh divider. They'd talked about the hazards of smoking. Lorraine knew a lot of the police in the force; they came by her stand on the way in and out of the courthouse to testify. This officer looked familiar, but she was pretty sure he'd never bought flowers from her. She was envisioning an enormous spring bouquet he could take home to his wife that would make him forget this whole thing. She was already imagining Ricky's application forms for colleges, checking the box where they asked if he'd ever been arrested. "Don't write this up, officer, please!" She leaned over and whispered so Ricky wouldn't hear. "He's special ed."

"That don't mean squat to me, Ma'am. It don't take a genius to know you can't cop stuff for free."

Lorraine didn't look forward to her next school parent conference. Although Dean had not attended these with regularity, she always consoled herself with the knowledge that at least Ricky's troubles weren't the result of a broken home. Ricky's teacher had made a point at their last conference of mentioning that her own two daughters were in the *gifted* program.

They met in her classroom, Lorraine taking a seat in one of the student chairs with an arm for a desk that she pulled up next to the teacher's desk. It was snug and so low that she had to look up to Ricky's teacher, who had permed blonde hair, a tan face, and a nice figure, everything plumb. "Ricky's been practically comatose lately," the teacher said. "Usually, he's popping off in class. I wondered if there was something going on at home."

"He goes through moods," Lorraine said, trying to shift her body position in the cramped chair. "Typical teenager, I guess." There was no way she was going to tell this woman about Ricky's shoplifting or the rift with Dean. Ricky's teacher was obviously more into justice than mercy. Even the waves in her perm were steely.

"There's nothing you'd like to share with me?"

Lorraine hadn't even told her mom and dad about the separation from Dean, telling them instead that the move into Mercy's apartment was an economy measure so they could save up for a down payment on a real house. If she hadn't been required to change the phone number she might not have told her that much. "Ricky has a loving home," Lorraine told the teacher. "No drugs or guns. I drill him on spelling words and help him with his math."

"Whoa! I'm not accusing you, Mrs. Hostler! I know about his attention deficit issues. He's got to be watched."

Lorraine squirmed to get out of the desk, put the strap of her purse over her shoulder, and excused herself. *Darn you, Dean*, she thought. *Where are you when I need you? Ricky's in free fall.* It was almost embarrassing how ineffective her parenting had been, but the last thing she was going to do was set herself up for criticism from someone she didn't even know.

6

Takin' the candy bars was small time, I know that. They had nuts and I don' even like nuts. I only eat 'em 'cause Mom thinks they bother my dopa mine. That's what makes me stupid. Good name for it, but I'd rather have plain Hersheys. Family size. I could have slid one of those hummers straight down the front of my pants. That's how they caught me. The candy bars stuck outta my pockets. That's how stupid I am. I'm not s'posed to eat chocolate either. Mom said I'll get zits. What's so big about zits? Everyone has zits. Braces and zits. It's all small time.

I shoulda tak'n some knives. Things that would make someone think twice. They'd think I'd freaked out. Or glue. Twenty tubes of glue. Mom'd have me at the clinic so fast it'd make your head swim. They'd give me pills to slow down my 'drenalin so I wouldn't 'lucinate. The candy bars were somethin' a dopa mine kid would do. I took the cigars for Dad.

The produce guy dragged me into the manager's office, up some stairs I'd never noticed. They had a regular fort up there with a kitchen and snacks, stuff they'd probably copped from the store shelves themselves. They could look through a secret window and see the checkout stands. They made me pull my shirt up like I might have somethin' in my belly button. Then my pants. I even had to drop my underpants.

I should have tak'n Dad's twenty-two. I saw it when we moved. Mom wrapped it in a towel and put it with her stuff. I was missin' Dad real bad. With his gun, I could have done like *Dog Day Afternoon* that Dad and I saw on video and laughed till we were stupid at the stuff the bank robber did. Al Pacino. I'd love to be like him. I could have made the checkers strip down and go in the cooler. Then they wouldn' jus' bawled me out and told me to be a good boy. That woulda meant hard time. I'd have been someone to reckon with. People at school would think twice about callin' me duckbutt.

I didn' tell Mom but when she kicked Dad out I stopped takin' my pills. It was easy. I just put my fist against my mouth and faked a gulp of OJ. Then I slipped 'em in my pocket and gave 'em away at school. Mostly to Skeeter Parker. He said he was collecting 'em. I didn't care. At least I had someone who'd sit with me at lunchtime 'stead of eatin' in the lavatory alone. Skeeter was dumber'n I was, but there was one big difference. Everyone liked Skeeter. I prob'ly gave 'way the pills 'cause I was mad at Mom. I knew if she wanted Dad back, he'd of come. What was so big about the trailer anyway? She didn' even like it. Besides, the pills were makin' me shorter and I was tired of bein' a midget.

I'm not givin' away my pills anymore either. Skeeter told me he crushes 'em up into powder and snorts 'em through his nose. Said it makes him feel like Hitler. Then he told some a his friends, so now they want 'em too. I told 'em they'd have to buy 'em, even Skeeter. Life sucks, so why not suck up some of their money while I'm at it.

The worst thing is Mom's visit with the Judge. I'm talkin' 'bout her dad, my supposed to be grandpa, who likes to be called Yore Honor if yore in a serious talk with him. Anyway, Mom said I had to go over there, so I did. All the Judge could talk 'bout was someone he said my mom should'a married. Like right there in front of me, he's talk'n bout how he knew all the time tha' my dad wasn' right. Like he was God, tell'n Mom he always knew it wouldn' work. An' I'm think'n, right there, he's talk'n bout me. Like I didn' work.

Like why didn' he make *my* dad Pres'dent of his Rotary Club 'stead of the real state guy. Like his Rot'ry Club has all the fancy people in town. How smart this other man was. An' so gen'rous for build'n a hospital for kids, 'cept it was just a gazebo in a park to cook hot dogs in the rain. Like his man's gonna know how to fix car wrecks. How to pound out dents in fancy cars. How to match the paints.

An' not once did he say anythin' smart or famous 'bout me. He could'a lied, but I 'spose judges don' lie. I could'n help but wonder if the Judge was really Mom's dad. They were nothin' like each other. An' I was nothin' like him. The Judge was from Mars an' I was on the moon.

7

Dean didn't know exactly what he was getting into when he made arrangements to board the horse and sleep in the stall with her. His family had raised wheat in Rosalia before his dad lost the farm and moved to Renton. The only animals Dean really knew were those mule deer who lived off the leftovers and found their own water in the draws. All Dean had to do was watch the salt block on the fencepost behind the barn and replace it when the deer had licked it to a nub.

Orphan's stall had a back door that opened into the field where she grazed, and she could come and go as she liked. Whenever Dean came into her stall, however, she would escape to the field. Dean filled the corrugated trough behind the barn with water each night and stuffed more hay into the rack in her stall. Next day, it would be spread all over the ground.

"Hey, girl, take it easy on the hay! I only look rich."

Dean exited past the Sprague's house with the headlights off on his way out at night and drove around Renton in his pickup like a burglar casing out jobs. Every time he stopped in front of someone's house he knew, he'd leave the motor idling, debating whether to get out, but he never did because he couldn't find the words to explain his predicament with Lorraine. And by not actually telling his story out loud, he could diminish the reality of it. Each loop through town usually ended up back at the empty space in the trailer park, with Dean listening to the Sonics on the radio, counting the roof antennas on the trailers, and imagining everyone else nestled in front of their televisions enjoying *Dallas*.

When the trailer disappeared, he figured Ricky and Lorraine had moved in with her parents, so he dropped a note in their mailbox one night, a first step toward begging Lorraine to come see the horse, and offer to meet her and Ricky after work somewhere:

> *We can fix this whole situation, make it just like the old*
> *days. Call me at the body shop. Say the word, Sugar.*

He wasn't sure if she'd gotten the messages because for a long time there was no response. Finally, she sent a note to the body shop. He recognized her handwriting and sniffed the letter front and back before opening it. Sliding his finger under the flap, he gently broke the bond she'd sealed with the moistness of her tongue, closed his eyes, and made a prayer in his head asking Saint Anthony, the patron saint of the lost, to help him get Lorraine back. There wasn't a scratched-out word, the penmanship was perfect, but the message was all wrong:

> *It's not a matter of a place to live, Dean. It's a matter*
> *of who I choose to live with. I'm sure you always meant*
> *well, but I let your affection mask the problems. Your*
> *irresponsibility is too hard on Ricky. You and I can*
> *forge on our own, but it's not fair to mess up Ricky. He's*
> *too vulnerable. It hurts me to say this, but I can't take*
> *you back, with or without the horse. Fortunately, my*
> *parents didn't open your note, but please don't send*
> *any further correspondence to them. No, fortunately,*
> *the Judge didn't open it!*

She signed it simply "Lorraine."

Dean drove out to the old Barbee Mill on Lake Washington that night, where he'd worked one summer in the mill pond rolling logs that were fed to the sawyer. He parked between the saw house and the lake so nobody would be able to see him from the street. Might as well have a view of the lake, he thought. People paid good money for waterfront property. Lorraine had always said she didn't care what they could see outside as long as the insides were nice, but Dean had dreamed of getting them a house on the hill someday so that everyone in Renton would have to point up to say where the Hostlers lived.

Alone at night, he couldn't help but think back to the way things used to be with Lorraine. In the earliest stage of their relationship, it was one hand clapping, before she knew he even existed. Dean even attended Sunday masses at Saint Anthony's just for the chance to see her from a distance. The Culhanes always went to the ten o'clock mass, with the Judge in his dark suit, diminutive Mrs. Culhane with a nice hat, and their daughters in tow. Dean would take the first pew in the choir loft so he could survey the whole church. Judge Culhane would lead the family down the aisle, then step aside and watch each of his ladies genuflect, bow their heads, and make the sign of the cross before scooting sideways into their pew. Dean imagined himself as the tip of Lorraine's finger as she touched her forehead, her breastbone and the point of each shoulder. Lorraine's younger sisters fought over their prayer books and poked each other during the mass, but Lorraine was all concentration. Dean imagined her lips moving as she followed the priest's prayers. She crossed her heart with both arms on the way back from communion. Dean had never seen such goodness, and it made him itch to think of it.

He'd daydreamed about the ranch-style house they'd buy, with everything on one floor, a recreation room big enough for a ping pong table, and a double garage, one for her car, one for his. It would have those flat, pale bricks, a wrought iron porch railing, and a huge picture window in the living room. Their bedroom would have a fireplace with a mantel where they'd put the pictures of their kids and the dogs. They had to have dogs, maybe a Golden Retriever and a Border Collie, who'd sleep on the oval rug at the foot of their bed. Dogs were creatures he understood. In the morning, he and Lorraine would sit in their bathrobes eating toast with marmalade from those fancy little packets with the peel off tops that restaurants used. In his imagination, the kids were never there at breakfast. The only voices were his and Lorraine's as they planned their day. Sure, Lorraine's family would come over for birthdays and holidays. At first it would be awkward, but then Dean and the Judge would start talking about internal combustion engines and the damaging effects of the Industrial Revolution, things Dean had learned from his own dad. What made Dean trust his vision was the fact that he knew they'd sometimes quarrel, they'd both get huffy, then Dean would let her win, and they'd hug. He had no idea where these visions came from. The only fights *he'd* ever witnessed had ended up with his mother throwing the nearest blunt object at his dad.

As anticipatory as their relationship was then, Dean believed it had all of the dimensions of real love - the highs, the lows, and the mystery.

He'd never experienced the sensation of wanting to give himself to someone the way he did with Lorraine. Privately, he tried to clean up his act, make himself worthy of her, inventing four-letter words that were as whistle clean as the Holy Ghost. When he had impure thoughts, he fought to make sure they didn't include Lorraine. He cherished her virginity. He wanted their first time together to be pure silk.

About two in the morning, Dean awoke to some commotion outside the car and realized he was still at the Barbee Mill. He wiped the steam off the window and noticed that the Pontiac next to him was rocking. He cracked the window and listened to the moans. He thought of Lorraine again, and there was the same ache he used to feel from the choir loft.

Next day, Dean's boss called him into the office, which had a one-way window that allowed him to keep track of what was happening out on the floor. Harold Bogle loved cars. He raced them, wrecked them, and rebuilt them. Along one wall of his office, there were two gunmetal-gray filing cabinets straddled by a plywood shelf full of trophies from the drag races at Spanaway. The body shop sponsored the car that Harold drove. After every race, it would be back in the shop for a touch-up or reconstruction.

"Opened it by mistake," Harold said, handing Dean a letter.

"That's all right."

Harold vacuumed the back of his hand with his nostrils. Lorraine used to call Harold when Dean was late getting home on paydays. Harold was hardly a role model, but Dean could imagine him taking her side. "Not exactly a satisfied customer," he said, pointing to the letter. "Hey, I don't want any garnishments served on me."

Dean took the letter to the lavatory, which was a pit. Guys who could buff the hood of a Buick until you had to squint to look at it couldn't keep the sink clean. Dirty footprints mottled the linoleum and there were urine etchings in front of the toilet bowl.

Dear Dean,

Even though you and I can't live together, you still have a financial responsibility. I now have a regular job, but you know how expensive Ricky is. I'm asking for support payments equal to 40% of your take home. I think you'll find that's normal for this sort of thing. Mercy was kind enough to take us in and Ricky now has his cousins Cory and Samantha. My eyes are wide open, Dean. It may take a while to find the path, but I take comfort knowing I'm not going to jump off any more cliffs.

Lorraine

Dean folded up the note and stuffed it into his overalls. Where was the sugar, he thought? Had she forgotten the Easter flour bunny tracks he'd made on the carpet with his fingertips that led to the nylon stockings with the tickets to Bob Dylan? Had she forgotten the time he sang *Lay Lady Lay* to her while they were making love? And hadn't he been supporting them since LBJ was President? What happened to the girl who trusted him with her virginity on the hood of his car? Of course, he was going to help support Ricky. He missed the hell out of Ricky. She didn't have to make him sound like a bum.

Back to work with the disc sander, Dean worked his way back and forth across the putty on a fender while scheming in his head how to get Lorraine back. In his mind's eye, he pictured himself this time coming in and out of one of those new apartments on Rainier Avenue with the sliding glass doors to the balcony. He'd buy one of those pole torches and invite Lorraine and Ricky over for barbecued chicken with potato salad and cheesecake. He and Lorraine would mix up a jug of Margaritas in a blender and get a little tipsy. He'd ask them to stay over and offer Lorraine and Ricky the two bedrooms. Then in the middle of the night maybe she'd get lonesome, tap him on the shoulder, and slide in next to him on the couch. He'd stroke her hair back behind her ears and kiss her cheekbones.

Sparks interrupted Dean's reverie. "Shit, shit!" He'd scoured clean through to the steel with his sander.

Dean stopped off at a tavern for a beer after work. He'd sworn since the night he'd come home late for Ricky's birthday that he'd abstain totally from hard liquor. Something he'd mostly succeeded in doing. He ended up sitting next to another guy who'd just separated from his wife.

"It was entrapment," the guy said. "I thought the sister was cool about it. Then she finds religion. Can you believe that? I think she just wanted to piss off my wife." The guy's eyes sagged from the weight of the bags under them and it was hard for Dean to imagine him seducing anyone's sister. "Whole thing started after a baptism for one of her kids and she said her toilet was plugged. She was in one of those shorty bathrobes. I plunged the toilet and she fixes me a drink. Then she asks me to rub her hands. *Bad circulation*, she says. Next thing I know we're doing it like banshees against the refrigerator."

The guy was buying the drinks, so Dean bought him a hot corned beef sandwich with cole slaw. The guy mostly watched *Cheers* on the shelf behind the bar while Dean told his story, which was admittedly tame by comparison. No wonder the wife had kicked him out, Dean thought, this guy had committed adultery, the big one.

"Must be some ass on that horse you bought," the man finally said at the commercial break, and then choking on his own joke. Dean had to pat him on the back. He didn't want to be responsible for this guy, but nobody else in the place seemed to care.

When *Cheers* ended, Dean asked him if he was paying child support.

"It's a scam," he said. "Pretty soon she'll be bunking up with somebody else. Let him pay her."

"My kid's a slow learner," Dean said.

"So's my wife," the man said, and started choking on his own laugh again.

As Dean patted him on the back, he wished there was a way to expose Lorraine to guys like this, to prove that she could have done worse. That was Dean's disadvantage, Lorraine read books and he talked to real people.

When he left the tavern, Dean hurried to the farm. Orphan would be starving. He thought of the dogs he had growing up, how no matter when he came home they were always wagging their tails in welcome, how they shared sandwiches on his bed together, how Dean covered for his dogs when they chewed things up or later became incontinent and peed all over the house. He'd wished for a dog his whole marriage, but Lorraine was allergic to the dander.

He slowed down and dimmed his parking lights when he came to the *Chuck & Jill Sprague* mailbox with the red rooster painted on the side. Dean didn't want to wake them up and cringed as his tires crunched the gravel like a homemade ice cream maker. The only light was the yellow bug bulb on the porch. Dean looked up at the house,

47

wondering which window was the master bedroom. Although he'd still never met Chuck, he imagined him shorter than Jill, with stubby fingers and risers in his shoes.

There was no electricity in the barn, so Dean had to use his flashlight. The hay bale he'd thrown into the stall had a ragged corner, but the rest of it was intact. The water trough was full. When he shined the light on her, Orphan turned away.

"Hey, girl, I was just kidding about eating too much." The warm air in the barn was leaking out the door to the pasture and Orphan started sidestepping toward the door as Dean approached her with an open hand. "Easy girl." Dean wanted to touch something warm-blooded. Orphan reared her head and flung a string of snot across Dean's arm. Discharge had crusted in the corner of one eye. Dean clicked his tongue, "Come here, girl."

Orphan backed into the side of the stall, panicked, and then bolted out to the pasture. Dean followed her with his flashlight. The ground was saturated from the rain and Dean sunk in up to his laces as he followed her along the fence. She acted like she was searching for an opening so she could return to the girl who'd doted over her. Dean aimed the flashlight at her body this time, avoiding the eyes. That's probably what had spooked her, he thought.

There was a Douglas Fir just outside the fence and that's where Orphan stood, underneath it, in the highest part of the pasture, where she could survey the terrain for predators, which at the moment amounted to a single rookie with a flashlight. Dean stopped about fifteen feet away and surveyed her hide for cuts or scrapes. She'd rolled in the mud and her coat was rumpled where the mud had dried. There were no wounds, but her nose was runny.

Dean headed back to his truck to get the bedspread and red Scotch plaid emergency blanket and pillow he kept in the toolbox bolted to the pickup. He shook the dust off the bedding, carried it back to the stall, and pulled it up under his chin. He could see his breath.

He was feeling very much the outsider, as if everyone except him was part of the intricate system called the human race; they'd studied it, mastered its rhythms, and merged with it like flakes in the path of a runaway snowball. No Hostler that he knew of had ever studied past high school. There were no licensed Hostler engineers or lawyers. As far as he knew, nobody in his family had ever been the boss of anything save their own house. But his dad had told him once about his grandfather Otto, who was a blacksmith and horseshoe farrier at the turn of the century, a craft that had been passed down to him by his father. When the United States joined World War I, Otto Hostler shipped overseas as part of a calvary artillery unit where he shoed and mended injured horses. They said he came back a changed man, notoriously antisocial, and feared in his own town because he practiced exorcism. The only demons he couldn't exorcize were his own, the burning images of soldiers and their dying horses. The country he helped save had industrialized and made the working horse nearly obsolete. Otto tried to transfer his skills to a steel mill, but he lacked the heart for it.

Dean got up and made the trek out to the pasture again, this time with a blanket instead of the flashlight. Orphan stood her ground as Dean let her smell the blanket, then flung it over her back and evened it up on each side. He waited to make sure she'd accepted it, then went back to his bedding in the stall.

The marmalade cat who lived in the barn studied Dean for a while from just outside the gate, then finally tip-toed in and took a place next to him. He didn't remember falling asleep until his nose awakened him to the scent of the barn in the morning. His face had slipped out of his makeshift mummy bag and onto the porcupine straw. The cat was still asleep on a corner of the bedspread. When Dean started to raise himself, there was a commotion behind him, and he turned around just in time to see Orphan's butt as she exited to the pasture. Dean untangled himself and rolled over. Dean knew that horses did most of their sleeping standing up but there was a large hollow in the straw next to his, and he felt it with the flat of his hand. It was still warm.

Dean tucked his shirt in after a gratifying leak in the pasture, shook his leg to make things sit right in his shorts, and headed back to the stall. Jill Sprague was waiting for him, her elbows over the gate and her chin resting on the folds of the bedspread.

"You look like hell," she said. The pointed toe of her cowboy boot was sticking through the slats. "Should have knocked, I guess. Saw your truck and came down."

"Yeah. I got here a little early."

"Bullshit. I heard you drive in last night. What's the story here, Dean? A man doesn't sleep in a stable unless he's rock bottom."

He didn't want to get into it. He liked it better living in bubbles. This was his horse bubble. The body shop was another bubble. There was always trouble when the bubbles bumped into each other. "I was married . . . I mean I'm still married, but we're going through something."

"That's called divorce."

"She's just mad at me. You know how some women are always getting their hair fixed, and have to sit under the sun lamp to get a tan, and color their hair, and buy new dresses, and read fashion magazines? Well, Lorraine's just the opposite of all that." Nothing seemed to be registering with Jill. She was still leaning over the gate with her elbows, waiting for the punch line. "What I mean is, she's not a perfectionist, except when it comes to me."

"Take a shower up at the house while I fix you a cup of coffee."

"Thanks but I don't want to intrude."

"You can't go public like this."

Dean looked down at his pants and checked the front of his shirt. Everything seemed normal except for the straw clinging to him. It must have been his face. He had a tendency to puff up a bit when he drank. He was expecting Jill to say something about the fact he was wearing the same clothes as the ones he'd met her in, but he beat her to the punch. "I guess I'm still in transition."

"See you up at the house." She turned away and headed out of the barn before he could really finish what he was trying to say.

The shower was on the main floor, in the middle of a cedar sauna that had benches around the sides. He slid the wooden dowel into the lock position. He loved the smell of cedar; his dad's cigar humidor had been lined with it, and Dean used to open the humidor, put his face across it and inhale Cuba. There was a row of white plastic knobs along the wall, one of them with a maroon robe, another one heaped with layers of female clothing hung in the order of undress -- cotton undies, a bra, jeans frayed at the cuffs, and a blue gingham shirt with a ballpoint pen clipped to the pocket. The shower head was mounted high, the stream was forceful, and it reminded him of when he used to take showers at the Liberty Pool to wash the chlorine off, knowing that on the other side of that thick concrete wall Lorraine was showering too.

Jill was sitting alone at the kitchen table when he finished showering. Her sleeves were rolled up and a blue barrette held the hair back on one side. She had those little bumps along the rims of her ears that his dad had told him were a sign of intelligence. Dean's coffee mug was poured and still steaming. There was no sugar or cream on the table and, even though he preferred his coffee with whitener, he wasn't going to impose.

"You need a vet to look at that horse," she said. "When's the last time she was wormed?"

It was hard for Dean to reconcile this woman's clear complexion and blue eyes with talk of worms. They should have been discussing strawberry fields and pools of cream, or whether she and Chuck showered together and soaped each other down in the sauna. "Where's Chuck?"

She looked at the large watch on her wrist, which had digital displays, luminous markers, and timer buttons on its circumference. "He's outta here before sunup. What's the matter, you nervous?"

"Just asking."

"Horses aren't as tough as they look," she said. "They need a little TLC, that's all. And it's better if they get a lot of small meals rather than one or two big ones. Give her a flake of hay, not the whole bale." She was criticizing him, he knew that, but he enjoyed listening to the huskiness of her voice, and the coffee was strong. "They're grazing animals. Their digestive systems are designed to keep small amounts of food moving through. They'll bulk up better that way and avoid the colic."

"How do you know all this?"

He could tell she didn't welcome his question the way she started tapping her fingers on the table. "I guess I read a lot of livestock magazines." She reached into her wallet and pulled out a calling card. "Here's my vet."

Dean studied the card. There was a "DVM" behind the guy's name and his office was in Auburn. "He's good, huh?"

"You've never owned a horse, have you?"

"Not owned."

"Lust doesn't count."

She was too quick for him, knocked him off-balance. He needed to study her remarks in his own corner and figure out what she meant before he answered. Lorraine always said that every conversation between a man and a woman had a subtext. Women wanted rapport and men wanted to report. That certainly didn't fit Jill.

At lunch hour, Dean told his boss he had to go to the Post Office, but he went to the feed store instead, bought some supplies on credit, and then drove out to the farm to check on Orphan. He didn't want Jill to think he'd ignored her advice. When he entered the stall, Orphan exited, trotting up to her usual place under the fir tree. *So much for TLC.* She treated him like a child molester.

Dean pulled the string on a bag of Equine Formula. The guy at the feed store said it was ideal for two-year olds, stimulated the immune functions and helped digestion. It smelled like the bran meal that Lorraine sprinkled with wheat germ for breakfast, and it stuck to his hands like there was syrup in it. Dean scooped out a handful and walked over to the opening.

"Got something for you, girl."

Orphan swished her tail, bowed her back, and stood her ground. Translation: I'm interested, but why don't you just put it down and scram. Dean sniffed it, and she pawed the ground. He turned around, put his head against the red siding on the barn, closed his eyes, and twisted his arm so that his palm with the food in it was behind him. He waited, listening to the crows squawking in the fir tree. His arm was starting to tremble. Then he heard the suction of hooves and her congested breathing coming closer. He could feel her heat as her lips nuzzled against his palm. It was a transcendence akin to prayer.

That night, Dean stopped at a Texaco to wash his hands and wipe the pasture mud off his shoes with paper towels from the dispenser. He put fifty cents into the cologne machine, gave himself a squirt of Brut, and headed off to see his cousin Mercy, who spoke to him through a crack in the door.

"Just leave her be, Dean!"

"Can't you put in a good word for me?"

"We're not marriage material, Dean. No table manners and we're sexually overloaded."

"That's unfair. I've never cheated on her."

Mercy was holding the door tight like she expected him to rush her. "I don't want to get in the middle of this. Lorraine's my friend. She's why I came back to Renton. I won't let you hurt her again."

"What about me?"

"You bounce."

"Just tell me where she is."

Then someone peeked out from the hallway behind her. "She works 'till ten, Dad! At the Ram." It was Ricky.

"Well, shit, that wasn't supposed to happen," Mercy said.

It was the first time he'd seen Ricky in weeks and the sound of his voice, his boyish directness, tickled him. That's what was so crazy about Lorraine's case against him. He and Ricky always got along like two mutts from the same litter. Dean waved at Ricky but he'd already disappeared.

Mercy looked almost sad. "I'm just trying to protect a friend, Dean."

A Rival

8

Lorraine did what she always did when she came home from the Ram: put her ear to the kids' door to make sure there were three of them. It was quiet. No radio or tape player. Her heart beat a little faster as she turned the knob slowly, disengaging the latch bolt, and then pushed the door in far enough so she could see two lumps under the covers in one bed and one lump in the other with his head on the pillow.

She closed the door, tip-toed to the living room, flipped off her platform shoes, tugged off her ankle socks with the big toe, and squirmed free. Then she walked barefoot across the carpet, grinding her arches into the pile. Nerve endings. Restoration. Between the flower cart and the restaurant, she was on her feet sometimes more than twelve hours a day. She worried that her legs would puff up the way her mom's had and she'd get varicose veins.

When she heard a knock on the door, Lorraine assumed Mercy had gone out for something and forgotten her key. She swung the door wide open before she realized it was Dean. "How'd you know where I was?"

"I got your note at the body shop." She thought she detected something on his breath like grain that had been pulverized with a pestle.

"This isn't a good time, Dean. I'm too tired to argue."

"What's to argue about? Here." He unfolded four $100 bills from his shirt pocket and pushed them into her hand.

"It's not payday."

"I wanted to be early."

If anything, her bitterness had deepened since separating from Dean, like tea bags left in the pot too long. It wasn't just the continuous parade of dirty dishes at the Ram, or the fact she had practically no time with Ricky, or the incessant questions from friends and acquaintances. That was all static. The maddening part was the irrevocable waste of it, the fact that she'd spent the prime of her life trying to build something with Dean. And here she was with dead legs, a sour marriage, and Ricky freaking out. The thing that was going through her mind as she stood there was the old cycle: Dean sweet, Dean romantic, Dean off the deep end again. Dean Hostler wasn't a relationship, he was cotton candy. In the time they'd been apart, she'd tried to put his record in perspective, the way her father would have done at a sentencing. If his losing the trailer had been a first offense, it might have been different. Yet, seeing him standing there downcast in the hallway, with early money for Ricky, it was impossible to do what she should have done. "Come on in," she said, "but just for a minute."

He kissed the tips of his fingers and tapped them gently on the backs of her hands. "I'll disappear the instant you snap your fingers."

"Don't do that, Dean."

"What?"

"That. What you've always done."

Lorraine turned off the lights, except for the one on the stove, so the kids wouldn't wake up and join them. They sat on the couch and split a can of Ginger Ale over ice. Dean put his hands on hers and she drew them away, something she should have done years ago, before they parked at the river and he spread her across the red-checkered tablecloth. Her mother had warned her that you can never go back down the intimacy ladder. But their problem hadn't been the sex, it was the confusion that resulted from the sex. Dean equated sex with personal fulfillment, and for a while so did she.

"You and Ricky gotta come see the horse" -- he held up his hand before she could interrupt him -- "I know you're mad. Just let him see her, then we can sell her and pretend this whole thing never happened."

She pulled her hand out from under his again, like they were in a game of stack-the-hands. "I told you, this isn't just about the horse."

"I can get a better job. I've practically quit drinking." He pointed to his mouth. "Last swallow from a leftover in the truck."

"It's bigger than that, Dean."

That's when he told her about his dream of a crippled boy with a peg leg that everyone teased because he smelled like tar. It was like one of the made-up stories he used to tell Ricky at bedtime. His knee was touching hers and she let it go. She also ignored the stick figures he made on her leg as he talked. "The remarkable thing about this boy was his dog. The dog would bring his lunch to school if the kid forgot it. Wherever the boy was, the dog was with him." Dean's story made her sleepy and she let her head rest against his shoulder. She was no longer listening to the words, but the sound of his voice must have softened her because she didn't stop him when he kissed her on the lips. She gave in to his kiss, rationalizing it as letting him down easy. She wasn't sure how far up the ladder they would have gone because the front door opened, the overhead light came on, and Mercy stood before them in an overcoat and tennis shoes.

"Oh, my!" Mercy said. "Am I interrupting something?"

Lorraine stood up, tucked in her blouse, and patted down her hair. Before she could say anything, Dean was starting for the door.

"I told you, I'm outta here!" He slapped his hip. "I almost forgot." He stiffened his arm, slid his hand into the front pocket of his jeans, and handed her a package the size of a bar of soap wrapped in a Peanuts comic strip from the Sunday paper and tied with a brown shoestring. "It's a present for Ricky."

Lorraine shut the door, slid the end of the safety chain into its groove, and leaned her head against the door to start the examination of conscience. She knew she'd made a mistake. Dean wasn't a person who could handle mixed signals.

Mercy was already in the living room with two jigger glasses filled with something peppermint, and she handed one to Lorraine. "Okay, tell me about it."

"It's nothing. You know Dean."

Mercy took hers down in two gulps. "Of course, I know Dean. I've felt guilty half my life because he screwed up yours. If I let you go back to him, I won't be able to live with myself. Give him hard edges, honey. No more *could of, should of.*"

"He brought me support money."

"For that you let him make out with you?"

"Stop it! I told him he should go."

"I had a little trouble letting go of the first one myself. He kept coming back, and somehow it made it more exotic diddling someone who wasn't my husband anymore."

Lorraine knew she just needed to get through what the books called the *second-guessing stage*, when you wondered if you should give it another try. "Don't worry, I'm not going to exacerbate the situation by having sex with him."

Mercy took the untouched jigger out of Lorraine's hands, set it on the phone table, and gave her a hug. "The mourning period's over. See someone else, sister. Take your mind off the past." She looked into Lorraine's eyes. "I have someone in mind."

Lorraine paced circles around the kitchen table as she watched for the car in the street below. Mercy had agreed to work Lorraine's night shift at the Ram, and they were letting the kids order in sausage and pepperoni pizza. Without vegetables. A neighbor across the hall had agreed to check on them every half hour. It had been ages since she'd gone anywhere that people wore cocktail dresses and suits. Mercy had lent her a black crepe pantsuit with scalloped lapels, French cuffs, and jeweled buttons. The pants felt flimsy, but Mercy assured her she looked hot. "Fluidity of movement," she said. Mercy also suggested she go braless. "Make a statement."

"Not with *my* equipment."

When Ricky asked where she was going, she told him it was a stage play, focusing more on the *what* than the *who*. If he'd pushed it, she'd have told him she was going out with a friend, and if he'd pushed it further, she'd have told him it was someone she knew from school. She couldn't imagine telling him it was a man, not this soon. She hated to be evasive with Ricky, candor was part of their bond. She was convinced, however, that despite his acting out with the shoplifting he was better off with Dean removed from the challenges of his daily life. Out there, in the great beyond, Dean's shortcomings were less influential on Ricky. Out there, she could let Ricky idealize him without fear of being proven wrong the next time Dean showed up with liquor on his breath or didn't show up at all. As simply a picture on Ricky's nightstand, Dean could almost be a hero.

She felt guilty going out because her nights off were so rare. She sensed that Ricky was starved for time alone with her, that he needed something to do besides watch TV in that long stretch of the day until bedtime when his pills wore off and he became so restless. Still, she had to do this. If *she* was more settled, she could settle Ricky. She had decided to go back to that juncture in her life where she still had choices, where she could find someone who made fewer promises but followed through on the ones he *did* make. She was tired of getting pumped up and then popped. She hungered for stability. Besides, her companion wasn't just anyone.

A large white car with tinted windows and a chrome gargoyle on the hood pulled up in front of the apartment and double-parked, its emergency lights blinking. "Goodbye!" Lorraine yelled toward the TV room, which was also Mercy's bedroom. "The pizza moneys on the table!" There was a muffled chorus of goodbyes. Now she just had to negotiate one flight of stairs in her heels and intercept her date before he could ring himself in on the intercom and start a conversation with one of the kids. This was strictly a tryout. If it didn't work, then it had never happened, so there was no sense in getting Ricky all wound up over nothing.

Her break with Dean finally offered the opportunity to set her life on its intended course. If it worked, she could start going to church again, she could ask for a general confession to erase her teenage and adult sins and resume receiving the sacraments again. Maybe she could also shake her depression, get off the cycle of anti-depressants. Most important, she could possibly find somebody to help mentor Ricky, somebody who showed up. She hadn't really ever given *him* a fair chance. A couple of innocent dates and the one night she let down her guard. She'd effectively betrayed him by going out with Dean and then never looking back.

Judge Culhane and her *companion* for the evening, Gifford Pomeroy, were in Rotary together. They'd co-chaired a committee to raise money for a log gazebo in Liberty Park. Gifford personally raised so much money they had to build two gazebos. "Now there's a man of substance," Judge Culhane had chided. A part of her was excited to be able to tell the Judge that she was separated from Dean and seeing Gifford. Of course, a part of her dreaded it.

Although they'd lived in the same town together, Lorraine knew very little about Gifford's private life. He'd never married and even Mercy was clueless who he might have dated. He had no relatives in Renton. His mother had passed away, but Lorraine couldn't have said when, and his father had been killed in an accident when Gifford was still a kid. How had Dean put it? "Gifford's old man was queer in the head and his mother was loopy, so what do you think that makes him?" Still, she'd always wondered. And now that she was extricated from the Dean Hostler circus, her appetite for someone very much unlike Dean was irresistible.

When she reached the ground floor, Gifford was already on the porch, scouring the faded list of tenant names under the plastic laminate. When she burst out of the entrance to the apartment house, he reared back. "My, don't you look nice?"

"Well, so do you!" And he did, in a double-knit Dacron blazer with silver buttons and slacks. Gifford Pomeroy was shorter and more compact than Dean, with worry lines around his eyes, but his carriage was good, like a man accustomed to respect. He offered his arm and escorted Lorraine to the car. Knowing he was a successful real estate broker, she expected the interior to reek of tobacco smoke, but instead it had the scent of new leather. She watched Gifford walk around the front of the car, while she listened to the classical music playing on the radio. Mozart, she guessed. She'd heard all the great composers at home, but she never risked interrupting her father's reading to identify the pieces. She'd not listened to classical music since marrying Dean. In the trailer, the little TV with rabbit ears was always on. The sitcoms were one of the few things that calmed Ricky down at night. Along with Dean's bedtime stories.

While Gifford was shedding his overcoat and laying it across the backseat, she impulsively pulled open the ashtray under the radio and stuck her finger in. There was what felt like hard candy wrapped in cellophane. Lorraine couldn't help but think of the last time she'd gone out on a date, when even though seatbelts were required she'd sat in the middle so Dean could put his arm around her and drive one-handed with the steering knob on his dad's Impala. The idea was to sit so close that, from behind, it looked like there was only one person in the car.

Gifford turned the music down. His fingernails were clean and evenly manicured, with white crescent edges. "Those pendants are perfect for your face," he said. She couldn't remember Dean ever noticing the shape of her face, which she always thought was too oblong.

She smiled. "Mercy lent them to me."

Gifford made a U-turn and headed back through the downtown. Lorraine peered into the Ram as they passed to see how busy it was. Mercy was standing over a couple of truck drivers with a coffee carafe cocked against her hip. Although she'd never confirmed it, Lorraine suspected that Mercy was behind Gifford's sudden interest in her.

They stopped at the light where she used to turn for the trailer park. "Do you like Arthur Miller?" Gifford asked. Lorraine racked her brain to think of the kids they'd gone to high school with. "The playwright," he added mercifully, "the one who married Marilyn Monroe."

"I'm sorry, of course! The slender fellow with glasses."

Gifford laughed. "Yeah, the slender fellow who gave a bad name to people like Willy Loman who go on the road to make sales for a living." Gifford alternated glances between the rear and side mirrors as he gunned the car into the northbound freeway traffic to Seattle and worked his way into the left passing lane. "I think I'm chasing a buck to prove something to my old man. Not exactly the American dream."

She was taken aback by his candor. "I didn't know your father."

"Neither did I," he said, abruptly. "He was a store clerk who brought home a modest wage when he worked, and hardly noticed Mother and me. A total loner." Gifford's hands were strangling the steering wheel. "Mom finally got fed up with him and moved out. I expected him to fight back, but he just let her divvy things up like it was a game of *Parcheesi*. When she asked him if he wanted to have me summers, he said he'd rather have the Buick."

"That's horrible!"

"I couldn't blame him. I was a jerk at that age."

Gifford constantly switched lanes to keep the car speed up, yet she trusted his driving, probably because she trusted his self-deprecation. "When I sold my first house at nineteen, I caught fire. For the first time in my life, I realized I didn't need my dad."

The play was Arthur Miller's *The Price* and they sat in orchestra seats, close enough to see the perspiration on the actors' faces. Two brothers, a policeman and a doctor, met in the attic of their deceased father's house to make arrangements with a Jewish pawnbroker for the disposition of their family's once classic furniture. As the play progressed, she couldn't help but think the play was a bad choice, something sure to gnaw at Gifford's pain from his own father's disappearance. She noticed that he didn't laugh at the pawnbroker, who she found amusing.

At the intermission, Gifford bought champagne and a cup of mixed nuts and ushered them to a high table surrounded by stools in a far corner of the lobby. A couple of people Lorraine hadn't seen since high school showed up at their table, and she kept thinking someone would ask her about Dean. Gifford introduced her to the friends she didn't know as Lorraine Hostler, which sounded strange in the presence of so many people who knew her as Culhane. He called her an old friend, which sounded surprisingly comfortable.

"See what I mean?" Gifford said on the way back to their seats, while the lights were flickering to signal the start of the second act. "I cover up my insecurities by sticking with people who owe me."

Gifford made no attempt to capture her hand in the dark or to put his arm around her, although he did brush against her flimsy pants with the back of his hand a few times. As the play evolved and the brothers quarreled, Gifford handed over his handkerchief, which was embroidered with a *GP* in the corner. She found herself identifying with the policeman who discovered that while he was supporting their destitute father on low wages his older brother was getting money from their father to finance his medical school education.

Afterwards, they went to the Four-Ten restaurant in downtown Seattle for a spinach salad, with warm bacon dressing, and zabaglione for dessert. The restaurant was lit with crystal chandeliers and votive candles that flamed at every table. Their waiter wore a starched shirt and tails and spoke with an endearing Italian accent. Gifford was at ease with the menu and the myriad of utensils.

"I'm enjoying this, Lorraine." His brown eyes sparkled in the candlelight and the palms of his hands opened softly towards hers. "But I hope I'm not intruding on something I shouldn't be."

She was ready to resist any premature advances, but she was unprepared to talk about her and Dean. Frankly, she was unaccustomed to communicating in the kind of measured way that Gifford was inviting. Talks with Dean had been more akin to bouts, where she could respond recklessly to a reckless proposition. "You're not trespassing, if that's what you mean."

"I want to do more than just obey the law."

Lorraine knew that he was fishing and she didn't want to be coy. "I'm ready to file a petition for divorce if that's what you're asking. I'm at that point. As soon as I can afford the attorney."

"This isn't twenty questions."

She watched him write her initials in the table linen with the handle of his spoon, then smooth it over with his hand. She knew she'd said too much. She hadn't even used the *D* word with Dean yet, and here she was blurting it out to Gifford, making her feel so calculated.

"I am a great admirer of Judge Culhane," he said. "I know folks he helped with down payments on their homes. I'd be honored to return the favor if that's the issue."

"Let's not talk about this."

Gifford didn't say much on the way home, and Lorraine was sure it was because she'd cut him off. Yet, sticking up for Dean at least once in the evening had allowed her to feel better about going out on him. In the lobby of the theater there had been no threat of running into him but, as they got closer to the Renton exit, they were returning to Dean's territory and although she didn't know where Dean was living, she could feel him. "My turn to ask a question," she said.

"Shoot."

"We're almost the same age. Why *haven't* you married?"

He thumped the steering column with his thumb and nodded his head up and down. "I almost did. A woman from Saint Cloud I met at a real estate seminar. We commuted back and forth for almost two years. I told her I'd move there if she wanted, but I couldn't pull the trigger. Actually, she asked *me*, and I still couldn't do it."

"Too much real estate for one marriage?"

"I guess I was just wary of the wrong fit."

She couldn't help herself from saying something she shouldn't have. "You would have made a good father."

He smiled and cupped her hand. "*There's* a leap of faith, but thank you, Lorraine."

When they reached Mercy's apartment building, he walked her to the door, this time with his arm loosely around her waist. They stood there under the glare of the motion light and Lorraine searched for a way to tell him how nice this had been. Her Catholic education had reinforced the notion of men as predators. So had *Ms.* magazine. Yet, here she was with one of the most successful businessmen in south King County and not wanting to say good night.

"Thanks, Gifford. I feel elevated by the whole evening!"

"Me too. Seventeen years was worth the wait, or was it longer?" He wrapped his arms around her and she pursed her lips for a kiss, but he buried his head against hers and just squeezed. He was thicker than Dean and it wasn't just his overcoat. There was more to him. He was a man who talked rather than flirted, and the effect was pure rapture.

Lorraine took off her heels and tiptoed into the apartment. She checked on Ricky and, as she stood next to his bed, indulged herself in a brief fantasy where she, Gifford and Ricky had just come home from the stage play. She stripped off her pantsuit and hung it on the back of the bathroom door. She was glad Mercy wasn't up because she wanted to savor the evening before the cross-examination. Strange as it seemed, she also wanted to talk to Dean, to flop out on top of the bedspread with a breadboard full of cheese and crackers, and once again hear his analysis of Gifford Pomeroy, how he was such a master of first impressions but someone not to turn your back on. This time, however, she wasn't going to give in to Dean's biases out of spousal loyalty. Neither she nor Gifford had said anything about the loss of her virginity or his.

She felt like a teenager in her corner bedroom again where she used to kneel down on a ragdoll next to the bed and pray for a good marriage, healthy children, and breasts. She hoped this feeling would last, that daylight wouldn't prick the bubble.

9

Mom must a thought I was stupider than she let on. Like I would'n see her go. I saw her get in tha' big Buick with a short guy in a sport coat and tie. Pretty damn fancy! Someone who opens the door for you. I didn' see him curtsy but it wouldn' a surprised me. And she'd said she was too tired at night to go places. Well, scratch that idea. So, yeah, I played a stupid game of Old Maid with Sam and Cory. Yippee! One a them won every game. It was like they were baby sittin' me. Like I heard Mercy tell 'em I can get excited so let him win if you can. Well, I didn' fall for it. After they left, I walked 'round the house till I found something I could slug. Hard. Again and again. I found a baseball bat in S'mantha's closet. A real one. Not one a them 'junior' versions. I'm tired a bein' junior.

So I carried that bat 'roun the house, jus' gettn' mad and madder 'bout my mom goin' out on Dad. Sneakn' behind his back. Probably lettin' some stranger feel her up and playn' diddle with her. I didn' know the guy in the Buick from siccum, but jus' the picture of him bein' all nicey nicey with my mom was enough. And behind my dad's back! My god, Mom, yore married! What kind of example is that to parade aroun'?

An' I'm gettn' pretty tired of my 'cousins' askn' me questions about my dad. What happn' to yore dad, Ricky? I heard he did somethin' real stupid again. Like his brain had exploded. Samantha kept remindn' me that she used to have a dad too. Said she knew how I felt. Crap, what'd I care 'bout *her* dad? He was long gone. Prob'ly never seen again. Maybe if yore a girl, it don' matter if yore dad disappears on you. But I liked my dad. We did things. Like shootn' his rifle and shootn' at squirrels. You shoulda jus' seen the junked up cars my dad hammered out an' fixed up like new.

Anyway, I couldn' get over bein' pissed, so I went back to the bedroom I shared with the cousins. Tha' was at least kid territory an' who cared what kids do. I closed the door. Didn' wanna give a bad example to the cousins. I was jus' itchn' all over to hit somebody. Like the guy who took Mom in the Buick. So I took a crayon and made a circle on the wall 'bout where his head might a been.

I never played baseball. All they had at my school was PE, which everyone said stood for *Plain Empty*. Like me. But I put that bat on my shoulder like I was Mickey Mantle. Someone powerful. The guy who took Mom out was on the other team an' he was pitchn' so I didn' wanna miss gettn' a hit. I closed my eyes, said to myself now or never hotshot, and waggled the bat 'roun just to get the feel of it. Then I closed my eyes tight an' jus buried the end a' tha' stick in the sheetrock! BOOM! Couldn' prob'ly done tha' in the Nashua, but hot damn, I buried the head a' tha' sucker in the sheetrock and made my own bat hole.

Of course, Mom balled me out big time when she saw what I'd done, said how disappointed she was. How it wasn't like me, blah, blah, blah. She said I was gonna hafta learn how to patch sheetrock and use my own money doin' it. I said wha' money. An' she said, tha's yore problem.

Tha's when she also got on her soap box 'bout a special school for screwed up kids. Who wants to live with a bunch of loser kids my own age? How's tha' gonna help fix what Mom thinks is broken?

I'm a teenager. Haven' you ever heard of late bloomers? Lots of famous people got what I got. Heck, jus' 'bout ev'ry teenager goes thru hell and back for one reason or 'nother. Cool it, Mom! I'm more like Dad. I'm an inventor. Someone with new ideas! I've got energy. But I sure ain't gonna spend it on other mixed up kids. You even told me this's somethin' I'm gonna grow out of.

I told her she's throw'n me under the bus. Now, me *and* Dad. What's wrong with this picture? Yore smart. You tell me.

10

Doctor Babcock, the vet Jill had recommended, was a rotund man, hardly the build of a horseman, with baggy fatigue pants tucked into his shiny black galoshes, and a wool plaid hunting shirt that tucked into his fatigues. He'd agreed to meet during Dean's lunch hour. He was late, but he wasted no time getting down to business. When he showed Orphan a handful of mash from a plastic bag in one of his pockets, she perked her ears forward, swished her tail, and sauntered over to him. Dean felt redundant, the same way he'd felt in high school when the girls only noticed the guys who started on the football team. Babcock walked around Orphan as he talked, the same way Jill had, lifting the tail, pushing back her lips to check the teeth. "Kind of late in the year, but look out for worms," he said. "Has she been eating her dung?"

"They do that?"

"Keep the manure shoveled up!"

"Of course!"

He circled Orphan again, picking up and examining each hoof.

"She lets you do that?" Dean asked.

"We smelled each other's breath. We're friends now, or at least not enemies." He chomped at Orphan's mane with his fingers bent against his thumb. "They like to be touched. Same thing you probably do with your wife."

"That's what Jill said?"

"It's worse in the fall when the botflies are out. They leave their eggs on the legs. Then they show up in the stools and you have to give them a paste or drench their stomachs with a tube down the nostrils. Keep the manure picked up!"

Dean's second thoughts were turning to third thoughts. *People with jobs do this?*

Babcock chuckled. "It's like cramming for a big exam. Once in a while you'll have to pull an all-nighter. Live like a horse. They sleep three, four hours a day and that's in short snoozes. And they do it mostly standing."

"That's no problem, I'm a night guy." Dean wanted to mention the fact that he and Orphan were sleeping in the stable together, but he wasn't sure how smart that was. Maybe he had worms too. "You can always hire a groom. Jill will know someone. She's forgotten more about horses than most vets ever know."

Without explanation, Babcock went out to his 4x4 and came back with a second black bag full of steel files, chisels, hammers and a pair of pincers. He stood with his back to Orphan, lifted the left front hoof and wedged it between his knees. Dean's job was to hold onto the shank while Orphan rotated her ears to listen to the groan of the nail as the vet pried the horseshoe off the hoof with his pincers. To Dean's amazement, she neither kicked nor fled.

"A lot of vets won't do shoes, but I look forward to the chance," Babcock said. "She's got a bad nail hole. Feel that."

Dean reached down and gripped the hoof where the doctor pointed. "It's warm."

"Feel the other side. See the difference?"

The vet pushed his thumb against the underside of the hoof. "There's your lameness. Somebody drove the nail in crooked."

With one of the tools from his bag, the doctor enlarged the hole and dabbed all around it with tincture of iodine. Dean kept looking at Orphan, whose ears were alternately alert, then pinned against her head. "Sorry, pal." While they stood face to face, Dean made a point of exhaling toward Orphan's nostrils and inhaling her breath, which was warm and surprisingly sweet for someone who didn't brush. Her brown eyes, which had to be more than ten times the size of a human's, kept looking at Dean as if to ask whether he was still up to the task. Dean looked away.

"You're going to have to soak this hoof in warm water and Epsom salts for ten minutes two, three times a day for a while. I'll fill the hole with Ichthammol. It's an old fashion drawing agent. I'll put a boot on to keep it clean."

The more he talked the heavier Dean's head became, and there was a pain at the base of the skull. He was wondering why someone at the auction hadn't bothered to point out the downstream implications of horse ownership. Even cigarettes came with warnings on the pack. In his mind's eye, Dean had likened raising a horse to driving a car, something a little tricky to begin with, but which quickly became second nature.

In order to up his credentials, Dean briefly entertained the idea of telling the vet about Otto Hostler, the blacksmith in his family. But, of course, the vet was an educated man. He'd know this kind of skill wasn't hereditary. "Tell me honestly, Doc. I'm not trained. I get queasy when I see blood. Do you think I'm going to be able to handle this?"

The vet finished pulling a black bootie up over the hoof, cinched it, and straightened himself up. There were beads of sweat on his forehead like the bubbles on water about to boil. Then he reached over and patted Dean on the shoulder. "Make the horse a priority and you'll be fine, sir. Keep her hooves trimmed for balance. Ignore her and she'll melt down on you as sure as a fudgesicle in the sun."

"I got her for my son," Dean said.

"My dad bought *me* an Appaloosa when I was a kid. White snow all over his butt. I wanted that horse more than a car." Babcock wiped his eye with the sleeve of his jacket. "That Appaloosa is why I'm a large animal vet."

"Ricky hasn't seen her yet."

"This isn't a pet, you know. A thoroughbred's an athlete, a creature made to run. Keep an eye on her conformation."

"Her what?"

"Her front feet turn in a bit. The forelimbs bear two-thirds of the body weight. You need healthy hooves. No hoof, no horse. You need a good farrier is what you need."

"A what?"

"A good farrier will keep the hooves trimmed right."

"Are they bad?"

"Borderline, I'd say." Dean knew borderline. He and Lorraine had taken up residence there with Ricky's condition.

The vet stayed until two-thirty talking horses, telling Dean how to break her, how to read her tail and her ears, the difference between a friendly nicker and a warning snort.

"The horse is a nomad," he said. "They avoid their oppressors by scattering, becoming centerless, staying on the move. It's part of being a prey species. Cooped up isn't what their genes are used to."

Dean decided he liked this man, and he wondered if this was how his own great grandfather Otto was. The more the vet talked horses the more Dean was drawn to Orphan, to her mysterious heart, to her ancestors and his own. Rather than risk bouncing a check, Dean told Babcock he'd pay him at the end of the week. "After payday."

"You get in any trouble, just ask Jill. She's gone to hell and back with horses."

Dean blew off the body shop for the rest of the afternoon and brushed Orphan with the curry comb the vet had left behind. When he was tired of brushing, Dean just sat down in the stall and watched how she moved, tried to read her tail. As dusk turned in the direction of night, he started to feel panicky. He had none of the equipment to soak Orphan's foot: no pail, not even hot water in the barn. He wondered again how he was going to blow antibiotics down her throat, paste her for worms, teach her to accept a bit, and still keep his job so he could pay Lorraine child support and convince her to take him back.

As he sat there with his back against the wall of the barn, he thought of the other night with Lorraine on the couch in Mercy's apartment, and how delicious that single kiss had been. You could have blindfolded Dean, put him in a room full of lips, and he would have still found Lorraine's. He'd memorized their grip and their give. He knew he shouldn't have kissed her at Mercy's. It was too soon, and too much like before. He could taste the hunger in Lorraine for something different. He'd given himself a talking to, all right. He was getting tired of sitting on the bench and begged the coach to put him in the game, but when Lorraine let him into the apartment the other night he ran the same old play.

He also shouldn't have stood outside on the sidewalk afterwards staring up at the second floor, watching the lights go on and off, but he had to know where on this spinning globe Lorraine rested her head at night. For almost eighteen years, it had been next to his and that marvelous brain had dreamed inches from his own.

When Dean looked up, Orphan was standing over him, her muscular neck blocking the moon rising over the pasture. Dean couldn't see her eyes, but he knew they were still asking whether he was up to the task. The black bootie was still on her foot. He rubbed the back of her knee and she relaxed her leg so Dean could pick it up. He was touched; she had no reason to trust him. Orphan nipped at his shirt pockets and tried to nuzzle under his armpits to see if his rank smell was something to eat. He pressed in on her midsection to see if he could feel the ribs. She sidled away like she was ticklish, then bared her teeth and ripped a big sliver off the top rail of the stall, frightening the scraggy orange cat, who jumped out of harm's way. Doctor Babcock had told him that horses were social animals. In the wild, he said, they organized in harems with one stallion and his mares. The stallion kept other males away. So what did that make Dean and Orphan Annalina?

It would have been a good time to bail out, but all avenues seemed closed. Dean had tried to find a buyer with no success and the girl who'd raised her said they couldn't take her back. He almost had to laugh. He'd bought a horse so a woman he didn't even know could fix her truck. *Not exactly sainthood*, Dean thought, *but I've done dumber things.*

Dean was in the stable soaking Orphan's foot in a mop bucket when he heard familiar voices approaching. Orphan heard them too and exited to the pasture. One voice was Jill's, and Dean took a quick look around to make sure he hadn't left out any sharp objects or toxic substances. She'd found his collection of 45 rpm records in the corner of the stall and told him to leave them up at the house. She'd also posted a note on his door about leaving an empty Coke bottle in the straw. "The horse could step on it and eat the chards," she said. He was steamed at first, taking it as criticism of his horsemanship, until he remembered everything else she'd done for him, lending him the sleeping bag and pillow, the water jug on a stand in the barn, soap and towels and, of course, water from the laundry room faucet. She'd even given him a key to her house.

"Dad?"

"Ricky! What are you doing here?"

Ricky looked down at his tennis shoes, and Dean realized he'd barked at him. "Rode my bike." His voice was apologetic.

"How'd you know where I was?"

He pulled a piece of paper from his pocket. "Your note had an address on the back."

Dean studied the note he'd scratched out on one of Jill's business pads and folded into the compass case he'd given Ricky and left with Lorraine. "I didn't think you'd . . . does your mom know you're here?"

"She thinks I'm doin' a paper route."

Dean knew he should have bawled him out. Lorraine wouldn't have believed that he could figure out a map or find an address. That was part of what they'd argued about, and Lorraine always took the side of what Ricky couldn't do. "I'm glad you came, pal!"

Jill peaked her head into the stall, "It looks like you don't need me anymore."

"I'm sorry," Dean said, turning Ricky around by his waist, "this is my son, Ricky." Jill's sleeves were wet with something up to the elbows. "We've met." She wiped her hand backwards and frontwards on her pants and stuck it out for Ricky. He wouldn't shake.

"Ricky?"

"That's all right," Jill said.

Jill went back up to the house and Dean sat down with Ricky on a bale of hay. The marmalade cat strolled under the gate and rubbed against Ricky's pantleg.

"How's school, kid?" Dean reached over and tousled his hair. "God, it's good to see you!"

"Sucks." His voice was subdued.

Dean bumped him with his elbow. "How's your digs at Mercy's?"

"That sucks too."

This didn't make sense. He'd pedaled five miles to get there and now he wouldn't talk. Dean tried to shake him out of it. "You gotta let me get a word in, son."

Ricky was engrossed in a piece of straw that he'd wrapped around his index finger. "You live with *her*?" He nodded toward the house.

"Jill? Oh, no. What made you think that?"

Ricky picked up another clump of straw and winnowed it down to a single strand. Then he did the finger wrap again. A light went on in Dean's mind, and he gripped Ricky under the armpits and dragged him over by the door to the pasture. He was still a flyweight. "Close your eyes." Dean reached through the slats in the fence and cupped a handful of oats from the open bag in the next stall. "Make a lake with your hands." Dean dumped the oats into Ricky's hands and positioned him next to the opening with his arms extended. "Don't move."

Orphan was in the upper corner of the pasture, under the tree. Dean whistled and her ears turned like radar dishes toward the barn. Doctor Babcock said a horse had sixteen muscles in each ear and could rotate them a hundred and eighty degrees. A horse could hear an earthquake before it happened. Ricky was new, something to be wary of, somebody whose breath she'd never sampled. Yet, there was a handful of oats sticking out there for the taking. Dean figured if an adult male horse could smell a mare in heat a half mile away, Orphan could smell those oats from twenty yards. Orphan drew back the corners of her mouth and opened and shut her jaws.

"Hold your hands steady, Rick. Just like I taught you with the rifle." Orphan was walking towards the barn now, her head at a jaunty angle so she wouldn't miss anything in the blind spot between her eyes. She was no longer limping. Her stride was even. She was five yards away. "Hold your breath."

Ricky's cheeks puffed out. Orphan made a straight line toward his cupped hand, blowing air through her huge nostrils. When she reached Ricky, she nuzzled and slobbered the grain out of the crevices between his outstretched fingers. Then Ricky opened his eyes, and that's when Dean heard the click that a horse must hear when the earth shakes.

11

I knew it was a horse all the time. I could smell 'im. Dad said it was a her, which at first I didn' like. When he said she was mine, I said he was lyin', but I must have believed him because I couldn' even keep lookin' at her. I closed my eyes and crumpled over in the mud.

I went to Dad because I was mad at Mom. She was so strict it made me feel even more stupid. Then sometimes she'd baby me and that felt even worse. I knew her plan was to make money and get a new house, which was better than livin' with Cory and Sammy. They didn' have a dad either, so I guess this was better than livin' with the Judge who didn't have a clue and was even more strict than Mom. Mercy wasn' so bad, it was just her kids. Mom could'a used some of Mercy's jokes. The only thing I hated was the way Mercy always smothered you against her tits try'n to make you feel better.

Mom and Dad were from different tribes, but I never thought she'd kick 'im out. She didn' even tell me at first. She never told me the important stuff. In a way, though, it was better than him just leav'n. I could see why he would, but it was better that Mom kicked him out, because that meant he didn' wanna go. Cory said he'd be livin' with another woman and we got in a fight over it and I made a big slit across his bike seat so the stuffin' oozed out and told him he was lucky it wasn't his brains. He tried to wreck my bike too, but I hid it in the dumpster behind the Seven 'leven til he cooled off. I knew he'd try somethin' else but that's when I decided to find Dad.

So guess what? Maybe he is livin' with that woman. I hope not. That'd make me just leftovers.

The horse made me think of the elephant Dad told me about. The one who loved the girl elephant in the same cage at the zoo. Reg'lar love birds, he said. Then the girl elephant got sick and the old man elephant jus' stood over her for six days 'til she died. Then he would'n eat or drink anythin' and his skin got droopy and he starved himself to death. Dad said all animals have bigger hearts than people do. He told me this when I didn' wanna go back to school after summer was over. He sat on my bed and cried and then I cried and asked him why he'd tell me a story like that when I was feelin' crappy about goin' to school anyway, and he said it was to show there was always someone worse off.

I must have inherited somethin' 'bout animals from Dad 'cause when I turned round, the horse was there lookin' at me and I could tell right away what Dad meant about animal hearts. I tried not to cry but I knew the horse could see right thru me. Whether she was mine or not I was gonna love that horse even if it meant quittin' school and not havin' a mom and dad. Well, I wasn't sure about that last part.

Dad showed me how to share my breath with Orphan and comb her and he swore me not to tell Mom, but I knew that was mainly 'cause he didn' want Mom to know about the woman. I loved that the horse was named Orphan. Just like me.

Dad hoisted my ten-speed into the back of the pickup and drove me back to Mercy's that first time. I didn' ask him about the woman at the farm because he'd been so cool 'bout Orphan the way he made it seem like she was really mine. I also didn' tell him 'bout gettin' caught swipin' stuff at the Freddie Meyer store or sellin' pills at school. Now that Mom thought I had the paper route, I had to have the pill money to prove I wasn' lying. Otherwise, I couldn' see Orphan. Dad didn' say much drivin' back either. He wasn't very good at saying important stuff, but who was I to talk?

He dropped me off a block away and brushed the mud off my pants and rubbed my head so nobody'd know where I'd been. He said it felt good just to be whackin' my pants again. And I didn' wanna spoil things by tell'n him 'bout the new man Mom was see'n.

12

It didn't take Dean long to find a groom. Ricky bicycled down to the Spragues' nearly every day after school as well as Saturdays.

"How you getting away with this?"

Ricky rubbed the insides of his pantlegs together at the same time as he rubbed his elbows against his ribs. "Kid at school told me 'bout his paper route, so I got one."

"But how can you do that if you're down here?"

"It's a fib, Dad." He pointed out to the pasture. "Orphan's my paper route."

Lorraine had worked so hard at honesty that it concerned Dean to see how easily her lessons had been lost on Ricky. Her insistence on honesty had been the steepest part of the hill for Dean, who'd grown up with a father who believed you had to make a choice between survival and the truth. It wasn't the lies that had banished his father to the garage; it was the truth. The day he told Dean's mother how he lost the papers for the patent on the wind deflectors, she chased him out the back door with an electric mixer that looked like it was still turning even after she pulled the cord from the plug. This was supposed to be the invention that was going to make *Hostler* a household name, like *Maytag* and *Kleenex*. "Are you comfortable with a fib, Ricky?"

Ricky looked at his dad wide-eyed. "You said me comin' here had to be secret!" This was probably exactly what Lorraine had in mind when she said that Dean was always working at cross-purposes with her.

"Something can be a secret and still not a lie, son." It was difficult to talk like Lorraine when he didn't think like her.

In truth, Ricky had already become horse-crazy the way Dean had been Lorraine-crazy. Every tidbit of horse wisdom that Dean learned from Jill and the vet he passed on to Ricky, who glommed onto it and put it into practice. By the time Dean came home from the body shop, Ricky had usually fed and watered Orphan, combed out her tail and mane, brushed her, and also curry combed the cat.

Then Ricky discovered the round pen, which was a corral with no corners on the other side of the barn. Judging from the weeds, it hadn't been used much lately. Ricky stood in the center of the pen with a lead on Orphan and made her walk and trot around him. By stepping towards Orphan, Ricky could make her speed up or slow down, like he was herding her, but she had no corners to hide in and had to keep moving. Orphan towered over Ricky, but he was fearless. Sometimes Ricky would run next to Orphan's front shoulder trying to keep up with her. He was smart about it; if Orphan got ahead of him, Ricky just made a shorter circle and caught up with her on the other side of the loop. They'd do this for hours, until both of them were sweating. Then Ricky added another wrinkle to their workouts, one that almost brought a halt to their playtimes. He started stepping in front of Orphan to make her stop, his hundred pounds and change against a half ton of horse. Orphan dodged him and kept going, but Ricky didn't give up.

One day, Dean came home and found Ricky in the round pen with a rope on Orphan slapping at her feet with a burlap sack while Orphan danced away. Ricky was studying every twitch of her tail and toss of her head. Dean had gone from worrying about Ricky to worrying about Orphan. He almost yelled at him to stop teasing the horse, but there was something going on that only the two of them seemed to understand. Gradually, Orphan stopped jumping away from the burlap and started marching in a circle around Ricky, bobbing her head up and down, her tail hanging loose again. Then when Ricky dropped the burlap, unsnapped the rope, and turned away from Orphan, she started following him around the pen with her muzzle over his shoulder like they were bosom buddies just walking home from school.

"What was that gunnysack thing all about?" Dean asked when he met Ricky at the gate.

"Jill said it'll teach her to handle anythin' thrown at her."

"I thought you didn't like Jill."

He turned away with no comment.

Ricky made up games to play with Orphan. One day he looped a long clothesline around her neck and drove her from behind in figure eights like she was pulling a buggy. When they were done, Orphan followed him back to the stall, chewing and licking her lips. Jill said horses were intimidated by someone taller. If you raised your hands over their head they'd cower. The reverse must have also been true too as Dean watched how comfortable Orphan was in the company of her sawed-off groom. But Ricky didn't just do the fun stuff. With a pitchfork and straight shovel, he loaded up the wheelbarrow with soiled wheat straw from the stall and dumped it into the dung bin behind the barn, then fluffed up the bedding, leaving it soft and springy for Orphan. He even shoveled up the dung in the pasture.

"Dung is our enemy, Dad."

Dean always had friends when he was Ricky's age. Except for Gifford, none of them worked, so free time was like natural gas, waiting for an errant spark. He remembered making a water ski rope out of a clothesline, tying it to the stem of his bike seat, and taking turns pulling friends around in the street on steel roller skates with clamps that hooked onto your shoes. The idea was to pedal as fast as you could and then make a sharp turn to crack the whip and dump the other guy off. Vibrating out of your skates was like jumping from a moving car because you had to get your feet going as fast as the rest of your body, but if you lost it you'd tumble like a piece of lint blown out of the dryer vent. Dean plastered himself against a picket fence once, and a week later his mother extracted a hardened crystal of dried blood from his left ear with a pair of tweezers.

One evening when Dean came back to the Spragues Ricky's bike was on the ground by the barn door, in too much of a hurry to use his kick stand. The stall was empty and so was the round pen. Then he noticed that the gate at the far end of the pasture was ajar.

Dammit, Dean thought, *the horse is loose.*

Ricky must have been messing with the gate and Orphan made a break for it. Jill had made a point of telling them to keep Orphan out of the cow pasture so it wouldn't get overgrazed. As he trudged up the hill, Dean wondered, quite frankly, what all the fuss was about. There seemed to be plenty of grass, also water, which was soaking through his work shoes and wicking up his socks as he headed toward the rise. *Where's your brain, Ricky?* Once he got to the top of the hill he thought he'd be able to survey the terrain. How hard could it be to spot a horse? There were hoof prints in the mud, but they were going in circles like Orphan was acting crazy. Then he heard a scream like a Comanche war cry from the horizon. He first saw the horse's head and then almost hidden behind her neck, hugging her with all his might, Ricky came barreling over the top of the hill on Orphan Annalina.

"Pull her up!" Dean yelled. Ricky was bareback. They were heading straight for Dean, and Ricky was leaning into Orphan. Dean turned sideways and braced himself to catch Ricky. "Jump!"

Ricky went by in a blur, his knees dug into Orphan's sides, a window of air opening and closing between the horse's back and Ricky's butt. Then Ricky pulled on the bridle, Orphan twisted her head to shake loose, and Ricky tugged until her jaw was practically against her chest. "Whoa, Lina! Whoa, girl!" Orphan's legs stiffened and stamped the ground as she rotated in a circle, snorting and puffing. Her eyes were inflamed. Dean raised his hands and calmly walked over and took a tight grip of the reins. Orphan nodded her head up and down like she was ready to run again.

"Dammit, you could've been killed!"

"No way, Dad!" Ricky was panting, and his eyes were wild too. "She runs like the wind!"

Dean wanted to abandon himself to Ricky's excitement, and if Lorraine had been there to put on the brakes, he would have, but this was different. He was going somewhere now without Lorraine.

Dean tried to honor Lorraine's request to stay away, but then the sap would overflow and he'd stumble into the Ram in the evening just to sit there and watch her work. She looked like a stewardess in her uniform and with his eyes he'd caress her rump and run his hands up and down the soft part of her calves as she carried plates, wiped tables, and took orders on the pad she pulled in and out of her apron pocket. And he'd order *a la carte* so she'd have to come back more often. His tips were almost as much as the price of the meal.

"Ignore me," he told her. "I'm just getting my fix."

"Don't, Dean."

"Why don't you let Ricky live with me for a while?"

"In your truck? No way."

Dean had to bite his tongue to keep from telling her where he was really staying, but there was no way she'd let Ricky sleep in a stall. He'd have to wait until he had something more traditional.

Some nights Dean drove into town and sat in his truck across the street from Mercy's apartment, waiting for Lorraine to come home. By the time she'd get there, he'd sometimes given in and taken a shot from the bottle in the glove box, which disqualified him from any rendezvous. One night, when he'd managed to stay dry by chewing through a pack of Juicy Fruit, he made the trip across the street, timing his entry to coincide with someone who had the security code so he wouldn't have to beg with Lorraine over the speaker. Instead, he begged with her through the safety chain on her apartment door.

"I won't start anything, Lorraine. Promise."

"If I thought it would help, I'd drag you through the keyhole, Dean, but we'll just get into it . . ."

"You set the boundaries. If I cross them, I go."

"I'm tired at night."

"How about breakfast then?"

"I'm seeing someone."

She could have said he was a lousy conversationalist, a clumsy lover, even a bad father, but to say she was seeing someone staggered him. He teetered, his lips went dry, and he thought he might even be shivering. "Jesus, Lorraine, we're still married."

"That doesn't matter."

"You're not sleeping with him, are you?"

"That's hardly the point. You and I aren't a good fit, Dean." He hated it when she said that. They fit like spoons. She could finish his sentences, and he hers.

Dean started wrapping his support checks with notes on a piece of tablet paper from the body shop or a napkin from whatever fast-food place he was in.

> *I hope you know that being away from you is the hardest thing I've ever done, Lorraine. Some days I pretend you've moved. Some days I pretend we never met. Sometimes I have to pretend you died. Because why else wouldn't you see me?*

Every day, Dean asked the receptionist at the body shop if he'd received any mail, but her answer was always the same.

The horse became Dean's primary source of intimacy. Orphan had started nuzzling and crowding him before her breakfast. At night, when it was just the two of them, Dean just sat there listening to her breathe until she conked out on all fours. They could be in the stall together for hours without having to talk about the family budget or a better job. He'd play with her ears, pull on her tongue, and slap her on the rump. She loved to be handled. They traded touches, nibbles, and pinches. Things worked with Orphan that never would have worked with Lorraine, but he ached for Lorraine.

One morning, Jill invited Dean up to the house for fresh coffeecake with brown sugar crumbled on top. He watched her smear the sides of her coffeecake with butter, holding the knife against it until the butter melted into the pores. Their conversation was going pretty well and Dean decided to venture into new territory. He'd still never met her Chuck, and he was beginning to question what kind of husband he was. Dean would have expected him to at least come down to the barn and pee in the corners of the stall to mark his territory.

"Do you and Chuck ever fight?" She didn't answer right away and he wasn't sure she'd heard him. "I'm trying to figure out what I'm doing wrong with Lorraine." Dean's cowpoke on the lam act had only lasted until she asked him about the gold band on his finger. She said she would have known without the ring. There was a certain bewildered look to married men.

"Chuck's not a fighter," she said.

"Neither am I."

"Do you sulk?"

"I don't think so."

"Do you cheat on her?"

"Not yet, knock on wood."

Jill cut her piece of coffee cake into squares, balanced one square on the blade of her knife, and lifted it to her mouth. "What do you talk about when you talk?"

He opened his mouth to answer and nothing came out. It had been so long Dean couldn't exactly remember. The only conversations he could recall were the ones when they were eighteen and she was pregnant. Then there was a big gap until the night she kicked him out of the trailer. "What should I talk about?"

"Talk about what turns her on."

"Teach me."

Her laughter made her drop a piece of cake that scattered brown sugar crumbs across the table.

"I'm serious. I need a woman's slant."

"Shit, Dean, I'm just a farmer. I like bulging udders with no blisters on them."

"Serious. You're a beautiful woman. You're smart. You can help me." Dean didn't know exactly what being beautiful had to do with it, but she'd already told him she majored in psychology and told him about the workshops she'd taken in Bioenergetics, Gestalt, and nude therapy. That last one shocked him, that someone as bright as Jill would be taken in by it. How could someone get in touch with their *id* when their private parts were hanging out? The more Dean heard about college, the more he was glad he hadn't graduated from high school.

"Psychodrama is what you're talking about," she said. "Role playing."

"That's what I meant."

She laughed and got up from the table, cleared dishes into the sink, brushed crumbs from the table into her hand, and stretched a plastic bread bag over the leftover coffeecake in the pan. She hummed as she worked. Dean didn't want to leave. He didn't want her to go back to her chores. He wanted to be a farmer instead of a dent man in a body shop.

"Why don't you ever compliment me?" Jill said out of the blue.

"Compliment you?"

"The sparkle in my eyes, the way I fix my hair."

What the hell, Dean thought. He tried to catch her eye to see if she was serious. "I do, don't I?"

"Women like to have their accessories noticed too. Like my earrings. It's part of our self-image."

He'd never seen her wear earrings, but he was catching on to the game they were playing. "You have a great body!"

"That's what men think will get them into bed or what they say when they're on the verge of coming. Every woman looks great then.

I want you to notice me when we're just passing each other in the kitchen." A piece of coffeecake was caught in the corner of her mouth.

"I don't always say it out loud. I touch you instead."

"Does your hand ever just say, *I appreciate you*?"

This was getting complicated. He didn't know who he was talking to anymore or whether it would make any difference if he did, but it felt so good to be talking to a woman again. He wanted to brush that brown sugar off her lips and put his arms around her the way he used to with Lorraine, to break the awkwardness of being trapped in two separate bodies.

13

Of course, Mercy had quizzed Lorraine about every moment and every conversation she'd had with Gifford on their *date*, including her telling him she was on the path to a divorce with Dean.

"Hell, girl, maybe he'll cover your costs for an attorney!"

Lorraine regretted her bringing up with Gifford the subject of divorce. It was too soon and it was tantamount to begging. She chastised herself for how far she'd strayed from her own principles. However, she couldn't help but feel excitement about having a second chance to get to know Gifford. The last time he'd come into the Ram, they'd talked for an hour about learning disabilities. She'd only mentioned Ricky's condition in passing but he'd already read several books on the subject and talked to a couple of his doctor friends. For the first time in her life, it felt like she had someone who took Ricky's condition seriously. A partner.

Gifford continued to take her to dinners in Seattle at restaurants Lorraine had never stepped inside of. Once they took the dinner train from Renton to the Chateau Ste. Michelle Winery in Woodinville. Some nights he'd just meet her at the Ram and give her a ride home to Mercy's. Everything was platonic. Hugs, kisses on the cheek. Lots of catching up with each other's lives. Adult conversation. Neither one of them wanted to go too far too fast. Whenever Lorraine slipped out with something foolish that she and Dean had done, Gifford refrained from criticism. There was no piling on. He remembered everything she told him. It was thoroughly different than any relationship she'd ever had. She stopped taking her anti-depressants. She was returning to normalcy. This was no longer an experiment. She was looking forward to telling Gifford the whole truth.

Ricky begged his mother to go with him to the SuperCross Motorcycle races in the Kingdome. As much as she hated that sort of thing, it was hard to turn him down, knowing what he was going through. She asked Gifford what she should do.

"I'll take both of you," he said.

She still hadn't told Ricky she was seeing someone, but she was ready to start down that road. First, she had to let Ricky and Gifford become friends.

Lorraine called Ticketmaster. She'd read the ads for the SuperCross in the Sports section. It sounded horrible. There was nothing she could think of less enriching than watching hyped up motorcycles racing each other over a dirt track with jumps and bumps and spewing exhaust onto the audience. She consoled herself that this was part of developing her masculine side, something else she'd have to do to make up for Dean's absence.

Mercy agreed to work Lorraine's Friday night shift at the Ram. "It'll be the perfect ice breaker for the three of you," she said.

Lorraine twisted herself inside out trying to decide the best way to tell Ricky they were going with Gifford. If she told him too far in advance, it would make it a date. It had to be spontaneous. She didn't want Ricky to consider it an encroachment on their own time together. She felt proud of herself for going. She couldn't imagine her own father, the Judge, ever doing something so frivolous. He preferred to spend his evenings reading Winston Churchill or Oliver Wendell Holmes while he listened to long-play Vivaldi records on the console.

In the end, she and Gifford decided they'd just run into each other at the Kingdome. She'd take a taxi to the Kingdome and avoid the parking fees. He'd just happen to have the seat next to theirs. Ricky deserved his own beginning with Gifford. Get to know him slowly, at his own pace. Ricky wouldn't think it was so strange. After all, she and Gifford had gone to school together and he was a customer at the Ram. Gifford had agreed not to mention their prior dates. They were adults, he was the kid, how hard could it be?

The noise in the Kingdome was deafening, almost frightening, as they scooted in next to Gifford. She did her best to act surprised and tried to make the introductions in the din. Gifford did a marvelous job, she thought, of trying to engage Ricky in conversations about the "whoop" sections on the course where the riders skimmed along the tops of bumps, sometimes jumping three in a row, staying upright over steeply banked turns, and how it had taken 500 truckloads of dirt to create the course. Lorraine was impressed with Gifford's research. He'd even told Ricky how he would love to see the world championship sometime in Paris, practically inviting Ricky and Lorraine to go with him. He bought them Cokes, pizza slices and a MotoCross sweatshirt for Ricky, which Lorraine had to retrieve from the floor under his seat when the show was over. Ricky seemed subdued on the way out.

"I guess I'm not that much into motorcycles," he told her.

Gifford took them to the Red Robin for a hamburger afterward, but Ricky wouldn't get out of the car.

"I'm not hungry," he said.

"We can get you something to go," Gifford said.

Lorraine was both peeved and crushed. Gifford bought her a strawberry Margarita, but Ricky's funk had numbed her appetite and wiped away the whimsy. Gifford, on the other hand, seemed energized. He ordered a mushroom burger with fries, tartar sauce instead of catsup, and it hurt Lorraine's jaw just to watch him put his mouth over it.

"He's doing this because I'm a threat to his dad," Gifford said. A mixture of mayonnaise, mustard and meat juices dripped out the bottom of the burger, down his fingers, and into the plastic basket. "As long as there are two options," he said, "people will wring their hands and equivocate. But once the decision's made, they'll find a thousand reasons to justify their choice."

Lorraine felt woozy. She'd been wrestling with this kind of equivocation like Jacob and the angels. The grease from Gifford's burger was upsetting her stomach and she yearned for the sight of clean, green vegetables. "A boy's not a real estate deal, Giff!"

Gifford put his burger down, wiped his fingers on the napkin, and enveloped her limp hand. His hands were warm, hers were cool. "All I'm saying is we need to bring clarity to the situation. Tell him we're seeing each other. Tell him the truth."

"Ricky's still in the car, I hope," she said. "Please . . . take me home."

One Saturday, Lorraine accompanied Gifford to what he called an "old-fashioned closing" at the title company's office in Enumclaw, where the buyer and seller sat at the same table and passed around the documents for signatures. The husband half of the purchasing couple was a slender man with a goatee who had last minute jitters about going through with the transaction because of the asbestos they'd discovered in the furnace ducts as a result of the inspection. Anyone else in Gifford's place, she thought, would have tried to cram down the deal, but Gifford just talked to him calmly for thirty or forty minutes like they were building a boat together. In the end, Gifford gave the man the names of three contractors and two hundred and fifty dollars of his commission for a second opinion on the furnace. After the papers were signed, they shared champagne on ice and Gifford distributed bouquets, white roses for the sellers and red for the buyers.

It was Lorraine's idea to go back to Gifford's house after the closing, so she could fix him lunch. She loved his house, a Victorian with a hillside view of Lake Washington. Gifford had completely refurbished the interior, restoring the original plaster, refinishing the window frames and hardwood floors, adding recessed lights, and adorning it with antique furniture and richly textured Oriental rugs. Her lungs expanded each time she walked into the kitchen, which he'd modernized with Saltillo floor tile, cream with Prussian blue ceramic tile on the counters, and acres of natural light that poured in through the double-paned windows and skylights. More light could find its way into that kitchen on the dreariest day of winter than had ever made it into the Nashua in high summer. *I could live and die in this room*, she thought.

She didn't want to appear over eager, but she felt drawn to Gifford's civility, his patience, his attentiveness. She had found herself trying out the idea of sleeping with him and wondered if she could be honest with Dean or Ricky if they asked about it. Maybe it was partly the champagne, but Lorraine knew that it was something deeper. After eating lunch in the Adirondack chairs on the front porch -- honey-baked turkey and Jarlsberg cheese sandwiches on dark rye cut into triangles, slices of muskmelon, unsalted potato chips, and sparkling cider -- she led him to the master bedroom. There was no music, but Lorraine danced a few steps with him in the space between the four-poster bed and the chifforobe. There was no rush as they unbuttoned each other. Everything was slow and soft, including Gifford, but Lorraine managed that too. There were no fireworks and the earth didn't move, but she felt exhilarated. She'd been the teacher this time the way Dean had always been hers.

To Lorraine's dismay, Mercy guessed what had happened without her saying a word. She said it was from watching the way they'd kissed in front of the apartment, the suppleness of her body. "It's no big deal, Lorraine. This isn't Iran! Nobody's going to stone you for taking your veil off. Besides, if you don't get a little with Gifford you're going to get itchy and want Dean again."

"Don't say anything to Ricky, okay?"

Mercy just shook her head and smiled as if to say, *Don't you know, girl? Everyone ends up knowing everything anyway.*

Coming from a Catholic parochial school where it was a mortal sin to imagine a man naked to a place where students talked about *doing it* in the bucket seats of VW bugs in the parking lot, Lorraine was petrified on her first day of high school. Her mother had made her wear a Saint Christopher medal around her neck and she took it off and stuffed it in her shoe under the arch of her foot before entering the building. The last thing she wanted was someone to pull it out from under her blouse and make her explain it. Belief in dead saints seemed so primitive in the company of people whose heroes were on magazine covers, sitcoms and cassette tapes. She wanted to change her personality, to be like the girls who teased their hair in the lavatories and weren't afraid to pucker their lips and give a pretend kiss behind the back of a good looking guy in the hallway, or wear Bermuda shorts and bare legs when it was snowing outside.

Lorraine figured that her own history provided an inkling of what Ricky must have felt. They'd mainstreamed the special ed kids for PE and Washington State history at his school, but everyone knew who they were. They might as well have worn sandwich boards. Even their books were different. Kids were always grabbing one of Ricky's at the bus stop or in the cafeteria, flipping it open, and reading it out loud in a Dick and Jane singsong voice.

"A guy in home room said I had shit for brains," Ricky said. "Out loud!"

"Ignore them," Lorraine said. "Kids who talk that way end up with criminal records and car wrecks!"

Lorraine tried to make a point of talking to Ricky about Dean. In fact, she talked about him more now than she ever had when they lived together. She wanted to gradually educate him to Dean's shortcomings, to help him understand why they weren't together. Instead, she found herself lionizing Dean in ways he probably didn't deserve, but Ricky seemed to need a father figure now more than ever.

Ricky liked her stories, especially those with Dean in them. She'd started referring to him as *Dean* rather than *your father* as often as she could. A subliminal message. So far, Ricky hadn't called her on it. One night she told him about the kid who lived in the tree at the park in a fort consisting of a plastic tarp and cardboard from a Philco refrigerator crate.

"The police came and tried to get the kid down. Nobody could shinny the tree," she said, "so they called Puget Power and one of their crews showed up with a cherry picker bucket seat they used to work on power lines. Your dad saw what was happening and stood up for the kid to the police. *People hit golf balls in this park, so what's wrong with a kid sleeping in a tree*? he said."

"Dad said that?"

"When they pulled the kid down, Dean went to the police station and talked them out of arresting him."

She could see Ricky replaying that one in his head as he pushed the remains of his dinner around his plate and she wondered if she should have told him the truth. That Dean was the kid in the tree.

Mercy was at the kitchen table in her bathrobe, with strips of white adhesive tape strategically placed on her face to lift the sags, and doing her nails, when Lorraine got up. Lorraine opened the shades to let some light into the apartment. She couldn't stand the way Mercy could live like a mushroom.

"So, have you let Gifford give you the money for the divorce yet?"

"I don't feel right about it, Mercy."

"Sweetheart, love's got nothing to do with money!" Mercy blew against the gelatin she'd painted onto her nails and held them up to the light. "Money's the stuff people sweat and spit on, from my cash register to yours. There's nothing personal about it. And Gifford Pomeroy's certainly got more of it than he needs."

"It feels unfair to Dean."

"Unfair to Dean? Hah!" Mercy waved her fingers in the air, keeping her neck rigid. "I don't care if he *is* my cousin. He's the guy who pulled the plug on your home. The guy who got you pregnant and then didn't show up in time for Ricky's birth."

There was an answer to Mercy's indictment but Lorraine didn't have the courage yet to share it with anyone. Not with her father, not with Gifford, and for sure not with Dean or Ricky.

14

The worst thing was the pretendin' . . . Mom pretendin' the guy at the Moto Cross was a surprise. I could tell they planned the whole thing. Like some guy in a suit and gold jewelry is going to jus' show up and buy me a sweatshirt. I mean who's that stupid? He whispered stuff in my ear like I was ten years old. Like if he bought me a Moto Cross shirt we'd be friends for life. I know what's goin' on. Mom's got a new boyfriend, but she knows how pissed I am 'bout what she did to Dad. How am I s'posed to respect a guy who wears a pin on his chest with the name of his company. Like that's such a big deal I should bow down and shine his shoes. Him trying to act like Mr. Rogers. This guy could tell you he shot Hitler. Why would Mom let Mr. Rogers make a move on her and kick Dad out? At least Dad has guts. Dad's spit could knock the new guy over.

There's no way I was gonna let this guy have Mom. He'll have to come through me first. I'll get weapons if I have to, steal 'em. I don't care if I get caught. Long as I keep him off'a Mom. Mom didn' really like the guy anyway. It was obvious she was jus' see'n him 'cause she was lonesome. If I have to, I'll teach the real state guy 'bout pretend'n.

Mom said I don't think before act'n sometimes. Well, I'm thinkin' now. I'm thinkin' lots of things and the scrips gonna change. You said I don' manage my emotions. I don't even know what you're talkin' about. I'm not made a plastic. I'm human and I have a brain with lots of ideas on my shelf. Not able to pay attention, you said. Well, I'm payin' lots of attention to Mr. Real State.

Yore the one who's actin' on impulse, Mom. All Dad did was get home late for my birthday. Big deal. Maybe he had a reason, a good reason. You'll see.

That's what I like about Orphan. She don' know how to pretend. You don' even know her, Mom, but Jill said you wanna train a horse you gotta *be* the horse. That's what I wanna be. The horse.

MOVING TO THE HOUSE

$\Diamond$

15

Dean must have mistaken the yelling of his name for something in his dream because when he finally woke up, Jill was shaking his arm and shouting in his ear. There was a battery lantern in the straw next to him and the light made the blood on her arms glisten. The first thing he thought of was Orphan. She'd impaled herself on the fence or been hit by a car. Jill dragged him out of his sleeping bag and he reached for the pants hanging on the sideboards. At the other end of the barn, in a stall lit with lanterns, an enormous mare lay on its side with its legs extended stiffly. A bloody froth bubbled out of its vagina. Dean was terrified.

"The foal's backwards," Jill said, "hold her head down!"

The horse was glaring at Dean sideways out of a bulging eye that looked like it would pop out of her head. All he knew to do was pet her on the neck, which was as hot as chicken broth.

"Don't toy with her!" Jill yelled. "Keep her head down!"

Against his own instincts, Dean pushed down hard on her neck. Jill's arm disappeared up to her armpit inside the horse as she dragged a strap inside. The horse was experiencing gigantic contractions, like dry heaves, as she arched her back and pawed the air. Jill grunted as she strained to get hold of something inside.

"Give me a hand, Dean. She's breached!"

Dean moved to the rear of the horse and she gave him room next to her. The ooze was warm and slippery. They pulled together until what looked like an animal trapped inside a huge opaque plastic bag started to emerge. Then a yellowish fluid and more blood followed. When the mare stopped her contractions and rested, they rested. Jill's face was sweaty, she might also have been crying.

"Come on, Didi, don't give up!"

After a few minutes, the mare started pushing again. A hoof poked through the sack. Then another. The rest of the glop followed, sloshing onto the ground. Jill peeled away the sack, revealing a nappy brown coat. Jill's shirt was smeared with mucus from the innards and wet tangles of her hair were plastered against her forehead and cheeks, but her jaw was firm, the teeth clenched.

When the foal's head finally appeared, Jill rubbed the membrane away from the nostrils and hooked her finger back and forth inside the mouth. The eyelids moved. Jill leaned over and put her ear next to the nostrils, then against the foal's chest. Dean looked down at the mother. Her eyes were closed. When she opened them, her irises were rolled up into her head so that only the veined whites of her eyeballs showed. Jill was crying and Dean walked over to her on his knees. He pulled Jill's head onto his shoulder and she shuddered. "Why does someone always have to get hurt?"

Dean stroked the hair on the back of Jill's head while, over her shoulder, he watched the foal struggle to lift its head and look back at the mare it was still connected to by the umbilical cord. Dean rubbed up and down on the shirt that was stuck to Jill's back, trying to take her pain away. He knew then that she'd fibbed, she wasn't just the woman who loved machines. She was every bit as much the new mother as the brown mare on the floor whose breaths were coarse and full of groan. This wasn't just her livelihood; that gooey new foal with the gangly legs and floppy ears was her kid. But why hadn't her husband been there to help?

Didi, the mare, died from the complications of foaling. Jill was stunned and full of recrimination. Dean had never seen her so distraught. She blamed herself for the death, said she should have gotten hold of Doctor Babcock sooner. By the time the contractions started, it was too late. All Dean had to do was imagine that Didi was Lorraine to know what she must have been going through.

Lorraine was not yet eighteen when she told Dean she was pregnant. It was summer and he was part of a crew that pumped out septic tanks. It was the most money he'd ever made in his life. After two days on the job, he had the business down cold. Back the truck into some god-awful corner of the lot, clear away the car parts and scrap lumber blocking the tank, shovel off the overburden, pry off the concrete lid, string the hose without kinking it, make sure the nozzle was deep enough in the tank to hold a vacuum, and flip the pump switch. Housewives offered him donuts and Coca Cola while the truck sucked the crap out of the tank. Driving between jobs, he added up the hours he'd worked and imagined what else he could buy Lorraine to celebrate the good news. Maybe he'd take her to the drive-in movie and buy stuff at the snack bar instead of packing a lunch the way cheap people did. Or they'd get cheeseburgers and root beer floats at the Dairy Queen and take them to the Barbee Mill yard. When they made trips like this, Dean always parked the car facing the moon so they could scrunch down and watch it rise until they were practically on top of each other and he'd pray that Lorraine would release them from the vow of abstinence they'd made after their first and only sexual intercourse.

She hadn't even peeled back the foil on her burger when she broke the news, which was abnormal because Lorraine always finished hers before he finished his and sometimes ate part of his as well. He knew there was something important on her mind the way she was trying to push down a smile, and he wondered if Judge Culhane had finally decided to give her the Cadillac as a graduation present.

"You might not think it's so good," she said.

"Come on."

The moment she told him she was pregnant, he knew she wasn't going to get the Cadillac her dad had promised and she wouldn't be going to college in the fall. She'd be lucky if her parents let her come home for Thanksgiving dinner. But a warmth spread from a gland deep inside him, a flood more powerful than any orgasm. Lorraine was wrong. It didn't scare him a bit. They were one for one. Although Dean had never really associated his passion for Lorraine with a baby, her announcing it made him realize that's exactly what he'd wanted all along. No more him and her, just *them*. He knew then they'd have to marry and there was no way her old man could do anything but bless them. The Judge's first grandchild was going to be the son of a reprobate.

"Mother of God, Lorraine, a baby! Culhane and Hostler in the same body. Can you believe that?"

She was weeping. "What are we going to do?"

From his knees, he said, "Marry me, Lorraine!" It was the fourth time he'd asked, but this time he had a case to make. Maybe he was just a septic pumper, but his sperm had fastened onto one of her eggs and it wasn't letting go.

Dean got fired a few weeks later for putting the pump hose into somebody's well instead of their septic tank. It was a simple mistake. My god, he was a new father. He was distracted. What was he supposed to do, dip his finger in and taste it first? But everything else was sweet in those days. Lorraine consented to their marriage and he got a job doing sprinkling systems, something more respectable to report when her friends asked what her husband did for a living. It was funny though how everyone used toilets but nobody wanted to be responsible for what came out of them.

Dean put a rack on the roof of his car to carry the sprinkler pipe, which ruined the lines of his used Impala and was something he never would have considered before Lorraine said yes, but now he loved doing sprinkler systems. He couldn't help but think of Lorraine each time he rubbed plumber's putty across the pipe threads and twisted them into a joint.

As winter came on, the sprinkler business dried up and Dean was pretty down until his dad suggested he sell weathervanes. "Weather's never out of season," he said. Heck, Dean thought, he already had the rack on the Impala for a ladder. He put an ad in the paper for *Dean's Weather Vanes and Chimney Sweeping*. As long as he was going up on the roof, he might as well do the chimneys too. He always loved the chimney sweeps in *Mary Poppins*. A lot of people would have been nervous working pitched roofs, but for Dean it came naturally. He was nimble on his feet and worked without ropes. When kids gathered in the yard to watch him walk the peak with a broom he always gave them a show.

The day their baby came, his show ended with a somersault onto the patio that knocked him cold. When they took him to Valley General, he couldn't tell them who was President. It was the first time he'd been in a hospital since his tonsils were taken out. By the time he was lucid enough to call home and talk to Lorraine, nobody answered the phone. They kept him under observation until about eight-thirty that night, when he walked back to the job site in the rain to get his car. Lorraine's note in the Nashua said she'd be at her parents' house so Dean drove to the Culhanes. The Judge answered the door and confronted his weather-beaten, slightly dazed son-in-law.

"Where the hell *you* been?" he asked through the screen. It was clear he wasn't going to let Dean come in and drip on their carpet.

"It's a long story, sir."

"You missed the birth!"

What the Judge didn't know was that he was in the emergency room at the same hospital as Lorraine when Ricky was born. So, technically, he *was* there.

Dean left the body shop early the next day and stopped by Woolworth's to buy a gift for Jill. He looked at jewelry, dresses, perfumes, even lingerie, remembering how unpretty Lorraine said she felt after Ricky was born. But none of that seemed right for Jill. He ended up choosing a wide-brimmed ivory hat with a maroon band and a feather that the clerk said would be flattering on a full-bodied woman. It came in a round box with a string handle.

"It's a portable milker!" Jill said facetiously, as she sat on the floor of the living room and shook the box next to her ear. Dean remembered her saying how a woman liked to be noticed even when you're just passing each other in the kitchen. "Oh, my God," she said as she stroked the brim, "I've never had a dress up hat."

"Get used to it, boss!"

She put the hat on and they both laughed.

Dean told her the story about falling off the roof and missing Ricky's birth, and how forever after he'd tried to make it up to Lorraine and pretty much botched that too.

"Your Chuck ever screw up that bad?"

Jill pulled the hat off and started tugging at the brim, mangling it with her fingers. "I have a confession, Dean. You'll think I'm a monster." Her voice was subdued, the way it was when she talked about Didi. "There is no Chuck."

"You mean he doesn't work at Boeing?"

"He doesn't exist!" She crossed her legs and put the new hat upside down in her lap. "Have you ever heard of laying a horse down where you tie up the front legs and sit on it until it submits? It's what some people think you do to an unruly horse." She was agitated, rubbing her thumbs hard against the velvet in the brim of the hat. "It creates such fear in a prey animal that their nervous system short circuits, the horse thinks it's going to die. She loses the will to live and her soul flees to spare the pain of the actual death."

"But what does that have to do with . . .?"

"It's the same as being raped!"

"God, Jill."

"I made Chuck up because I didn't want to go through that again. I thought men would be more apt to leave me alone if they thought I was married."

"Geez, Jill, I feel stupid. All this time . . ."

She put the hat back on and adjusted it so that it covered one eye. "How would you feel about moving into the house?"

He repeated her question out loud, a habit he'd developed when he didn't know how to answer. The idea wasn't something he was a hundred percent opposed to. "Are you doing that role-playing thing?"

"Never been more serious."

"You're okay with that?"

A slow smile broke out on her face and she slapped Dean on his leg. "Oh, God, Dean! I didn't mean you and me . . . I'm just talking about the guest room."

After bragging about how hard he'd worked to get back in Lorraine's good graces, he felt stupid. He pulled the hat off her and did something a kid would do when he'd just been tricked. He reached his arms around her from the back and gave her a bear hug. He could feel flesh where her blouse had come unbuttoned.

Then she reared back and pushed Dean to the floor on his back. That's when Dean caught a glimpse of a silhouette in the side doorway and tried to pull himself out from under her. Chuck would have been bad enough, even Lorraine, but this was worse. It was Ricky.

By the time Dean reached the door, Ricky was on his bike and heading down the access road. Dean ran as fast as he could in his stocking feet, cutting through the garden, leaping over the vegetable trellises trying to shorten the margin. Ricky was standing on his pedals, pushing down hard on one side then the other. By the time Dean reached the mailbox, Ricky was at the first curve of the county road.

16

Now that Lorraine was a regular waitress for the Ram, she abandoned her flower stand so she and Mercy could trade off the night shift duty and thereby each have a chance to see their kids in the evening. On a busy night, they'd both be on duty at the Ram, which meant they'd have spells where they could catch up with each other's news of the day. Lorraine missed wheeling her boxy green contraption with the spoked bicycle wheels and canvas canopy to the Mecca Tavern where they had let her store the buckets of fresh flowers overnight in the walk-in cooler. Her *rent* for the storage had been a daily bouquet for the bartender, who put it next to the cash register to *class up the place* for happy hour.

With Gifford's help, things were moving forward on the divorce front. He'd arranged for the law firm that handled his business affairs to represent her in the divorce. Gifford accompanied her on the first visit with an attorney who, of course, had a molded glass *Pomeroy Realty* paper weight on his desk. Gifford asked as many questions as she did, but it was a relief to have a helpmate, someone who could treat this as strictly a legal problem. Thankfully, she thought, there was no bad-mouthing of Dean, although the attorney did raise the possibility of using an investigator if things *got messy.* Lorraine couldn't imagine how that would ever be necessary with Dean, who for all his faults, wasn't a philanderer and didn't keep secrets from her. In fact, it was his inability to filter information that had caused many of their problems.

As the evening shift slowed, Mercy and Lorraine talked. "I'm considering moving in with him, Mercy. See if this is for real. Get him used to being a father."

"Do you want me to be your cheerleader or tell you what I really think?"

"Do I have a choice?"

"If the samples are free, why would he ever buy the real thing?"

"That's *passé*."

"Hold out for the whole schmear!" Perspiration darkened the underarms of Mercy's uniform and there was a drop of barbecue sauce from the lunch special on her shirt pocket. "First get the ring and your name on the deed to the house."

"A marriage license is no panacea, I've tried that. Besides, Gifford's not that way. He respects me."

"You need more than respect, honey."

"I thought you'd say I was being pragmatic for a change."

Mercy looked away through the blue neon coils of the *Open* sign suspended in the window of the Ram. "I'd also miss the hell out of not having you and Ricky around."

Lorraine reached across the table and squeezed her forearm. "So would I."

Mercy's gaze was still fixed on the traffic outside. "Does Dean know what you're doing?"

"Not yet. You know Dean."

"Yeah, I know Dean. He'll go nuts. So will Ricky."

"Dean seems to be handling things. In fact, I'm surprised he hasn't missed Ricky more."

Mercy returned her gaze to the table. Her eyes were wet. "At least get the divorce started, so it won't feel like bigamy."

Gifford came by the Ram for coffee before his evening meeting with the Board of Realtors. Lorraine sat with him in the booth while he endlessly stirred his powdered creamer and sugar substitute into his coffee. Gifford was hardly ever down but, when he was, Lorraine always assumed it was because of something she'd done. She couldn't remember that kind of self-recrimination with Dean, probably because Dean's failures were so transparent, but Gifford had layers she hadn't peeled away yet. He stared into his swirling khaki-colored coffee, and it felt as if there'd been a change of heart.

"You okay, Giff?"

As he reversed the direction of his spoon, she watched the undiluted residue from the creamer coagulate in his cup. "You know that two-year old sale topper I bought last winter at the sale?" He didn't even look up to see her reluctant nod. "Finished as a racer before he ever raced."

"I'm sorry."

"He was my *Futurity* horse, Lorraine!" She didn't know what a *Futurity* horse was or why it could mean so much to him. Horse racing was one of the layers she hadn't peeled away yet. She'd known of his interest in horses from the outset of dating him and, at first, it had troubled her. The irony of it being horses made her feel guilty initially about banishing Dean, but it wasn't as if horses were going to disrupt her and Gifford's plans. With Gifford, horses were strictly a business. They could have been shares of stock as far as Lorraine was concerned. An investment. She tried but failed to follow Gifford when he jabbered on about breeding charts, nicks, and earnings per start.

Gifford stopped stirring, put his spoon on the table next to his cup, and looked up at her. "A couple of the guys want me to go to Santa Anita some weekend and shop for a replacement. You wouldn't mind, would you? I'll make it up to you. Promise."

"Oh, stop it. Nobody's keeping score! Of course, you should go. Find your *Futurity*." Relieved that they'd found a cure for his despondency that was disconnected from her and amused at her use of this new horse term, she chuckled out loud.

Gifford laughed too and grabbed her hand. Then he looked at his watch, jumped up from the table, and gave her a peck on the cheek. "I'm gonna be late."

Maybe there weren't as many layers as she thought.

Business was slow, so Lorraine closed the Ram early that night. She counted out eight dollars in tips for the day, four of them from Gifford. Refusing Gifford's offer to help, she had paid the $1,000 retainer for her attorney by taking an advance on the new credit card she'd put in her own name. "Don't worry about a little debt," Mercy had told her, "you're entitled to a bankruptcy every seven years. Also a new husband."

On the walk home to Mercy's, Lorraine passed Walton Auctioneers, Parker Paint, Utter Clutter Collectibles, Pioneer Loan, and a pet shop with cats sleeping in the window. Every store was dark. The traffic from I-405 droned in the background like a perpetually breaking surf that never experienced the relief of retreat. Hardly anyone came to downtown Renton at night anymore. Instead, they went to the multi-screen theaters, fast food outlets, and covered corridors at the Southcenter Mall. The Ram was an anomaly, a retreat for its increasingly geriatric clientele.

Lorraine remembered walking downtown the night she told her dad she was pregnant. She'd waited until he'd gotten up from his reading chair to slice Swiss cheese onto a tray of saltine crackers and put it in the oven before she said anything. Their talks always happened in the kitchen. The kitchen was their business center. His face reddened and he steadied himself with one hand against the ledge of the sink as she told him. The veins in his neck bulged like someone had applied a tourniquet and, for a moment, she thought he might be having a heart attack. Her mom had always told her how stressful his work was, how it was their job to relieve him from the rigors of deciding who went home to their loved ones and who was sent to jail. He gasped for air.

"How . . . could you?"

"I love him, Daddy."

"You were our best hope." He stumbled over to the refrigerator and grabbed the door handle like he was on a ship foundering at sea. "The Hostlers aren't our kind. You'll be dirt poor. You'll never go to college."

"There's a baby inside me. Can't you say something nice about the baby? It's a human being, Daddy! Your first grandchild!"

"Get rid of it!" Spittle chased his words. "Get rid of the baby and get rid of your Dean Hostler! I'm not going to be an accomplice to this!" Lorraine couldn't cry, she couldn't even back away to the other side of the kitchen like she wanted to. "Marriage is a sacrament, not some back alley assignation."

"I don't want *your* kind of marriage," she said, "the way you've treated Mom!"

He slapped her hard on the cheek, and she was astonished. He'd never even spanked her. Her cheek burned and she touched it to see if she was bleeding. She looked up at him, hoping for a hint of regret, but his teeth were clenched like he might slap her again. Gray smoke wafted out of the crack in the oven door, but he made no move to rescue his precious cheese on crackers. She ran out the side door, without a coat and without a goodbye to her mom who'd tip-toed into the circle of light from the kitchen in her bathrobe.

The most irresponsible place she could think of going that night was downtown, to the old section her dad said to stay away from because of the vagrants. It had started to rain so she ducked into Slider's Bar & Grill, a one-story establishment with a brick facade and soiled green awnings. She asked a man on a stool at the bar for a cigarette, and he cupped the flame of a match in his hand and lit it for her, which set off a coughing spell when she inhaled the first puff. His teeth were tarred and his breath had the coarseness of spicy sausage. She just stood there next to his stool mouthing the smoke and she almost took up the man's offer to have a drink with him in a booth. Maybe she had screwed up her life.

When she emerged from the dankness of the tavern and took a deep breath, she felt the fabric of her insides tearing. What she'd always visualized as the Culhane family quilt -- her parents, her sisters, their big house with the stairway bannister and laundry chute, the Catholicism, even her shyness -- was ripping apart. Through the split, however, there was daylight and the sensation of breaking out energized her. She realized for the first time that she didn't have to turn out like her parents. She didn't even have to be a Catholic. She could form her own bond with God. She'd prayed that her child would be special, someone magical, because that's really what she'd seen in Dean, the ability to produce something out of nothing.

Her mother and sisters attended the marriage ceremony, which was in the rectory because the Judge wouldn't allow the embarrassment of a public marriage in the church of someone who was already with child. The morning of the wedding the Judge told everyone he'd 'come down with something' and stayed home. Her parents' wedding gift was a set of knives, with a card signed by her mom. The Judge came to the hospital once after Ricky was born, but he never set foot in the repossessed Nashua trailer that Dean's father had given them. Judge Culhane had more faith in the stain of original sin than in the power of the resurrection.

As Lorraine walked across the Cedar River bridge after closing up the Ram one night, she leaned over the concrete railing and watched the muddy waters of the Cedar River swirling their way under the Renton Public Library toward the Lake Washington inlet. Her father's unconditional dismissal when she announced her marriage to Dean eighteen years ago had stung her, but now she'd also rejected Dean

Hostler in favor of a businessman who wasn't religious, played the stock market, owned a big home, and raced horses for money.

A pickup rushed in next to her and stopped so fast she felt the wind whoosh around her bare legs. As the window on the passenger side rolled down, she recognized the voice of Waylon Jennings. Dean had often put on Waylon Jennings when he wanted to dance with her in their cramped trailer kitchen. Ever since the lawyer had given her the draft Summons and Petition for the divorce, she'd dreaded running into Dean. Never mind that it was all for their own good, she didn't want to see him suffer.

"I'm looking for Ricky," Dean said, and swung the door open. "I gotta talk to him!"

She climbed into the cab.

Neither of them said anything on the way to Mercy's while Lorraine replayed her last seventeen conversations with Ricky. Maybe he'd run away, but how would Dean know that? The guilt of working such long hours flooded her. The peer pressure, the aching to be noticed was so hard for a kid on the margins.

Mercy was sitting on the kitchen counter in her nightie and underpants with her feet braced against the back of a chair, painting her nails, toilet paper coils separating her toes, when Lorraine burst into the apartment with Dean following. Lorraine ran down the hall and rushed into Ricky's room without knocking. The light was off, there was no radio playing, and no battery games going, but she could see the lump in the bed. Ricky pulled the covers up around his neck as she came closer.

"Where have you been?" She shook his shoulders through the bedspread.

"Nowhere."

"Your dad's here." She couldn't help but fall into the old nomenclature.

He pulled the sheet up over his ears and mumbled something she couldn't understand.

"Enunciate, Ricky."

"I don't have a dad."

Lorraine was taken aback. She'd never seen him do anything but venerate Dean. He was miraculously blind to Dean's flaws. "He's here, and he wants to see you!"

Ricky didn't budge.

In the passage from Ricky's room back to the living room, it came to her the way a simple truth sometimes comes in the shower. Gifford was right, she'd equivocated. The worst place was in between. Besides, her intuition told her that something else was going on. "Ricky doesn't want to see you," she said to Dean.

"He doesn't?"

"I don't know what you did, and I don't really care, but I want to show you something." She walked over to her space on the bookshelf where she kept her bills and her check stubs, an opening between Mercy's stack of Vogue magazines and the wooden elephants that were supposed to be bookends. She picked up the manilla file and handed Dean the papers stamped *"Draft: for review and discussion."*

Dean slowly fingered the sheaf of papers. His vertebrae must have compressed because he slumped. "You don't need to do this, Lorraine. Please . . . I've changed."

"Every time you get near Ricky, things go dark and I get scared."

"Your father wouldn't want this."

"Don't you dare bring him into this and don't be so sure whose side he's on!"

"He's a stout Catholic! Divorce is a big no-no!"

She took the papers back and pushed him toward the door. Dean lodged himself in the doorway. There were tears in his eyes. She pushed against his chest, averting her eyes. "Go, Dean! Get out of here! Please."

He let go and she shut the door, pressing her forehead against the peephole. Her face muscles contorted as she tried to hold back her tears until she was sure he was gone. She couldn't let him know how much this hurt. She couldn't jump the chasm in two steps. She had to stretch herself out and hope for a soft landing. When she turned around, Mercy was standing there in her shorty nightgown, arms open, the tissues still between her toes.

17

After Lorraine showed Dean the divorce papers, he stopped at the Mecca and ordered a few boiler makers with tequila chasers, something he hadn't done since Lorraine kicked him out of the trailer. He stopped at the Mecca again the next night, and the bartender put a long-stemmed orange rose in his last drink, what he called a nightcap. Dean carried the rose home to Orphan Annalina, who was asleep on her feet in that trance-like state of hers. He let her smell it, then slid the stem into her mane. Orphan must have sensed how needy Dean was because she just stood there and let him wrap his arms around her neck, putting one cheek against her warmth, then the other. She had a healing quality: her mass, the absorbing silence, and the eyes. It was like she spent hours in some kind of expansive meditative state, thinking about her handlers.

Dean brushed her from forelock to flanks, all the time thinking of Lorraine's slim hips, the soft baby hair on her thighs, the way she turned her head sideways and arched her neck when they made love. Her hold on him was like the earth's hold on the moon. He could come up with the stupidest ideas imaginable, and she had a way of tethering him back, extracting the joy and chucking the rest. She'd bawl him out, they'd have a good laugh, maybe get naked and watch a video in bed, and fall asleep with the movie still going. Then, another day and another stupid idea. He didn't have to be responsible; Lorraine did it for him.

Each night Dean turned in at the Sprague mailbox he crossed his fingers on both hands and tapped them on the steering wheel, hoping he'd see Ricky's metallic blue bicycle in the yard. He was dying to tell him about his plan to take Orphan to Longacres and race her. It had come to him like a vision. His dad had always told him if you can see it in your mind, you can do it with your hands. It was as simple as a circle: he'd carted Orphan away from Longacres, now he'd take her back there. The idea wasn't fully formed yet, but that didn't matter as long as it was in motion. That's the way his mind worked. He never backtracked. His only gear was forward, same as a horse. If buying Orphan was a tangent, taking her to Longacres was a tangent on a tangent. Lorraine would croak if she knew what was running through his brain. She'd take out a calculator, list the expenses and tell him all the reasons it wouldn't work. She'd remind him that their first responsibility was Ricky. And that's where *her* tangent intersected his.

Maybe it was good that she'd shown him the divorce papers. It had thrown a scare into him, no question, but it had also challenged him. He'd prove to her he was a good father. This was five-card draw, and she'd just raised him. He couldn't show his hand. If he raised her high enough, she'd fold and he'd never have to. He'd beat flushes with a full house plenty of times. She didn't have to know about Ricky coming to the Spragues, and she didn't need to know about Longacres. Not yet. If it worked, he could win with zilch.

Orphan munched her breakfast from the hay rack, while Dean and Jill watched. Dean draped his arms over the gate behind him like an overcoat on a bent hanger. "I'm toast, Jill. Her attorney's got the papers already written up."

"I smelled you come in last night," she said. "You must have tied one on. Where's Ricky?"

"He saw us on the floor together. He probably thinks we're . . . well, you know . . . you were there . . ."

"You're a physical man, Dean. When words fail, you grab, like you did with me."

He couldn't look her in the eye and instead watched her chest while she talked. There seemed to be no rhyme or reason to when she wore a bra and when she didn't. Today she wasn't. With any other woman, Dean would have assumed it was a come on; with Jill, it was more likely defiance. She looked good, though, with freshly washed hair, and she was always lit up after working with her animals. Maybe Ricky *had* seen something.

"Do you still love her, Dean, or are you just missing her?"

"There's a difference?"

"You can miss someone out of habit like you miss your own bed. Love means you'd choose her over everyone else in the gymnasium even if it meant you had to live in a stable."

"I'll move back to the barn!"

She laughed. "God, listen to me. You'd think I was an expert or something." She backed away from the stall and brushed off the front of her jeans. "Hey, I like the muscle on your horse. Look at that rump. Ricky better come and work her before she loses it."

Jill invited Dean up to the house for waffles. He was supposed to be at work early, but he didn't feel much like working. He was only staying with the body shop so he could make the support payments and impress Lorraine. *A lot of good that had done.*

Ricky's absence disheartened him. He couldn't remember Ricky ever turning him down, for anything. He thought of just telling Lorraine the truth, that Ricky had run off after seeing him with Jill, but that was the rub. If he told her that much, Lorraine would assume he was sleeping with Jill. She knew how bad he was with abstinence. *I don't want to get nailed for a crime I haven't committed. I'm only trying to do something fatherly. Why does everything have to get complicated?*

Dean watched Jill lift a pitcher of syrup out of a pan of warm water and wipe off the bottom with a dish towel. "I'm thinking of racing Orphan, Jill," he said. "That would get Ricky's attention. I could go to trainer school."

She laughed. "There's no school. It's hunt and peck and listen to the horse."

Dean was seeing that white light again, the hot one that flashed through him at the horse sale. *Maybe I can't do anything about Lorraine but, by God, I'm not going to divorce my son.* "Ricky would be proud of me, wouldn't he?"

"You'd knock him off his feet."

Jill spread her butter, making sure it melted into each hole in the waffle. "Longacres is not that far out of your way into work. I can help you set things up. Take the money you're paying me to board Orphan and apply it against a stall at the track."

"No, no, I can't take a handout!"

"Work it off! There's always crap to do around here."

"How do you know so much about horses anyway?"

She half-closed her eyes and glared at him. She wasn't one of those women who liked to talk about herself.

Dean insisted on trailering Orphan to Longacres on his own. Jill lent him her horse trailer, but this was something between him and Orphan. The stall they assigned her was in the same barn where Dean had first met her, where the pretty girl with the ponytail told him that Orphan had lungs like a locomotive. He was holding onto that thought as he led Orphan from the trailer past all those thoroughbreds poking their heads out of their stalls that first morning and gawking at the newcomer. Orphan stepped smartly, looking from side to side, making sure everyone noticed. Her ears were erect, her head bobbed up and down like a boxer's, and she snorted. Dean, on the other hand, experienced the same paranoia that always plagued him in new surroundings. He kept thinking someone would pop out of nowhere and ask him what college he'd attended or what was the lineage of his horse.

The grooms and stable workers were busy brushing their horses, wrapping ankles, pushing bales of hay in wheelbarrows from the hay pyramid at the end of the aisle to the stalls. Dean noticed that many of the horses coming back sweaty from the track had matching red saddle towels with *BH* logos and their names engraved on the brass plates attached to their halters. Dean passed a tack room that had more leather than a Harley Davidson picnic. Then who should drop by but Bud Holliday, the trainer whose logo was tacked to most every stall in the aisle. He followed Dean into Orphan's stall, where he studied her anatomy as they talked, pushed his hand under her head and into her air pipes and rubbed the back of the legs. Dean could feel Bud's gaze and his hundred unasked questions.

"You can put your gear in my tack room if you want," Bud said.

"Oh, yeah, thanks. My gear." Except for the halter, a bridle and a lead rope, there was no gear.

Dean had this same feeling the day he had to quit messing around building villages out of tin scraps on the floor of his dad's garage and go to kindergarten. His dad pronounced it "kind-a-garden," which turned out to be a lie. It was anything but. Dean's mom tried her hardest to scrub the oil marks from the pipe shavings off his pants, but they still showed, and one kid started the rumor they were shit stains. Then his mom dyed the pants with brown shoe polish to cover the stains, but that only made it worse. When he finally got a new pair of pants from Penney's, he wouldn't let his mom snip the *Wrangler* tag off the pocket or wash them for fear of losing the label. That's how he felt on the backside at Longacres. Everyone else had new pants.

But Dean quickly became attracted to the people who inhabited the backside. They were people like himself who didn't fit in anywhere else. The trainers and jockeys, of course, but also the veterinarians, farriers, agents, suppliers, security guards, tractor drivers, counselors, chiropractors, soothsayers and just plain drifters. Everyone had a story. Many of them were gypsies who moved from track to track as one closed for the year and another one opened somewhere else. The only thing they all had in common was love of horse. They were people who dared to dream that the animal they worked on could be the next *Man o' War*. Most hadn't gone to college and everyone spoke in words that Dean could understand, even when he had to ask the Latinos to translate. Reading the newspaper meant *The Daily Racing Form*. The backside was largely a community of Spanish speaking people, the gifted men and women who served as the grooms and exercise riders, some of whom lived in cramped temporary dormitories scattered amongst the barns. They worked the horses in the morning and guarded them at night, making no distinction between those owned by millionaires and those owned by paupers like himself. Some of them schooled their children right there on the grounds. There was also a chapel on the backside and day care. Nobody could enter the backside without a pass. It was like the world had quarantined this pack of misfits and made them citizens of a shining city upon a hill.

Dean watched what the other trainers did with their horses and copied them. He wrapped Orphan's legs with bandages whether they needed it or not, pushed her around in the stall, picked her feet, changed the straw, and sometimes tied her to the ring on the back wall. The other trainers had exercise riders, some who were real jockeys, stubby guys no taller than Ricky, hundred pounders with weathered faces, piercing eyes, and a riding crop that stuck out of their back pockets.

The track was open every morning from five-thirty until ten for workouts. Horses paraded back and forth between the barns and the track with pony escorts, some with blinkers that matched the color of the wraps on their legs, all of them with flimsy saddles and short stirrups that allowed the rider's to float like a monkey above the horse. Dean watched them through the fence in the turn closest to the barns until he had to go to the body shop. The riders jogged their horses clockwise along the outside of the track to the far end, then turned around and took off galloping counterclockwise toward the finish line. Dean memorized the way the jockeys' butts bobbed in the air, their backs parallel to the ground, heads tucked against the horse's neck. *Hell, how hard could it be? The horses did all the work.*

Dean became fascinated with Pedro Garcia, one of the jockeys who worked horses in the morning and rode on race days, a beautiful rider, a mere grasshopper on the back of his mounts. After a few days of watching Pedro, Dean followed him back to the barn and waited until he had dismounted and lit a cigarette from the pack under his vest.

"Buenos dias," Dean said. Pedro's eyes lit up and Dean extended his hand. "I like your style. How'd you like to ride my horse?" He must have spoken too fast because Pedro just stared at him. "My horse," Dean repeated, pointing in the general direction of his stall, "Orphan Annalina."

"How many?"

He'd goofed up his English, Dean thought, he must have meant how much. "What's everyone else paying you?"

"How many horses?" Pedro said.

"Oh, horses . . . just one. One horse."

It was like a curtain had been pulled over Pedro's eyes. "Not enough horses. I ride for Senor Holliday."

"Yeah, yeah," Dean muttered, "I know."

Frustrated, Dean went on a grapefruit diet. He remembered Lorraine doing that -- God knew why, she was spare as a horse whip to begin with. Dean added hard-boiled eggs to his diet until the eggs gave him heartburn so he just ate grapefruit and toast. He came home from work each night and sweated for an hour in the sauna before weighing himself on Jill's scales.

"New girlfriend?" Jill asked.

"I want to ride."

Jill laughed. "How much do you weigh?"

"A hundred and fifty or so in my skivvies."

"Too much for racing! But you're not going to break her back. The extra weight in morning workouts will strengthen her."

Dean missed not having Orphan at Jill's but Longacres wasn't that far away. He could stop by to ride her, put her on the hot walker and feed her in the morning on the way to the body shop and visit her again after work. Evenings, when the barns were abandoned to the stable workers, Dean would sometimes take Orphan out and walk her around the grounds, to let her get comfortable in her new home and scare the spooks out.

With the feed and vet bills, Dean struggled to stay on a cash basis. Of course, the support payments to Lorraine came off the top. The day before his next payday Dean asked around the barns to find a cheap jockey's saddle. Within twenty-four hours, he had four offers, one for fifty bucks that he bought from a Bud Holliday groom. There wasn't that much to it, no more leather than a flattened out first-baseman's glove.

"No steal," the groom said, in case Dean thought otherwise. His brown eyes were beautiful, unblinking and Dean believed him.

Jill came to the track one morning and noticed that Orphan was pawing the ground and neighing at the other horses going by. "See the way she's moving her head in circles? She's barn sour. You gotta get her more action."

"I've been riding her every day since Ricky went AWOL!"

Dean had ridden a lot of horses in his life, but never a thoroughbred. There was a kid in grade school in Rosalia, Jesse Devine, who always smelled like manure. That's probably why they'd befriended each other. Jesse's dad owned a string of broken-down riding horses they rented by the hour. In exchange for the cigarettes that Dean copped from coffee tables and lunch counters, Jesse let Dean ride as much as he wanted. "Just show 'em you're the boss," Jesse said.

Dean waited until most of the other horses had finished their morning workouts to put on Orphan's racing saddle. She pranced her way past the other stalls as Dean rode her out of the barn, swinging her rump from side to side, making sure nobody missed the show. They made the long walk to the track past the other barns, past the horses on hot walkers who'd already had their workouts. People stared at them and Dean wondered if it was because of the crack in the helmet he'd dug out of the dumpster or his loafers they'd noticed. Dean held his butt up to keep his teeth from chattering as Orphan cantered toward the track. He didn't remember Jesse's horses having this much bounce in their step. The muscles on the top of Dean's legs were starving for oxygen by the time they reached the entry gate and he stood straight up in the stirrups the way he'd seen other riders do.

"Closes in ten minutes," the guy at the gate yelled.

Dean gave him a high sign with his index and shortened middle finger. Orphan was getting racy as they stepped onto the rich topsoil. Dean reached down and patted her on the neck, which was already moist, and turned her toward the far straightaway. Dean reined her in, and Orphan cantered sideways, her back legs trying to pass the front ones. He let his body bob with the rhythm of the horse. Away from the glare of the experts, he sucked in half of the air in the infield and his exhalation startled Orphan. Dean patted her on the neck to settle her down. *I'm the boss, I'm the boss,* he kept saying to himself.

With every new item they passed-- the tractor plow, the starting gate, a cigarette pack on the track -- Orphan's eyes bulged and her ears went rigid. This was the wide view the vet had talked about, the vision that encompassed everything. Reading someone's or something's intent at a distance was a survival strategy for a horse. Despite weighing more than half a ton with hooves that could shatter a bowling ball, a horse treated a candy bar wrapper blowing across her path as a mortal threat.

When they reached the far end of the backstretch, Dean turned around and let out some rein. With Jesse's horses, he always had to dig his heels into their flanks. Not Orphan. As soon as he relaxed the reins, she was off. No more up and down, she pinned back her ears and moved to a new gear, overdrive. Dean guided her over to the rail, compressed his body, and held on for dear life. Jesse was wrong: Orphan was the boss. His job was simply to settle in and defer to her flow. People were always trying to fix each other but with Orphan it felt like she was connected to some deeper force that preexisted people. There was nothing to fix. The saddle was groaning and squeaking with each monstrous stride. Dean's eyes watered. He was on a motorcycle without a windshield. No, it was better than that. Waylon Jennings was cranked up to full volume on the tape deck, he'd entered Lorraine, and they were racing toward climax.

Dean couldn't sleep that night and started fiddling with Jill's Black Forest cuckoo clock, which had stopped its cuckoo about the same time Ricky stopped coming to the farm. He had the works spread out on a card table and, as was his habit when he was alone at night, Dean thought of his marriage. He thought of the weeks following Ricky's diagnosis when Lorraine dragged home shopping bags full of library books and tore strips of paper to mark the *good parts* for Dean to read and stacked the books on his side of the trailer. "Ricky can't stay on task," Lorraine said. "He gives up on himself when he can't quickly figure out the answer." For Dean, the talk of damaged chromosomes acted like a tongue depressor on his libido.

Somebody rapped hard at the door and Dean set the clock's cogwheel on the card table and answered the knock. It was Ricky, in a suit and tie, dripping wet, with a streak of mud that ran forehead to crotch from the rooster tail of his fender-less bike. Dean hadn't seen Ricky in weeks. He was panting and bending in the middle like he had a side ache.

"You gotta come, Dad . . . now!"

Dean figured Ricky had a friend who'd been in a knife fight or gotten shot. Maybe Ricky had shot him. He was good with a gun. There was nothing wrong with his hand-eye coordination. From being around Orphan, Dean had gotten better at reading body language. No further explanation was necessary. Dean changed his clothes and put on his boots and the *Bogle's Body Shop* windbreaker he kept by the back door. They put Ricky's bike in the back of the pickup and jumped into the cab.

"The Holiday Inn, Dad!" was all Ricky said, as he took his place on the edge of the front seat, glaring through the swipes of the windshield wiper, rubbing his thumbs hard against the inside of his index fingers. The mottled glow from the streetlights rolled across his face as they reached Houser Way and turned south. He moved his lips the way Catholics did when they prayed the rosary. Maybe Ricky thought his dad would bail on him if he knew their true mission. Whatever it was, he was on task.

The only empty parking space near the entrance to the Holiday Inn was a handicapped stall, but Ricky pointed to it and that's where Dean pulled in. The electric doors slid open as Ricky led the way into the lobby. Clusters of people mingled in front of the fireplace, toasting champagne and laughing. It was a party atmosphere and, for a moment, Dean's spirits lifted. Ricky stopped them in front of the registration desk.

"Dad, it's Mom's engagement party!"

Dean grabbed him by the shoulders and shook him. "The what . . ."

Ricky pulled himself loose and led Dean past the concierge stand, down a corridor with red wine carpet, and past meeting rooms with tree names. There was a band playing *Georgia On My Mind* in the

Evergreen Room. The chandeliers were dimmed and hundreds of pretty people in suits and silk dresses sat at or stood around tables littered with dirty plates, coffee cups and stemware. The aroma of ham and pineapple slices warmed the air.

Dean felt like hired help. Nobody noticed him standing in the doorway, his body swaying, his mouth agape. When Ricky had told him Lorraine was engaged, it didn't matter with whom any more than it mattered what kind of bullet they were going to put through his brain, but when he saw Gifford Pomeroy standing on the edge of the dance floor holding Lorraine's hand, Dean's head practically exploded.

He was vaguely aware of Ricky tugging at his sleeve as he moved in a straight line toward the dance floor, bumping people and chairs out of his path. Someone grabbed him by the arm and he twisted sideways to escape, but his eyes remained fixed on Lorraine, who was standing there in a black satin dress, a silver tiara in her hair, and nothing except spaghetti straps across her bare shoulders.

"You can't do this, Lorraine!"

"Oh, Dean!" There was compassion in her voice and, for a moment, Dean thought she'd just forgotten she still had a husband, and now that he'd reminded her everything would get straightened out.

Gifford stepped between them, his hand on Dean's windbreaker. "This isn't a good time, Dean." He was maddeningly calm.

Dean pushed him aside. "You've been waiting your whole frigging life for this, you scummy goddamn scab!"

Someone jumped on Dean's back, then someone else. Dean spun them off and swung at Gifford, catching him hard on the neck. Then Dean swarmed him with punches until the people behind dragged him away by his belt, with his fists still beating the air. He could hear women screaming as a gang of folks smothered him against the floor, but he saw Lorraine at the edge of the crowd with her hands covering her mouth. He'd embarrassed her again, but their eyes met and he believed with every fiber of his being that she was making a mistake and that both of them knew it.

"Where's Ricky?" Dean kept saying. "I want Ricky, goddamit!"

Two squad cars arrived, probably the whole Renton night shift. It took three officers to handcuff Dean and escort him out of the Holiday Inn. Every bottle washer, waiter and patron in the place watched as they dragged him out the front door. The red lights were flashing on the squad cars, which were parked all helter-skelter in the lot, with some headlights high-beamed into the lobby of the hotel. They stuffed him into the backseat of one of the cars.

As his squad car backed away from the entrance, Dean saw Lorraine standing next to Ricky, wiping her eyes. Jill Sprague said if you loved someone you could pick them out of a whole gymnasium full of pretty women. Well, by God, hadn't he just done that?

18

Lorraine was anxious for daylight to arrive so she could finally get out of bed and busy herself in the kitchen, put something else into her head. Gifford knew better than to talk about the fight when they got home from the hotel. There's just no way she could have managed that. He fell asleep snoring with one hand draped across her hip, and she kissed it, lifted it back to his side of the bed, turned over, and struggled until she found sleep.

In the morning, she unplugged the coffee grinder and carried it into the bathroom so she wouldn't wake up Gifford. He'd converted her to fresh-ground coffee from the beans he bought at the food cooperative, which was owned by one of his clients. Growing up, she used to beg her mom to be the one who turned the key on the can of Folgers. That whoosh coupled with the husky aroma of coffee filling her nostrils was almost indecent.

Once the water had dripped through the beans, she poured the coffee into one of Gifford's Italian pottery mugs, which were hand-painted with clusters of grapes against green vines and dusty stucco. Lorraine preferred the mugs because they kept the coffee warm longer than the bone China cups she and Dean had managed to salvage through their nearly eighteen years of marriage.

Like the bud on a house plant, Lorraine sought natural light and turned her chair sideways in the nook so she could watch the fog burn off Lake Washington. When she was the first one up, she read a magazine or made headway in a book, but this morning she didn't have the energy to digest a single new idea. She watched a propeller plane rise from the Renton Airport, heading toward the fog bank that hovered over the lake. There was a make-believe character to the flight because, although she could see it moving, the engine drone did not penetrate the double pane windows. Normally, the sunlight and coffee were enough stimulus, but this morning she would have welcomed the noise.

As a surprise, Gifford had bought them tickets for a honeymoon trip to Acapulco, which he had showed off at the engagement party to the same effusive praise and astonishment that her four carat diamond had received. Gifford wanted a September wedding, after the racing season was finished and, of course, after the divorce was final. That would also fit with the schedule for completion of the house he was building for them on a waterfront lot on Lake Washington in Medina. They wouldn't just see the water, he'd said, they would be able to wade into it from their front lawn. The other surprise he'd whispered in her ear as they danced the first dance. "The Ram's going to have a new waitress for swing shift," he told her. "I've arranged it all with Dillard, and you won't have to push flowers or wait tables anymore." But she loved her flowers and working at the Ram with Mercy.

Gifford emerged from the bedroom in his bathrobe and slippers, his hair still mussed, his face puffy with the beginning of a shiner in one eye. Usually he was showered, shaved, and smelled of Old Spice by the time she saw him in the morning. He'd peck Lorraine on the lips, pour himself coffee, add his non-dairy creamer, rip the top off a pouch of sugar substitute, and stir it on his way back to the nook. It was like they'd already married and retired, there was no work for Lorraine to run off to, and Gifford could go in as late as he wanted. They had all morning to sip coffee, munch on croissants, and talk, except that everything she could think of saying was a horrible reminder of last night. So was the sight of Gifford's swollen face.

"This is the life, huh?" Gifford said, reaching over to pat her on the arm.

"It's foggy."

"I'm not going in today."

The thought of not being alone for the day panicked her. "But you always work Saturdays!"

"I've turned the page."

"What about your open houses?"

He smiled and ruffled her sleeve. "Make me a better offer."

When Ricky failed to show his face by nine-thirty, Lorraine went upstairs to make sure he was okay. Gifford had given Ricky the room with the windowed turret and spiral staircase so he could climb up and enjoy the view in every direction. Gifford had also given him permission to tape posters and pennants on the walls, but after three weeks of sleeping in the turret bedroom the walls were still bare. Lorraine sat down on the bed and brushed Ricky's hair back, the same way she'd always done.

"Hey, sleepyhead, it's almost lunchtime."

Ricky turned away from her. He'd given her and Gifford the silent treatment on the way home from the reception, a silence that had deepened when Ricky asked if they could go to the police station and see his dad. "Dean made his bed and now he can lie in it," Gifford had snapped. Lorraine could understand Gifford's anger. The party had meant so much to him. Lorraine had lobbied for an engagement dinner out with just the two of them, a few friends and, of course, Mercy and Ricky. For her, their marriage was a private matter, but Gifford had his herd of friends. It was part of what sustained him. Now his friends must have been wondering what kind of mess he was marrying into.

Gifford was peeved that Ricky had brought Dean to the Holiday Inn in the first place. From his vantage point, it was an act of betrayal. "I'm not expecting adoration," Gifford had told Lorraine, "I'd be happy with common courtesy." Until last night, she had thought things were improving. The three of them had been eating meals together. Ricky had even played frisbee with Gifford in the street in front of the house once and reported afterward that Gifford was *pretty good at it.*

"I hate this place," Ricky mumbled into his pillow.

"Everything takes getting used to," Lorraine said. You have a beautiful room." She was trying to think of something more persuasive, but it eluded her.

"Remember the story about that kid in the tree?" Ricky asked.

"Of course."

"We've got to rescue Dad!"

"It's not that simple, Ricky."

"I been see'n Dad, you know." There was a belligerence in his voice. "I don't have a paper route, Mom. I been bike'n out to see Dad and my horse!"

She was stunned. This was the boy she'd rearranged her life for. Since the moment she'd found out she was pregnant, every decision she'd made put Ricky first. She had vowed they weren't going to go through that adolescent estrangement other people did. "Why didn't you tell me?"

"You would'a tried to stop me."

"Where does he live?"

"Ask him yourself."

Lorraine felt her throat tightening. Maybe it was providential that she stop working so she could spend more time with Ricky. *He's right. I should at least know where Dean is living.*

"Don't you even miss our old trailer, Mom?"

After the fight at the Holiday Inn, they confined Dean to a holding area about the size of Gifford's Town Car. His jail mates consisted of a crewcut guy who'd beat up his girlfriend, a crane operator from Boeing with the top half of his ear missing, and a punk with hair wax who said he'd knocked off a Seven-Eleven.

There were so many reasons, Dean thought, why Gifford Pomeroy should be the one in jail instead of himself. Lorraine had always made excuses for Gifford, saying he probably regretted as much as Dean did the *caper* with the teacher's car in high school. Another thing Gifford had gotten away with. How could he make her understand that people like Gifford planned every move of their life? Gifford could be falling out of an airplane without a parachute and he'd be calculating the insurance recovery on the way down.

Dean stayed awake the first night in jail, hoping that Lorraine would come by. Maybe she'd bring Ricky with her. He knew she'd feel the need to first explain herself to Gifford. She wouldn't just walk out on the guy. She'd let him down easy. She'd finally let him know she wasn't for sale. Of course, Dean knew how dazzling Gifford could be. He'd made the mistake once of believing they were playing on the same team. It had taken Dean most of his childhood to figure Gifford out, but Lorraine was smarter. She'd get there quicker, before their proposed marriage.

The people in the holding area came and went. A guy in a shirt and tie who fiddled with his fingers and looked like a child molester replaced the girlfriend beater. A bearded guy with watery eyes took the crane operator's place. Dean sat on the floor with his back against the wall so no one would try to cornhole him. He drank all the liquid he could so they'd let him go to the bathroom more often and get away from his cellmates.

In the morning, they brought trays with miniature boxes of cold cereal, plastic spoons, cylinders of orange juice, and lukewarm coffee in paper cups. Dean traded his Corn Flakes and a packet of sugar for Wheaties, and the guy ripped open the sugar and poured it down his throat.

After lunch, Ricky came by. They had to talk to each other through a plastic window with a blowhole. Ricky's hair was mussed up and the front of his shirt was one buttonhole off. He looked like *he'd* been the one in the fight.

"Aren't you supposed to be in school?"

"It's Saturday. I jus' wanted to see if you're a'right."

"I'm fine."

"How's Orphan? I miss 'er."

"Okay, kid, you gotta take care of her while I'm tied up here."

"Wha's gonna happen to us, Dad?"

There were so many things Dean should have said, but he couldn't mount a decent account of himself. He forgot to thank Ricky for coming down and taking him to the Holiday Inn. Neither could he muster the energy to tell him there was nothing going on between him and Jill, or how sick he'd felt that Ricky had stayed away. He wanted to tell him he'd taken Orphan to Longacres, but he wanted to surprise him once he was out of jail. Dean's tongue was paralyzed and his heart was numb. He still couldn't get past the idea of Lorraine engaged to someone else.

Ricky left in a mumble and Dean's mind drifted back to the first time he'd been imprisoned, when he'd done time for Gifford. For joy riding their teacher's car. That detention had shunted him onto a dead-end track and lessened people's expectations of him. Worse, it had lessened Dean's expectations for himself. He no longer imagined becoming the Boeing engineer; he would be somebody's grunt instead. And now Gifford had the only precious thing that Dean had salvaged from his childhood. Lorraine.

On the second morning, one of the guards in squeaky black boots came by with a clipboard. "Which one of you is Hostler? Your bail's been posted."

There were no goodbyes, no high fives, no handshakes from his cellmates. Those who were awake looked like they wanted to spit on him, as if his release was in lieu of their own. On the elevator ride up, the guard said a woman had posted his bail and Dean brightened. He tucked in his shirt, parted his hair with his fingers, felt around for cowlicks, and wiped the crust out of the corners of his mouth as he stepped into the glare of the lobby. But it wasn't Lorraine. It was Jill Sprague, in the wide-brimmed, ivory hat with the feather in the band that he'd given her. She was dressed for church.

"I would have come yesterday if I'd known," she said.

"You didn't need to do this."

"I know."

Jill's bail was pure, unexpected sugar, but he couldn't turn the corner. He dreaded the prospect that he might run into Lorraine and Ricky on the street with Gifford. Maybe it would be better if he disappeared, went back to the Palouse and started over. His dad had always told him the worst thing was to be assimilated into the culture, but that's what had happened. He'd gotten swallowed up, he wanted the same things that everyone else wanted, and he wasn't any good at getting them.

On the insistence of Gifford and his attorney, Lorraine obtained a restraining order against Dean after the fight at the hotel. He was prohibited from having personal contact with Lorraine, Gifford *and* Ricky. Any violation of the order was punishable by incarceration. Lorraine realized that this was Gifford's way of getting back at Dean for the fight, but it was legal, and frankly she couldn't stand the idea of another confrontation.

Word spread on the backside that Gifford's syndicate was bringing his new horse up from California, "A colt with pedigree that wouldn't quit," they said. The purchase of the colt, however, set off another legal dispute. They wouldn't let Gifford license him in Washington. "Because some bastard has questioned his lineage," Gifford said.

Lorraine asked him, "Don't you have papers or something?"

"That's the trouble. They think the papers have been dummied up."

Gifford rattled on about his new colt while they ate breakfast and again while they got ready for bed. The horse was named *Nicanora*, which Lorraine thought sounded pretty until Gifford told her it meant "victorious army" in Spanish.

"My attorney came up with a plan though. We're going to take a blood sample and do a DNA match with his sire. It's foolproof. That'll teach those dummies to fool with me!"

Lorraine dropped Ricky off for a show with Mercy's kids and went to her mother's to finally bring her up to date on her evolving marital status. Her mother had perked a fresh pot of Folgers and spread some Oreo cookies out on a plate. Despite her mild dementia, she hadn't forgotten how to receive house guests.

Lorraine had purposely picked a night when she knew her dad would be with his bridge group, an event that both her parents used to look forward to. She took her mother through a sanitized version of the separation from Dean, then her renewal of an old friendship with Gifford, spiking her description of Gifford with the compliments Judge Culhane had paid him.

"I remember him," she said, something Lorraine doubted.

Her mother may have been under the Judge's thumb but she always revered him. Lorraine knew her mother still considered her marriage with the Judge to be the gold standard.

"I wish you'd come by more often," her mother said, "go to church with me sometime."

Had her mother understood any of this? "God's not just in church, Mom."

"You know. I mean religion."

Given her condition, Lorraine wouldn't have been surprised if her mother had abandoned regular attendance at mass. For her mother, however, attending mass was like ironing shirts. And, of course, the Judge still insisted on it, the ironed shirts and Sunday mass. "You understand why Dean and I are divorcing, don't you, Mom?"

"He's not right for you, honey."

"It's for Ricky."

"You shouldn't be working, Lorraine. Your father doesn't let me work."

"Gifford feels the same way."

"Who's Gifford?"

"My fiancé."

"Oh. You said that."

Just at that moment, someone opened and closed the front door and the Judge joined them in the dining room. "Oh, Lorraine, I didn't expect to see you," he said, as they gave each other an almost hug, the kind where you lightly grasp each other's arms but never make it all the way in. And then, taking Lorraine by the elbow, he escorted her into the living room.

"What happened to your bridge," she asked.

"Ah! Somebody said it was past her bedtime and left. You can't play bridge with just three people at the table! That's when I said sayonara!"

"Sorry Mom couldn't come to the engagement party."

"In your mom's condition, huh! I didn't want to put her through it. Being with people whose names you don't remember. Giff told me about it. Wow! Hostler finally got what was coming to him."

Lorraine didn't want to talk about the engagement party. Ever. With the fight and all, it was something to forget. And inviting the Judge into that discussion would have just ramped up his lifelong disappointment with her marrying Dean.

"But, hey, Lorraine, I'm glad you're here. With you divorcing Dean and marrying Gifford, it puts you into a bind. You can't take communion! You're excommunicated! But there's a way around it. You still want to be Catholic, don't you?"

Lorraine is already shaking her head, wanting to escape. This conversation was going exactly in the direction she dreaded. Even though she'd not attended Sunday masses regularly, except for Easter and Christmas, with the stress of taking care of Ricky's ADD and Dean, she'd drifted.

"I called the Bishop," the Judge said, "and we've come up with something!"

"Dad, let's not . . ."

Holding his hand up to shush her, he said, "Unless you annul your first marriage to the Hostler guy, you're ostracized! Excommunicated! No more sacraments. I don't want that to happen and neither do you or your mother."

"Please, Daddy . . ."

"I've already started the process. The Bishop's on board. We just need to put together a diocesan tribunal. I know some people close to the Bishop who can pack the tribunal. Hell, if we have to, we'll get the Pope to rule on it."

Lorraine has covered her face with her hands. "Daddy, daddy . . ."

"Daddy! Whose Daddy? This is a legal matter and I'm the Judge!"

"Gifford isn't even Catholic! Why are you . . ."

"I don't give a damn if he's Catholic! I want you to still be able to take communion with your sisters!"

Lorraine walked to the dining room with the Judge following her, finger waving all the way. She gave a quick hug to her mother. "Sorry, Mom! I'll be by again soon." And then she exited with the Judge still talking to her.

Lorraine scheduled an appointment with Dr. Kobler, a therapist for Ricky from the list of names Gifford had given her, another gesture that had impressed her. She was determined to cut away the tension between Gifford and Ricky and replace it with a foundation of trust. She had to first get them to the point where they liked each other. Every book she'd read on the subject stressed the difficulties of blended families. They just needed a little counseling to prime the pump. Of course, Gifford had assumed that the counseling was for Ricky.

"This is for you too," she said.

Gifford kissed her on the forehead, like she'd just shown him a not very good finger painting. "Whatever your pretty heart wants," he said.

She grabbed him by the arm. "Don't pretty me! This is serious, Giff!"

Doctor Kobler's office was in a house with a meticulously pruned rock garden in the front yard. As the three of them ascended the steps to the porch, she wondered if Gifford knew anything about the people he'd put on his list. He'd probably had his receptionist call around for names. She was afraid he'd be put off. Anyone who ran a business out of his home had to be bush league in Gifford's eyes.

"Thought he was s'posed to be a doctor," Ricky mumbled from behind them.

The sign on the front door said, "Quiet, please. Session in progress." Lorraine hushed the men with a finger across her lips and shooed them inside. The room smelled of Nag Champa, the same incense she used to burn when she meditated. Lorraine and Gifford sat on the sectional, Ricky took a seat on the ottoman, and she watched him crane his head around to look at the art. There was a black swan in a pond with blurry orange fish, a voluptuous Madonna with a wolf nursing at one breast, and a shrine with crystals scattered at the feet of a carved Buddha on the coffee table. Doctor Kobler had covered all the bases. Everything but a crucifix. She imagined him being Jewish with a goatee and wire-rimmed glasses. He probably smoked a pipe.

A woman in a mini-skirt and white leather boots that covered her calves emerged from the inner office, sniffling and wiping her nose with Kleenex. Her male companion -- Lorraine guessed they weren't married -- pushed her toward the exit door. Ricky couldn't take his eyes off them. Then Doctor Kobler appeared.

"Giff! Good to see you. Long time no see." The two men hugged, and Lorraine was relieved they knew each other; maybe she wouldn't have to defend the benefits of counseling afterward. Doctor Kobler was a tall, well-built man with a clean-shaven head. He wore a dark green turtleneck sweater, loose tan slacks, and sandals.

"And you must be the Mrs?"

"Not yet. I'm Lorraine Hostler. This is my son, Ricky."

"I'm sorry. Ron Kobler." He extended his hand to Lorraine.

Doctor Kobler ushered them into his office and pulled a fourth overstuffed chair into the arrangement and everyone sat down. Lorraine thought he had to be in his mid-50's but he was in remarkably good condition. He must be working out, something else she would like to be doing. He went over to his desk and came back with a plastic bag of Hershey's kisses and handed it to Ricky, who immediately passed it to Lorraine.

"They're fresh," Doctor Kobler said. "I live off them."

Gifford helped himself to one and the foil crinkled as Doctor Kobler sized up Ricky with his eyes. "Tell me what's going on, friend."

"Ask them," Ricky said.

"Maybe I should explain, Doctor," Lorraine said.

He waved her off. "You'll get your turn."

Lorraine squirmed as Doctor Kobler worked with Ricky. Question, glare, silence. Ricky acted like they didn't speak the same language. There was bitterness in Ricky's voice, and she suspected it was aimed at her as much as Doctor Kobler. It took every bit of her will power to keep from screaming and calling off their session.

"Maybe you all need a timeout," Doctor Kobler said. "I have an idea if you want to hear it." He was looking at Lorraine.

"Sure," she said.

"How about Ricky going away to school? I've had success with Delphian. It's a little boarding school in Oregon on the grounds that used to be a Jesuit novitiate. Seven hundred acres with individualized curriculum, sports, and a great teacher to student ratio. They specialize in troubled adolescents."

"I'm not troubled," Ricky blurted out, "but they are!"

When their fifty minutes were up, Doctor Kobler asked Ricky to wait outside. "I want to talk to your mom and dad separately for a minute." Even Lorraine could feel the pain of that one, but before she could say anything Ricky was out the door with a slam.

"He'll come around," Doctor Kobler said. "I do a lot of remarriages. This is your standard Oedipus complex. Gifford's taking away his lover. He'll fight until his mother makes it clear he can't have her."

"That sounds horrible," Lorraine said. "He needs me!"

"Honey, we paid for this," Gifford said, "just hear him out!"

"I've been married for eighteen years, Doctor Kobler. There's no Oedipus complex."

"He's also fighting the war for his biological father. You have to let him know that . . . what's your ex's name again?"

"Dean."

"That's right . . . Dean. Ricky has to know that Dean's over."

"I'm living with Gifford. I'm engaged. What do you want me to do, throw darts at Dean's picture? And what good is banishing him to a boarding school?"

The way Doctor Kobler looked at Gifford aroused Lorraine's suspicion. "Wait a minute, whose idea was this?"

Gifford broke the silence. "It's just one alternative, dear."

"Normally," Doctor Kobler jumped in, "there's a period of romance before the children enter. It's the natural rhythm of marriage." He looked at his watch, then leaned over and cupped Lorraine by both shoulders. "Let's talk about it more next session. I've got another appointment. Don't worry, it'll all work out."

She wished she'd gone with her original instinct and found a female therapist, and someone who didn't know Gifford. She was tired of everything being reduced to sexual paradigms. Where was the rest of the psyche? Wasn't it possible Ricky was just mourning the loss of an important relationship in his life with Dean? Why did everything have to be a sexual rivalry? And why hadn't Gifford told her about his idea of the boarding school?

Lorraine didn't feel like rehashing the counseling session on the way home. Especially in front of Ricky. She was afraid she'd say something she'd regret. To heck with them. Let Gifford and Ricky duke it out on their own. She asked Gifford to drop her off at the Ram.

Lorraine hadn't been to the Ram since before the engagement party, hadn't even said goodbye to her customers. Mercy had taken back the swing shift while they looked for Lorraine's replacement. Bernice Dillard, the owner's sister, was behind the counter and anticipated Lorraine's question when she came in.

"Mercy's not working tonight," she said. "One of the kids is sick."

She probably should have just called Gifford for a ride home, but she didn't want to go home. If Mercy had been there, they would have sat in the waitresses' booth. Instead, she took the table with the loose leg by the gum ball machine. The screw had gone in and out of the leg bracket so many times the hole was stripped, and the table wobbled when she leaned her elbow on it. When the bells on the back of the door jingled, she knew without looking that it was five forty-five and it was Abner. He could wander the streets aimlessly all day long collecting aluminum cans, but he was punctual about his coffee, and he always came to the Ram directly after dinner at the Mission. She could smell the wet cardboard and feel the heat as he arrived at her table.

"Care to join me?" she said.

He sat down across from her, resting his wrists against the edge of the table. His fingernails were chewed to the nub and the creases in his hands were visible from the grime of handling the town's throwaways. Hurrying back and forth from the tables, she'd never noticed how strong his eyes were, the corners of the sockets etched with laugh lines, although she'd never heard him laugh. He brushed back the wisps of gray hair on the dome of his head.

"Where you been, Miss Lorraine?"

"Oh, boy, where haven't I been?"

His eyes crinkled as he reached down, pulled out a silver pocket watch, and popped open the lid. There was a black and white photo inside that had been worn as thin as newsprint from being handled. Lorraine had seen this almost every time he came to the Ram. He wiped his brow with the back of his hand. "Isn't she something?"

"She has your eyes."

"She's my daughter, you know."

He snapped the watch shut, put it back in his pants, and picked up his coffee. He steadied the cup with his lips, took a loud sip, and managed with both hands to put it back on the table. "She's who I look for out there . . ."

Lorraine tried to dam up her eyes with the palms of her hands. He reached over with a dirty hanky and she took it.

Ricky slouched in his chair at dinner. "What's this stuff?"

"Liver paté," Lorraine said. "It's good for you. Spread some on a cracker and put a sweet pickle with it."

She'd made a point of the three of them having dinner together again. Gifford had agreed not to take any appointments before seven p.m., and she tried to make the dinners special. Tonight was tomato bisque soup, meat spreads, olives, celery and carrot sticks with garlic dip, seedless red grapes, and sparkling mineral water. She'd gotten used to the delicatessen Gifford had introduced her to on Grady Way.

"This is a nice meal your mom fixed," Gifford said. "Show a little appreciation!"

Ricky dipped his bread in the soup, nibbled at the soft part and then dropped the crust onto his plate. "I'm goin' for a bike ride."

Gifford put his hand up. "Hold it, Mister! Don't you think you should ask first? Where you going?"

"I don' know."

"That's a lie!"

"Gifford . . ."

"Your mother worries her tail off for you. I'm not going to have you disappearing into the night. Your grades are in the toilet. You're hardly someone who can play catch up. Are you going to your dad's?"

"Gifford! I can deal with this."

"You shouldn't be seeing your dad until this thing is settled!"

Ricky slumped into his chair again and played with the grape on his plate, rolling it around the outside of his soup bowl with his finger, until they excused him to his room. Nobody finished their dinner, and Lorraine didn't bother with the chocolate eclairs she'd bought.

"Sorry, dear, but he needs some discipline," Gifford said.

Lorraine later tried Ricky's door, but it was locked and his tape deck was playing, one of those punk rock groups she'd tried to discourage him from listening to. She knocked, but there was no answer.

About two minutes after Gifford's Town Car pulled out of the driveway, she heard Ricky tiptoe down the stairs and into the kitchen. At first, she thought he was going to fix something to make up for starving himself at dinner. Then the back door opened and closed and she snuck into the kitchen nook and watched him go into the garage. He came out walking his bike. He wasn't moving fast, and it would have been easy to catch him as she watched him swing onto the seat and lean over to grip the handlebars. His legs were too long for the pedals, growth she'd noticed since the separation. There was a light on the front fender and she wanted to run out to make sure it was working, give him a rubber band for his pantleg so it wouldn't get caught in the chain, but she was too conflicted to move. How did you hold on to someone? Tie a rope to them or let them run free?

19

No one knows what I'm thinkin'. I don' even know sometimes. I've learned one thing though, I'm never gonna have a kid. 'Cuz that would mean I'd have to marry someone and marry'n sucks like a jellyfish. Plants its mouth on you like a suction cup. If yore swimmin' it bites on your leg and you walk 'round with a crutch the rest of your life. When you marry, it gets you on the head and sucks your brains out through your ear hole. You don't even know it's happen'n. Then you start doin' stupid stuff.

Like Mom's turned into a jellyfish with stingers. All her new man had to do was show her his house and she went gaga. Since when does Mom care about tubs with claw feet and beds with gauze curtains hangin' over 'em. Shouldn' she pay more attention to who's on the pillow? Doesn' she feel the suckin'? I'm not goin' to some dumb school for stupid kids in Or'gun. Where'd that come from? Doesn't she see how she's doin' things like eatin' potato chips and junk food she doesn't even like? Then serves it to Mr. Wonderful when he comes in the door at night. Mom hated it when Dad drank and she cranked on him when he did. Now, she makes martinis and giggles and asks Mr. Won'erful if it's dry enough. I can tell he wants me out of his house. Outta his life really. Go to your turret room, he's think'n. He glares at me out the side of his head. It's pretty obvious I cramp his style. I wonder if he'd be that way with his own kid.

I don' min' the turret room. Though I'd never tell him that. With binoculars, I can watch the squirrels goin' into the attic on the house two over. They carry junk in an' out of there. Regular little party house. A whole family of 'em. Sometimes a gang of crows squawk at 'em for stealin' their food. I keep thinkin' one of the crows is gonna try grabbin' a squirrel and pick him apart to get the stuff outta its stomach. That's what Skeeter Parker and some of his friends tried to do to me. They didn' have enough money for pills this week, so they jus' held me down and took 'em outta my pocket. They're 'fraid to do anything 'less there's a whole gang of 'em squawking. 'Course eagles are differen' than crows. Eagles don' have friends. I'd rather be an eagle any day.

I can also see the upstairs of tha' house where the squirrels go. There's a girl who sits on a chair by the window play'n a violin by herself. I can't hear the music 'cause the window's closed, but she's beautiful the way she moves her head and lets her hair fall down over the strings. I see her playin' even when other people are sittin' at the kitchen table downstairs eating. That's *her* turret room.

I've made up my mind 'bout the shrink. I'm not goin' anymore. Period. I'll stand up to 'em like Dad did at the hotel. Turn into a windmill if Mom's guy tries to lay his soft real state hands on me. They want me to see Doctor Gobbler, they'll need a police force. Whose biz'ness is it what's in my head? Am I s'posed to be a sitcom or somethin'? Change channels, Doc. It wasn' my idea to get the divorce. Like I said, I'm not gonna get married. The Gobbler tries to act like he's on everyone's side, but he's a bumble bee flittin' 'round wait'n to sting. If I went to that school, I wouldn' be able to see Orphan. No way. I'd shoot someone first. I'm not pay'n him, so why's he gonna take my side? They always kick me out early while I wander 'round his house looking at his statues while they talk 'bout me. The real stuff. I thought you weren' s'posed to talk behind someone's back. I don' need to tell anyone what's inside me. Mom thinks she knows, let her tell 'em.

Actually I feel sorry for Mom. She's still all twisted up and miss'n Dad and just trying to make it look like she's fine. But you can see it all over her face. She's only smilin' and eatin' pate' on the outside. Some mornin' she's gonna wake up and come get me in the turret and we'll chuck this house with the spokes on the porch. One of my plans is to take her to the farm and show her Orphan. But what if we walk into the kitchen and find Dad wrapped around tha' Jill woman with her pants off? Not exactly what Mom'd be wishin' for. Even makin' martinis for the real state man would be better'n that. An' I'd be back in the turret watch'n the violin girl.

I won' let 'em take me away from Orphan. She makes all this crap not matter and she doesn't even know she's doin' it. Like she's seen it all before. When I'm touchin' her and she's look'n at me with those big eyes, I feel like she's see'n every show ever made inside me and I don' care 'cause she's not trying to change anything. Just look'n.

Dad totally wigged out after the fight. I snuck over there the second day he was in jail. I didn' care 'bout any trainin' order. He was a zombie with a Hall'ween mask. Just staring at me through the scratched plastic window like someone gave him a deadness shot. When he asked if Mom was missin' him, I lied. If I'd done anythin' else, he might have just hanged himself. I asked him 'bout Orphan wonderin' who was gonna take care of her, but I might as well been talkin' with my head in the toilet 'cause he wouldn' even say her name. A strange feelin' came over me though while we were talkin' like that. How all the time he'd said he'd gotten the horse for me, I never believed him. In the jail though, with that little hole in the plastic and the smell of everyone who'd been there before, I felt the reverse of suckin'. Somethin' was pumpin' into me, somethin' better than air. A juice was spread'n through me like warm blood. I didn' know what it was 'til I was leavin' the police station. Maybe Dad didn' mean it, maybe it just leaked out of him but I knew after that visit Orphan was mine. I was her guarding angel and I had to make sure nobody sucked out my brains and made pate' with it.

20

Still smarting from the news of Lorraine's engagement to Gifford Pomeroy and his arrest for losing it at the engagement party, Dean couldn't help but fixate on the injustice of it all. It plagued him when he was awake and it became the focus of his dreams, which had turned into nightmares. He'd considered Gifford one of his best friends in high school. Dean had stupidly tried to cover for him by changing seats with him as the police raced toward them on the railroad tracks after Gifford had taken his high school teacher's car on a joy ride. But it was Dean who was arrested and Gifford who skated free. And now, Gifford was trying to steal Lorraine. In front of everyone. In Dean's face.

Dean also missed being able to tell Ricky his bedtime stories. When Ricky was little, he was scared of the dark and insisted on having a night light on next to his bed. But Lorraine worried that he'd get distracted with the light on, shortchange himself on sleep and lessen his ability to focus on his school classes. So on story nights, Dean would lay flat on his back next to Ricky in the dark and they'd make up stories together, taking turns choosing the story, the characters in them, and the places where they happened. They had one rule, no story where the good guy dies.

Dean would often fall asleep before Ricky in the middle of the story and that was one of their rules too. Whoever fell asleep, the other guy couldn't wake you up. Since Lorraine had kicked him out of her life, it seemed like all his dreams were nightmares. With Gifford playing the villain. And Dean trying to get even.

In one of his dreams following the fight at the engagement party, Gifford brought his Town Car into the body shop with a crease in the front door on the driver's side where it looked like someone had swung the door too hard against a parking meter. While he waited for Shorty to raise the entry door to the shop, he pulled down the visor on the driver's side and a sales slip from Ben Bridge Jewelry fluttered down. Gifford had paid more for Lorraine's engagement ring than he'd paid for Orphan. Mad as hell in his dream, Dean went out to the scrap pile in the alley and found a piece of leftover angle-iron about the height of a door panel, duct taped it to the passenger side of the car and swung a twelve pound sledge hammer against the angle iron as hard as he could. In his dream, Dean had already taped the iron to another door when Harold Bogle pinned him against the car and said, "You just spent this week's check, asshole!"

When Dean woke up from his nightmare, he felt like he was coming off a sugar high. His head ached. He had a fever. And part of him wished it had really happened the way it did in his dream. So that Lorraine would know how painful this separation was. He didn't mind taking the rap, but when was he going to get credit for purity of motive?

When he heard Jill go outside to do her chores, he flipped on the Discovery Channel. There was a show on about miniature penguins, showing how the fathers abandoned the mothers and babies in the winter and came back with the food stored in their throats. It felt good to be watching the tube. Jill had encouraged him to spend more time in the main part of the house and told him he could help himself to whatever he wanted. His plan was to repay her with a freezer full of steaks when he got back on his feet, maybe throw in a king salmon.

Dean didn't hear Jill come in, but the next thing he knew she'd punched off the TV and was glaring down at him with her hands planted on her hips.

"Hey, I was learning something!"

"Don't 'Hey' me, bub! Look at you."

"It was a good program."

"Good thing you didn't see your horse this morning. You don't want her drinking in all this angst. You damn well better keep your job or you ain't gonna have a wife or a kid!"

Dean returned to his bedroom, where he'd covered the windows with dark towels so he couldn't tell the difference between night and day. It was a womb. He could eat snack food, play solitaire, and feel sorry for himself without interruption. Then a hard knock woke him up.

"Ricky's here!" It was Jill's voice and she was standing next to his bed.

He bolted up. The light from the open door was blinding. "What time is it?"

"I'll tell you what time if you'll tell me what day."

He paused. "Thursday?"

"It's Saturday and quit feeling sorry for yourself!"

"Ricky's here?"

"Standing in the kitchen."

Dean kicked his dirty underwear and socks into a pile in the corner, pulled on his jeans and dragged a comb through his hair. He thought he should be doing something productive when Ricky saw him, so he took his checkbook off the nightstand, opened the register, and started reading the entries. Some were without dates, some without dollar amounts, and some without both.

The shirt and pants Dean had hung on the knob fell in a heap on the floor when Ricky opened the door. Ricky surveyed the dirty dishes, potato chip bags, garlic dip canisters, and crushed soda pop cans scattered throughout the bedroom. Dean hadn't seen Ricky since the day he came by the jail.

"Why aren't you takin' care of Orphan, Dad? She misses you."

Dean fiddled with the pages in his check register, fanning them with his thumb. "I've been feeling kind of crappy." Dean mucked around in his brain, trying to reconstruct the history of the tug of war he was in with Ricky, but he couldn't remember who'd started it or whether they were even on different sides. "You've been over to see the horse?"

"Jill takes me. I've been workn' and feedn' her every day."

Ricky was backlit against the illumination from the next room. "I thought you were pissed at Jill?"

Ignoring the question, Ricky said, "We took Marmalade over too."

"The cat?"

"I've been exercise ridin' for other trainers too." This was unsettling for Dean, the collaboration between his son and strangers. "You gotta get outta here and do somethin' Dad!" With that, Ricky did an about-face and left the room.

Dean could hear Jill and Ricky talking in the kitchen and he strained to make out their words. Then the front door closed and the screen door whapped against the house. No more voices. Dean went to the window and parted the towels to watch them going side by side down the walk. They got into the Blazer, made a U-turn in the barnyard, and drove away.

Dean fell onto the bed and stared up at the tongue and groove knotty pine on the ceiling. Some of the knots had shrunk away from the boards and looked like they were ready to drop. He could smell the musk from his own armpits. When he turned his head to find his boots, his whiskers scratched against the pillowcase. He could feel the magazines between the sheets and the bedspread.

He got up to go to the bathroom, shading his eyes as he passed through the dining room. The bird in the cuckoo clock chirped. He pulled the toilet seat up and sat down, wishing he'd brought along a magazine. Ricky's backpack was hanging on the door and he reached over and pulled it onto his lap. When Dean was young, he used to go through his mom's purse, siphoning off the spare change and cigarettes. He unzipped each pocket in the pack and felt around inside. There weren't any cigarettes, not even matches, just cookie crumbs and Babe Ruth wrappers.

The main section of the pack had a spiral notebook and a hardcover textbook. *United States History.* There was masking tape holding the front cover on and Ricky had printed his name along the edges of the pages in blue ink. Dean flipped it open to a picture of George Washington standing in a boat full of soldiers, with a beard that someone had drawn. A folded piece of paper fell out of the middle of the book, and Dean picked it up off the floor.

> *Mom, your no fun anymore and your kill'n Dad. Don' let em send me away to that school in Or'gun. That would kill me too.*
>
> *Ricky*

Dean took a deep breath and wiped his eyes on his sleeve. He read it one more time and it socked him like a sledgehammer. He couldn't stand the idea of Ricky hurting his mother's feelings. He refolded the note and carefully put it back into the book. There'd just been a change of plans.

Type B

21

Lorraine was starving for the company of Mercy Kirk, and she didn't want just a booth at the Ram with food crumbs in the seams of the vinyl upholstery. Mercy knew about the men in Lorraine's life and Lorraine knew about hers. They'd groomed each other, dressed in each other's clothes, and forgiven each other's sins. Everything she'd ever told Mercy, Mercy had already done.

"I want to take you some place nice," Lorraine said. "One of those seafood restaurants at Shilshole where they spread the napkin across your lap. Just you and me."

"Oh, God, honey. Just come over to my place and we'll fix a cheese omelet. I'll spread *your* napkin." She laughed.

"I'm buying. It's part of Gifford's *allowance.*"

Gifford had agreed to move the monthly poker game to his house so he could watch Ricky on Lorraine and Mercy's night out. The counseling sessions had gotten them nowhere; Gifford and Ricky came home more worked up than when they'd started. She thought it would be good for Ricky to see Gifford with other men, in his real milieu, so he could see how Gifford was respected by his peers.

Lorraine chose one of the dresses Gifford had bought for her. He'd picked it out himself, using the average of the sizes from the outfits hanging in her closet. It was an equestrian styled suit, with houndstooth checks and velvet trim. The single-breasted jacket was shaped at the waist and the skirt was pleated in the front. She didn't have shoes to match but she made do with a pair of oxblood heels.

When she looked at herself in front of the full-length mirror in the master bedroom, she lamented how skinny and white her legs were without panty hose.

"My God, look at you," Mercy said, when she opened the door of her apartment to let Lorraine in. "I didn't know we were going as sex objects. I'll change."

"Quit it! You're fine."

"With pants? No way."

They went to Mercy's bedroom, where she slid the hangers back and forth on the clothes rod and held outfits against herself. Lorraine okayed a half dozen of them before Mercy finally pulled on her nylon stockings and secured them with a lacy garter belt. She stretched her leg out behind and looked over her shoulder.

"Are my seams straight?"

"You're the only person I know who still uses garters."

"Honey, men like to get a glimpse of flesh above the stocking."

Mercy wriggled into a snug plum dress with buttons up the front, a slit in the skirt that ended well above the knees, and a plunging neckline. "A bodice ripper, huh?"

"You'd look sexy in a gunny sack!"

Lorraine had told Mercy their reservations were at seven, just so they wouldn't be late, but they arrived in time to park at Golden Gardens next to the restaurant and walk the beach. Lorraine had always admired those scenes in the movies where elegantly dressed people took off their shoes and walked barefoot in the sand. Mercy didn't require a lot of encouragement and undid her shoes at the first picnic table. Then she twirled toward the water with the shoes dangling by the straps in her hand. Lorraine sat down on the table bench, pulled off her nylons so she wouldn't get them dirty, and stuffed them into her purse. There was a breeze that made her feel naked from the waist down as she ran to catch up with Mercy, staying on the higher, dry part of the beach. It was high school again, the sorority of two, Lorraine hoping that some of Mercy's sauciness would spill onto her. Once she caught up, Lorraine steered Mercy over to a log so they could sit down, watch the sunset, and dry their feet off before dinner.

Mercy had trouble steering her bottom to the half-buried log. "Not sure I can get down that far with my garter belt," she said, laughing.

Lorraine sat down next to her and twisted her bare feet into the sand to find the heat from the daytime sun. She could picture the people who'd sunbathed there, little kids playing catch, and wicker baskets with sandwiches wrapped in foil. Real families, with parents and kids who lived peacefully in the same house.

"How did you ever have the courage to remarry, Mercy?"

"I think it was the thought of being a single parent with no sex," she laughed. "I left Cory with his grandmother and went to the Club Med in Martinique. A guy with a good tan named Buddy bought me a Mai Tai. Not exactly badge of courage stuff."

"I remember Buddy."

"I wanted someone who'd never set foot in Renton. He had a college degree, he was in a divorce, and he told me how much he missed his kids. I thought, perfect, a daddy for Cory with a degree. We moved into his beach house in San Diego, married, and I got pregnant with Samantha. That's when I found out he was diddling our babysitter. And the babysitter's mother wouldn't report him because he was diddling her too." Mercy flicked sand into the air with her toes. "I asked him what they had that I didn't have, and he said, 'forbidden fruit.' That's when I moved back to Renton."

"I'd of sworn off men altogether."

"It's hunger, honey. Us Hostlers are cursed with an insatiable hunger."

In some ways, Lorraine envied Mercy's history, because it was so clear-cut. It would have been easier if Dean were an addict or a wife beater. Instead, he just acted like a kid, the kind who played catch in the street and managed to get out of the way in time for the fast cars. "I miss living with you, Mercy."

Mercy reached over and jiggled Lorraine's leg. "Bring your clothes over to the apartment sometime and we can do laundry together."

"How do you ever know you're doing the right thing?"

"Marrying Gifford or leaving Dean?"

"Both." Lorraine could feel Mercy's toes under the sand.

"Before you took Gifford off the market, I kind of had my eye on him myself."

"He's not enough of a hunk for you, Mercy."

"Hey, I'm grown up now. I look at the bulge in their wallet instead of their crotch."

They laughed and put their arms around each other.

"I just wish Gifford would ease up on Ricky."

"Men are so possessive. They can't stand the idea that you might have slept with someone else."

Wind surfers with scarlet, violet, and indigo sails crisscrossed each other in the bay. A flock of seagulls followed a barge being towed seaward. The sun was already low enough to ignite the clouds on the horizon. But Lorraine had lost her appetite, so instead of dinner at Ray's Mercy went into the cocktail lounge and talked the bartender into *loaning* her a bottle of Irish Cream and two carry out glasses with lids. Then they stopped by Mercy's car, grabbed two blankets out of the back seat and went back to their spot on the beach and looked out at Shilshole Bay, which was now vacant of watercraft and full of melancholy in the moonless night. They wrapped themselves in the blankets and planted their drinks in the sand. Lorraine could feel the warmth of Mercy's cheek against her own. She was wearing the same perfume that Lorraine had borrowed when they were living together.

This was her chance, thought Lorraine. She didn't know it at the time but this was why she had ached to have this evening with Mercy. She was bleeding internally, every organ cross-hatched with knife marks from her duplicity. Mercy would have every right to be hacked off at her. "You're going to hate me, Mercy, for telling you something I should have told you a long time ago, but I'm going crazy." There was water leaking out the corners of Lorraine's eyes and she knew it wasn't from the breeze that had kicked up. She was trying to navigate around a secret that had grown like a cancer in her fallen away Catholic soul. "This is family business. Jilted woman to jilted woman. You can't breathe a word of this to anyone. Cross your heart and hope to die!"

"My god . . . of course . . . we're family."

Lorraine took two deep breaths and then dove in. "I was a practicing Catholic way back when . . . in high school, remember?"

"How could I forget. Little Miss Perfect. God's worker bee on earth!"

"People were afraid to swear in front of me. I was stuck up. I was a religious fanatic. I so desperately didn't want to end up in hell, but I have anyway." Lorraine inched herself closer to Mercy and grabbed her hand. "You have to swear yourself to secrecy!"

"Cross my heart."

"I *was* a good student . . ."

"Understatement!"

"But I was also waking up. I wanted to come out of my bubble. Everyone else was going out . . . you know . . . doing crap that kids do. I wanted some of that."

"I was just the opposite," Mercy said, "but go ahead . . . I'm tracking."

"Out of the blue . . . in senior year, Gifford Pomeroy asked me for a date and I said yes."

"*The* Gifford Pomeroy?"

"I didn't even know him that well!"

"Yeah, straight A's, I hated him for that!"

"And he had a car, so what the heck? Go, I said." Lorraine looked around to make sure nobody was lurking within earshot. "We did it, we fucked! Excuse the French, but that's what it felt like. On our first date!"

"Oh, my god, we *are* related! But now you gotta tell me the whole story . . ."

"We went to his place."

"Nobody home, I'm guessing."

"Nobody home. And I still remember him turning the thermostat up and giving me a beer from the refrigerator. Another first. There was a quiz show on TV, which was our only light."

"Yeah, yeah . . ."

"I was so tired of living off the stories other girls told in the lavatory. I knew what the *it* was but I wanted to taste it. So when Gifford took off his shirt and unbuttoned mine, we moved to the couch. I still remember saying a *Hail Mary* and smelling the warm dust from the forced air of the furnace as we did it. Or, I guess, as *he* did it."

"Really . . . you said a *Hail Mary*?"

"I wasn't sure he'd even gotten his thing all the way in."

"Front door is far enough for most guys, honey."

"It was more like a business deal . . . you know, slam, bam, thank you ma'am!"

"So, holy shit, you fucked the most successful guy in our class! While I was diddling the losers."

"Shh! I don't want everyone on the beach to hear us."

"It's a deal, but . . ."

"We went out twice more . . . safe stuff . . . once to a movie and a candidate debate . . . then he disappeared. Totally. Zip. AWOL. I never went out with him again."

"Okay, this is starting to turn out more like my stories except Gifford didn't know I existed."

"He wasn't your type, Mercy!"

"Hey, don't sell *me* short!"

"Anyway," Lorraine said, "about two weeks later, Dean asked me out. Next to the pop machine."

"By the cafeteria," Mercy added.

"Well, I said yes, and I'd never had so much fun in my life. No alcohol, just Coca Cola and non-stop conversation and laughs . . . he was so open and adoring of me. I felt like I already knew him from the jillions of love notes he'd sent me."

"Okay, I don't need footnotes!"

"We went to a place out on the Cedar River . . . roasted wieners and marsh mellows on a stick over a fire that he'd started with a splash of gas from the spare can in his trunk. I was warm . . . it was what I imagined heaven would be like . . . in a cove surrounded by towering Douglas Fir." Lorraine stopped to adjust the blankets and spill it all out. "We did it on the blanket he spread over the hood of his car! The earth vibrated and he went in all the way!"

"Oh my god, Saint Lorraine! On the hood of a car!"

"The hood was still warm! And I was looking up at the boughs of the Douglas Fir."

"So who wore the rubber and who didn't?"

"God, Mercy, I didn't even know what a *rubber* was. It was dark. I didn't want to act like a nun!"

Mercy put her hand up. "Okay, time out!" She grabbed her glass off the sand. "This calls for another drink! You shock me, cousin . . . premarital sex . . . back to back?" She poured and they clinked their 'take out' glasses again.

"Dean and I started dating."

"You mean more fucking!"

"Oh, god no! I wanted to marry Dean, we were madly in love! But I told him we had to save ourselves until the wedding."

"He was okay with that?"

"Of course! He was an angel!"

"Remember, I was *at* your wedding."

"In the rectory instead of the church. The Judge's idea, of course. He said I didn't deserve a church wedding."

"You shouldn't have told him you were pregnant!"

"I wanted to tell him the truth! He didn't want me to marry the Hostler guy!"

"I'm still mad about that. My god, 'We're human I told him! Even *you* came out of someone's womb!"

Mercy raised her glass and they clinked again. "I'm proud of you, honey!"

"I was with child! With Ricky!"

"Excuse me for being real here, but with all this sleeping around how did you know who Ricky's father was?"

Lorraine visibly slumped. "Oh, god . . . I wasn't sure at first. So I prayed over it. Then I confessed it. The intercourse, well intercourses. Two of them. To Father Feist. And he made me pray a rosary for each one of them." And in a deep voice, she imitated Father Feist, "*Stay away from the occasions of sin, young lady.*"

"But how did you know?"

"I was sure Dean was the father! Absolutely. The earth moved! With Gifford, it felt like we were just going through the motions. It was more for him than me. With Dean I was attracted to his mussed hair, the hole in the knee of his jeans. I told him I could live in a bomb shelter with him. Most of all I loved the idea that he was totally nuts about me."

"So you didn't really know who the father was but you *wanted* it to be Dean."

"Sort of . . . I guess, but then I found out. For real. When Ricky's ADD surfaced."

"Jesus!"

Lorraine slapped both of Mercy's knees, "You know about Ricky's attention deficit disorder."

"Old news, dear."

"His teacher recommended we see a doctor or a counselor who dealt with this." Lorraine paused and held up her drink. "God, love this Irish stuff!"

"Anything to keep you going!"

"You're better than a priest, Mercy."

"When the Irish Cream runs out, we go back to the bar, okay?"

Lorraine stood up, then Mercy. They straightened their clothes and wrapped themselves together with the blankets from feet to neck.

"Talk about sexual," Mercy said.

"Well, anyway, we, Dean and me. We ended up seeing a doctor about Ricky's ADD. They told me it can be hereditary. So we each gave him a blood sample and a swab, to see where it was coming from. Ricky gave samples too as part of a routine physical. He had no idea why we made him give a sample or really cared."

"A swab?"

"It's spit! On a little ball of cotton."

"My god, that's gross!"

Lorraine took a deep breath. "Anyway, I'm a type *O* and Ricky's *A*." She stopped to let it register with Mercy and took her by both hands. "Dean's a *B* so the doctor said it's impossible for Dean to have fathered Ricky. Biology 101, he said!"

"You'd never done it with anyone else?"

"No, of course not! I told you. I'd done it twice. Swear to God!"

Mercy put her hands over her face, "So Ricky's not a Hostler! My God, I thought you were going to tell me you'd shtupped one of my husbands." They both laughed. "Who knows about this?"

"You!"

"Honey, doesn't this solve your big puzzle?"

Lorraine let out a deep sigh. "Ricky hates Gifford's guts! I was going to wait until we'd broken the ice and gotten Ricky used to the idea of another man in his life before I told him."

"So . . . what . . . you're going to wait and tell them in your Will? This is the passkey, babe! Gifford's not stupid. He'll put Ricky on a pedestal, make him president of his little company."

Lorraine finally let go of her knees and her legs dropped to the sand. "You haven't seen Ricky's fury. I've started to have visions of him stabbing Gifford in his sleep or putting poison in his ear. He misses Dean's bedtime stories."

22

The next night, Lorraine took Ricky out to dinner at a sit-down place, with the intent of making summer plans for him. Gifford was working late again, and Lorraine let Ricky choose the place.

Lorraine held her finger on the next summer class she'd circled in the Renton Park Department flyer. "How about archery? There's one for beginners and one for intermediates. I'll tell them you're intermediate."

"Nah," Ricky said, as he bit into the end of a roast beef au jus sandwich, squirting juice onto his plate.

"How about electric guitar? It says the teacher plays in his own band. That's cool."

"I don' have a guitar."

"We can get you an early birthday present." She stared at him. Instead of his face she saw the top of his head. "What if we got a dog? You could pick it out."

Ricky didn't look up. "It'd mess up his house."

"It's not just *his* house, Ricky. I'm trying to meet you halfway on this."

"I don' have any rights."

"Rights? Sure you have rights. What kind of rights do you want?"

"I don' want him. He's all *wrongs*."

She huffed in frustration. They'd gone over all this in therapy. "I don't want to go down that road. This divorce is between me and Dean."

"No it's not."

"Well, Ricky, it *is*."

In frustration, Lorraine bought herself a used ten-speed bike. Ricky had a bike, so she'd have a bike. She'd never ridden a bike with gears. When she was growing up, if you wanted to go uphill, you pedaled harder; when you went downhill, you coasted. There was a flat bike trail on the abandoned railroad right-of-way that ran down the center of the Green River Valley that she thought would be perfect. Gifford suggested she get a bike rack for the top of the car so that they could also do the Burke-Gilman and the Sammamish River trails.

Ricky didn't want flat and safe. Instead, he showed her the Maple Valley Highway, which was narrow, frighteningly busy, with no marked bike lanes and Lorraine vowed not to play mother. They started out together, Ricky in front with her following, and it was a thrill to see how strong he was and adept at handling the gears. Then the gap widened, they lost voice contact, and gradually he got so far ahead that Lorraine couldn't even see him.

She'd always worked, at least part-time, as the safety net for Dean's jobs, so she didn't have the luxury of free time with Ricky. The problem was finding an activity they could both enjoy. Conversation was certainly not one of them. He'd become suspicious of her questions. All roads led back to the great divide in their lives that was the dissolution of her marriage with Dean. She didn't know Ricky anymore.

In her desperation to reconnect, she took on another persona: Dean's. She stopped picking up after Ricky. She ate in the living room and left dirty plates on the floor. She stopped fixing his lunches. She stopped telling him where she was going and what time she'd be home. When she gave him a time, she made a point of being late. If he bothered to ask her where she'd been, she'd say, "Places." She started fixing herself Seven-Up highballs before dinner.

"I didn' know you drank, Mom."

"There's a lot of things you don't know, kid."

She signed up for shooting lessons at the Auburn Gun Club. In the first lesson, she learned how to disassemble a twenty-two rifle, clean it, and load it. She was afraid of the bullets, certain they'd explode if she dropped one. For the second lesson they took her to a shed with paper targets attached to clips on a wire that she could reel back into her assigned cubicle to see how she'd done. She learned to nestle the rifle into the muscle of her shoulder, hold her breath, and squeeze the trigger. Twice she set the rifle down without putting on the safety and her instructor, a thin man with wiry arms and a mustache, said, "What are we forgetting?"

The instructor stood behind her, with his arms alongside hers. His breath was a cherry lozenge. He had a pack of cigarettes in his front pocket that he never smoked on the range. If she turned around to ask him a question, he quietly pushed the barrel of the rifle down until it was pointing at the ground. They'd given her ear protectors, but she still flinched at every crack of the rifle.

The instructor whispered, "Follow the bullet into the target with your eyes."

When she got to where half her shots landed on the paper, she decided it was time to drop the idea on Ricky. It was a weekday afternoon and he'd come home with a broken bike chain.

"Drive me downtown, Mom."

"Can't. I'm going to the shooting range."

"The what?"

At his mom's suggestion, Ricky had organized his summer. He'd told her his routine was going to include early morning bike rides to the Maple Valley golf course where he'd comb the rough looking for lost balls that he'd sell to golfers waiting to tee off. Whenever he could, he'd also caddy. Whether he caddied or shagged balls, he'd come home, devour a meal of his own making and disappear to his room. She felt helpless. The more she tried to find out what made Ricky tick the more she didn't know him. She stopped asking him what he was doing with his mornings. It was too painful. And it was obvious he was lying. The giveaway wasn't the fact he diverted his eyes and mumbled under his breath. The giveaway was the smell of horse.

While Ricky disappeared in the mornings, Gifford disappeared in the evenings. "In a flat market, I just have to work each deal harder," he told her. Still, Lorraine always got up when she heard Ricky leave, but she saved her breakfast until Gifford woke, poaching his eggs and serving them on whole wheat toast, with a spoonful of jam on the side that he could slide his squares of toast and egg through. She ground coffee for herself and rinsed off the frozen blueberries she put over her granola. Gifford always drank a cup of black tea, followed by a second cup of mint or licorice herbal.

She wanted to tell him the truth about Ricky, but she wasn't sure yet how he'd handle it. Worse than Ricky rejecting him would be his rejecting Ricky. That would kill her. And, of course, once she told Gifford, she'd have to tell Dean and, of course, the Judge. The thought of connecting that circuit conjured up visions of anarchy, more *mano a mano* between Dean and Gifford, with the Judge as referee. She wasn't ready for that again.

Since moving in with Gifford, Lorraine had a lot of time alone, whole afternoons and evenings when she spoke to no one except her house plants. She bought shopping bags full of books on second marriages, alternating these with books on attention deficit disorders and genetics. There was too much time to take information in, and not enough opportunity to disgorge it with another human being. It would have helped if Gifford called once in a while between appointments, to tell her he'd made a deal, or even lost one. He was so purposeful that she often felt useless. Dean had no purpose. Gifford was all purpose.

The activity she'd taken on as a hoax that summer had turned out to be what she looked forward to most - the kick of the rifle, the sulfurous smell of gunpowder, and the sing of the bullets. She saved her targets, brought them home and put them under the stack of books next to her nightstand. The steely smooth trigger had become the most sensitive instrument in her life, certainly the one over which she exerted the greatest control, and she began to relish how it gave way and exploded under the pressure of her finger. She stopped telling Gifford about her gun lessons. She liked them so much it was almost embarrassing. It wasn't who she thought she was.

On Saturday, Ricky caddied or said he caddied, so Lorraine made a pizza and took Mercy and her kids to Liberty Park for a picnic. There was a Lutheran church group playing softball on the field next to them, boys and girls on both teams. Mercy went over to see if they'd let Cory and Samantha play. Lorraine couldn't tell what Mercy was saying, but she could see the man's eyes feasting on her body. Cory and Sam just stood there next to her, waiting. And waiting. They'd seen her do this before. That's what a single mother had to do. The man with the baseball cap turned around and said something to his players in the dugout and they reluctantly handed over two mitts that he gave to Cory and Sam. Mercy said something else and pointed to the kids in the dugout. The man turned around and pretty soon he handed her two baseball caps.

"Nice man," Mercy said, when she returned.

"He was hitting on you!"

"Thanks, honey, but I think he's a minister."

Their blanket started in the shade, but the earth turned, exposing their legs and then their backs to the summer sun. Mercy took off her shoes and rolled her jeans up to her knees, then she tucked her blouse into the bottom of her bra. Mercy's skin had a built-in tan that

Lorraine guessed was the result of time spent in the sun growing up. Lorraine had never sunbathed when she was young, out of shame for her underdeveloped figure. Finally, she had medical science on her side. Sunlight was carcinogenic.

"You think they'd mind if I took my top off?" Mercy said.

"Don't you dare!"

Mercy unbuttoned her blouse, rolled over, and reached back with one hand to unclasp her bra. "Sunbathing is like sex with God," she mumbled. Then she pulled the blouse up over her head and wiggled herself into a comfortable position against the blanket, breasts down. "Okay, wrong! It's full out intercourse."

Watching the kids running and yelling at each other, Lorraine couldn't help but think of how Ricky had ostracized himself from his peers. He didn't even get along that well with Mercy's kids, who were family. She always thought she could compensate for his isolation by forging an incomparable maternal bond, an umbilical cord through which she could pass a sense of self-worth. Instead she had passed him her apprehensions.

"Rub me, honey," Mercy asked.

Lorraine sat up on her knees and spread her hands across Mercy's back, which was warm and pliable. Lorraine tried to follow each rib from the spine outward, in slow, nourishing strokes. Mercy gave in to the pressure. Lorraine's mind kept going back to the same haunting thoughts, and she started to cry again. She tried to wipe her eye with the corner of her shoulder so that she wouldn't have to let go of Mercy.

"Okay, what's going on?"

"I still haven't told Gifford he's Ricky's father."

"Sweet Jesus!"

"It's just going to start a big ruckus."

"So don't tell 'im."

"I finally told the Judge about my divorce action against Dean."

Mercy and Lorraine raised their hands and slapped them together. "Finally!"

"He was all over it! Started talking about how he knows some Cardinals in the Vatican. How he can get my marriage to Dean annulled."

"Wow, he can do that?"

"He said once it's annulled, my marriage to Gifford will be the only one on the books. I told him it all sounded a bit phony and he said, 'That's how the law works!'"

23

Dean called Mercy to find out how Lorraine was doing, to see if he could postpone the divorce hearing, to find out how much time he had left. She was jumpy and evasive on the subject and sounded like a travel agent when he asked about the wedding. The dresses for the wedding party had arrived from New York and been fitted and tailored. Lorraine's veil from Zurich was at the dry cleaners being starched. Finally, she told him, "They've set Saturday the thirtieth of September for the wedding, Dean."

"That's less than a month after the divorce hearing!"

"They aren't wasting any time for mourning, Dean. Sorry, Cousin."

"Are they still gonna send Ricky to that school?"

"They specialize in troubled kids, Dean."

"He's not troubled."

"Troubled rich kids, Dean. Ricky'll love it."

Dean had rearranged his hours with the body shop so he could spend the morning at the track with Orphan and start his day at 1 pm at Bogle's and work a swing shift. It was another new start. He was bored with sleeping. His body was honeycombed with adrenalin. He wanted to go to the track every day. It distracted him from thinking about the divorce.

He reminded himself that this was the first day of the rest of his life and he was going to turn over a new leaf. The air was already warm and muggy. There was an aroma of discarded orange rinds in the cab of his pickup that Dean inhaled while he worked the gas pedal up and down to clear the air bubbles from the fuel pump.

He was in a heightened state of consciousness as he drove to Longacres, anticipating the cycle of every signal, hitting each intersection without using his brakes while the cars that raced past him got hung up in the wrong lane at the light. Dean stared at the places he'd gone by thousands of times before – the Texaco, Pickering Appliances, the Donut Shop. He thought of the day his dad brought him home from juvenile detention after his arrest for joyriding with Gifford, and they drove down Rainier Valley, past Sick's Stadium, along the lake shore to the perimeter road that ran around Renton Municipal Airport, where you could look across the runway and see jet planes fresh from the Boeing factory waiting to be flown. His dad had treated their trip home as a victory ride, never once lecturing him or wagging a finger. Dean remembered them pulling into one of the entry ways to the Boeing plant that day, about ten yards short of the guard house. His dad shut off the engine and the two of them just stared at those monstrous mud gray hangars behind cyclone fences with coiled concertina wire along the top, and Dean could only imagine the secrets they concocted inside those windowless edifices. In large block print, the sign on the highest part of the hangar read: *BOEING.*

Dean flashed his ID to the man in the guard shack at Longacres, who waved him onto the grounds. He passed barn after barn, finally pulling into an empty parking stall in the last row, where he shut off the motor, punched in the light knob, and pulled the emergency brake. *End of the line, Bub.*

A man with a weather-beaten face was scrunched down in the corner of a stall reading a book that was pressed against his knees. Dean's sense of conquest wavered. He felt anxious. It was one thing to not tuck your son into bed because his mother had yanked the rug out, but he had no excuse for not seeing Orphan every day. He stopped in front of a stall that looked like all the others, patted his empty pockets, edged over to the gate, and rested his arms on the crossbar.

Orphan was lying on her side in the stall. As soon as she saw Dean though, she lifted her head. There were pieces of straw stuck to her mane, her ears were perked, and for what must have been a full minute they just stared at each other. Then Orphan unfolded herself, shifted her weight over her legs and rose, front legs first. Orphan shook her head, gave Dean another skeptical look, and then moved toward the gate. Dean was stock-still on the exterior, but his insides were quivering. Jill had told him how delicate a horse's digestive system was, how sensitive they were to apprehension in the people around them. Stress a horse and it'll colic, she said. Dean didn't dare make eye contact and looked at her nostrils instead. He could feel her warm breath on his hands.

Jill had renewed her training license and had entered Orphan in a series of claiming races. Taking advantage of his summer vacation, Ricky had been regularly showing up in the morning to exercise Orphan. She'd broken her maiden second time out with Pedro Garcia riding.

Orphan's daily exercise reminded Dean of when Lorraine bought Mercy Kirk's old running shoes for a dollar and taped a workout schedule to the refrigerator in anticipation of her running a 10K race. Dean jogged with her the first two days, then developed blisters on the balls of his feet that split open and bled. Lorraine was faster, something that Dean attributed to her being lighter. She wore a sleeveless shirt and running shorts, and when Dean quit running to let his blisters heal he asked her to switch to sweats so guys wouldn't ogle her. Prepping Orphan for the track reminded him of the time Lorraine developed her own shin splints and Dean had to paint her legs with a liniment of wormwood oil and white thyme.

Orphan nibbled on Dean's shirt, bunching it up in her front teeth, and Dean could feel it tightening through his arm pits. He wasn't going to stop her even if she chewed it off him. Dean's eyes were inches from hers and he could see his reflection stretched across the curve of her eyeball.

"You're the horse I came in on, girl."

Dean was surprised to find a glass of Old Grand Dad waiting for him on the kitchen table when he came out of the bathroom at Jill's. There was another one in front of Jill, who'd taken off her boots and put her hair up on one side with a barrette. He'd never had a drink with Jill, didn't know *if* she drank. Dean's equilibrium was jangled. He'd given up drinking. Hadn't she been harping on him to get up and do something? Why hadn't she joined him when he was sulking in his tent? He would have welcomed a drink then.

"Here's to Chuck!" Jill said, raising her glass.

"I thought there was no Chuck."

"It's a metaphor." Her words slurred, this wasn't her first drink of the night. "Have a drink with me, Dean."

"Naw."

"Scaredy-cat."

Dean couldn't remember a woman ever demanding that he drink. His dad had and, when he was twelve, Gifford had. Jill poured another one for herself, they clinked their glasses, and Dean downed his out of a sense of camaraderie.

"I never trusted men," she said. "That's why I dropped out of college. To work with horses." She was making Dean nervous. Jill was one of those people who became down in the mouth when they drank. She picked up the bottle by the neck and topped off their drinks. Then she set the bottle down hard between them. "I went with a guy once who marked my periods on his Day Timer so he wouldn't get blood on his dick. Never heard from him in between."

She was making Dean uncomfortable and he wanted to excuse himself. He hated to hear women rail against crappy boyfriends or unfaithful husbands because he knew they were directing it at him too. It was a conversation women have been engaged in since Adam and Eve. They were still pissed at the male species for not picking up their dirty underwear, for wanting sex, for watching sports on TV, for forgetting to buy toilet paper at Safeway.

Jill didn't stop talking until they'd finished off the bottle, mostly Jill's doing. Then she suggested a sauna, and Dean declined, but next thing he knew he was following her down the corridor, stopping off at the bathroom to strip down to his jockey shorts and wrap himself in one of her Turkish towels. Jill was already stretched out naked on her back on the upper bench when he entered the sauna. It was as if she didn't know she was naked. Dean slipped his pants off under the towel and wadded them together into the corner.

"Put some more water on," she mumbled.

Dean looked over to see if she was watching, but her eyes were closed. He scooped the ladle into the bucket of water on the floor and poured it over the stones, which hissed back with a vapor cloud. It made him feel woozy. He'd only taken one other sauna, with Lorraine, but it didn't last long because Lorraine became claustrophobic. Dean didn't know sauna etiquette and figured the safest thing was imitation, so he spread out his towel on the bench under Jill's. Lorraine would kill him for what he was thinking.

Neither of them spoke and Dean wondered what it would be like to do it in this suffocating heat. If someone got worked up they'd blow a fuse. It made him think of matches in an oxygen tent and exploding dirigibles. She couldn't have been more than twenty-four inches from him. Her right arm dropped off the bench and flopped awkwardly into the air. Her fingers were limp. She tried to say something, but her voice was sloppy, or maybe Dean's hearing had faded. He reached up and put his little finger into the cradle of her hand, and the last thing he remembered was her squeezing it like Ricky used to when he was a baby.

He woke up in a strange room, on the edge of a high bed with tapered posts that thrust themselves toward the ceiling like harpoons. He was surrounded by an acre of pin-striped bedspread and piles of pillows, and he slid his hands around under the sheets to see if he was alone. A television was playing in the next room. He spied a half-full glass of water on the nightstand and crawled across the bed to reach it. The water was room temperature, but it felt like a glacier-fed stream as it ran down his throat and pooled in his stomach. His head ached and he rubbed his forehead with the palm of his hand to massage the arteries.

Jill burst in with a mug of coffee that she set on the nightstand. "Good morning, stud!"

Dean pulled the sheet up under his chin. "I'm sorry, Jill."

"What's there to be sorry about?"

"Didn't we . . . you know?"

Her knees leaned into the bed. "What's better for you, that we did or we didn't?"

With a splitting headache and dry-mouthed, it was hard to get his mind around that one. There were so many things to consider. She was the same old Jill again and he should have been relieved, but instead he felt a wave of guilt. He was a screwup just like his dad, inventing ideas in his head like love and redemption that he couldn't make happen in real life. Than he looked at his wrist watch. "I'm late for Orphan's workout!"

The pickup creaked when Dean opened the door on the driver's side. There was a half-eaten Twinkie on the seat that he couldn't remember starting. He tried two keys before he accomplished ignition. The windshield was mottled from last night's raindrops and so was his brain. Lorraine's lawyer had sent Dean a copy of the restraining order at the body shop. He'd shown it to Jill, to see if she thought it meant the same as what he thought. "Don't mess with it," she'd said.

"Not see my own son? No way!"

Dean hoped he'd find Ricky at Longacres, but Orphan was alone, methodically rubbing one front leg against the other, trying to shed her wrap. Dean unlatched the gate and joined her, with tears in his eyes. He put his hand around the shin bone and lifted her leg. Orphan made no effort to put her hoof down and Dean slowly planted it for her. Then he scratched hard against the outside of the wrap with his fingernails.

"I know the feeling, girl. Like a bug's eatin' you."

He scratched her other foreleg, then worked up to the shoulders and chest, the neck, the face, back to the butt and down the hind legs. Orphan leaned into the pressure of his hand.

It was Saturday, a race day at Longacres, and there were messages coming over the PA system paging vets and trainers. People in business clothes, strangers to the backside, wandered through the barns looking at their entries for the day. Dean interrupted a groom several stalls away who was taping his horse's ankles with light blue tape. "Do you know Ricky Hostler, my son?"

The man pointed toward the track. "Try the cafe," he said with an accent.

Dean checked again on Orphan, then zigzagged his way between the barns toward the racetrack. There was a shack near the entry gate to the track with vertical siding and no sign indicating that it was the backside café. Except for the smell of meat cooking, you wouldn't have found it.

People turned to look at Dean as he entered the cafe, and he wondered if there'd been talk about him. The guy who'd abandoned his horse, the guy being cuckolded, the guy who'd holed up at Jill Sprague's place. He took long steps and planted his heels firmly as he aimed himself toward the table where Bud Holliday, the trainer, was sitting. He wished he had a plug of chewing tobacco under his lip or a double wad of bubble gum. He shoved one fist into his pocket to put some bulge in his pants. There were four people at Bud's table, another guy who looked like a trainer and a couple of exercise riders. The guy picking his teeth with the prongs of a red plastic fork looked Dean up and down. There were no more chairs, so Dean just stood next to the table.

"Bud, you remember me? I gotta talk to you."

Bud dragged a chair from the next table over and gave it to Dean, who sat down just outside the circle. Then Bud went back to the conversations at the table, talking about who could go two turns, bleeders, faders, jockeys who didn't switch sticks, and trainers who ran their horses into the ground. Dean watched their faces. They knew the horses at the track like you knew the kids you went to grade school with. Dean skidded his chair over behind Bud, tapped him on the shoulder and whispered, "What's the biggest race left I can put my horse in, Bud?"

"For two-year olds, it's the Gottstein Futurity. One of the biggest races of the year. Last weekend of the meet."

"How much can I make?"

Bud chuckled. "Purse's fifty thousand. Winner's share is fifty-five percent."

It was the first time since he'd won the bid for Orphan that Dean had thought of her as a vehicle for revenue. A beautiful horse was its own best reason for being, like a piece of art. In the back of his mind, Dean realized that all of these trainers, jockeys, grooms and exercise riders were supported by some kind of economic system, but if you'd asked him out of the blue he would have told you that the only money that changed hands was at the betting windows. The horses and people on the backside were the trapeze artists and fire eaters who entertained them.

"Maybe I can throw the dice . . . one last hurrah," Dean said.

"It's the best two-year olds on the grounds," Bud said. "Colts and fillies. Not everyone who wants to gets in."

A new vision had formed in Dean's mind. He'd show Lorraine who was the better parent for Ricky. The one who banished him to some ritzy school where he'd end up with needle marks in his arm, or the one who made his horse a champion. He'd enter Orphan in the Gottstein and put the winnings into a savings account for Ricky's college. *Then* he'd let Lorraine decide what kind of parent he was.

Dean headed over to the grandstands to see if he could find Ricky and tell him the good news. Jill said Ricky had befriended some trainers on the backside who let him watch the races from the owner and trainer boxes on the upper level of the grandstands. Like Jill said, the track was a farm. Age didn't matter. They let kids do anything they were capable of doing. Dean didn't have enough for a cup of coffee, but after he overheard someone cussing because they'd thrown away a winning quinella ticket, he started picking tickets off the ground and sorting them out by race in the men's room. All he wanted was enough to buy Ricky a hot dog and a Coke so they could celebrate his new plan.

Somebody had wedged their racing form into the toilet paper dispenser and forgotten it. Dean locked the stall door and was paging through it when the name *Pomeroy* jumped out at him. Gifford Pomeroy owned one of the entries in the feature race that day, a horse with a name like *nicotine*.

Dean's heart raced as he walked the concourse above the owner's boxes. If Gifford was there, maybe Lorraine would be with him. All he wanted was a look at her, to see if she was happy. If she was, he'd leave her be. If she wasn't, he'd swoop down and take her away. He'd know by the slump of her shoulders. He moved aisle to aisle, checking people out from the top row to the bottom. He knew Gifford wouldn't be far from the finish line. Maybe they'd gone up to the Turf Club. Gifford probably had a company membership. Lorraine's engagement ring was probably also paid for by the company. He searched the men's restrooms near the Turf Club. If he found Gifford, he'd follow him to Lorraine. *Screw the restraining order.*

While the horses were saddling up for the feature race, Dean took the stairs up to the next level of the grandstands, where there was a landing with a view of the paddock. This was perfect, he thought. He'd let Lorraine reveal herself.

Owners and trainers were entering the paddock and gathering in clusters to wait for their horses to be saddled. Women in high heels tiptoed across the lush grass. It was a series of family reunions, with babes in arms, little boys in blazers and ties, yawning teenagers, and men with canes. *Rich bastards*, Dean thought.

Gifford Pomeroy and a man Dean didn't recognize joined a group on the opposite end of the paddock just in time to shake their jockey's hand and give him a hearty pat on the back before he mounted his horse. Lorraine was not with him; in fact, there were no women or children in Gifford's group. Just men in suits and sport jackets.

The horses paraded out of the paddock with their jockeys aboard and the groups in the paddock quickly dispersed like it had started to rain. Gifford waved his arms and was yelling at someone. Dean didn't pay a lot of attention at first. It was probably someone he'd sold a house to. More schmoozing. Then he saw Ricky flying out of the paddock in a sprint with Gifford chasing him.

Dean spun around, knocking someone's hot dog to the ground, and pushed his way through the people still packed near the windows overlooking the paddock. He took the stairs, coming down so hard on the landing that his legs buckled and threw him against someone's midsection. Dean bounced off and kept going. He ran along the fence next to the track, dodging spectators, looking sideways toward the betting windows under the grandstands. They'd ditched him.

Dean's head was jumbled. He'd always prided himself on the fact that he could think fast on his feet. He was someone who could shoot a pistol from the hip and hit a beer bottle floating down the river, the one who pulled the other guy out of the fire, the one who righted the overturned car. His brain worked better when everyone else was panicky. But this was Ricky, and that meant Lorraine. And where Lorraine was involved, he'd lost his sense of reckless abandon.

He ran all the way back to Orphan's stall in the barn, but Ricky wasn't there either. He walked up and down the aisles, peeking into stalls. Then he ran back to the grandstands again and made a pass by the booths at the entrance where people were selling the next day's Racing Form and tip sheets. That's when he saw the Town Car pull up, the same one he'd dreamed of pounding with a sledgehammer. The valet stepped out and two people emerged from the waiting line. It was Gifford, with Ricky in tow.

Dean yelled at them through the turnstiles, but the valet slammed the passenger door and the car sped away through the parking lot spewing blue exhaust.

24

Lorraine found a bottle of Chardonnay in the refrigerator and poured herself a glass while she cooked. She used one of their good stemware glasses that hung upside down in the cupboard. She'd watched chefs on television sip wine while they cooked, but it always seemed like drinking while driving. As she worked her way through a Julia Childs shrimp creole recipe, however, she realized that the simple act of imbibing transformed the whole act of cooking from something you did for other people's pleasure to something you did for yourself. She pinched instead of measured the parsley and salt, she eye-balled the cayenne. How many meals did a person have to cook before they could trust their own judgment? Besides, weren't spices a matter of taste? What was so magic about one bay leaf, they weren't even all the same size? How bad would too much butter be? She couldn't even remember if Gifford liked creole dishes. She knew Ricky liked prawns if they were breaded and deep-fried. Mercy's advice had been to play hard to get. "Mother them and pretty soon they'll forget your name," she said. Shrimp creole wasn't exactly a mutiny.

When nobody showed up by five o'clock, she turned the sauce down and put the bowl of de-veined shrimp into the refrigerator. At least Ricky should have been home. She corked the bottle of Chardonnay and put it back in the same spot in the refrigerator. She squirted soap into her wine glass, scrubbed it out by hand, dried it with the hand towel and carefully hung it by its base again in the cupboard. She put the bread on a cooling rack and covered it with a dish towel, changed the napkins from cloth back to paper, and returned the candles to their same places on the mantel. She didn't want to be disappointed. She didn't want to lose that feeling from the wine. But she couldn't help herself and started thinking of Dean, wondering why he hadn't understood the reasons for their disconnect. Maybe Dean *had* sensed it and that was why his paternal urge was so ramshackle and unreliable. But she believed Gifford was different. His whole life had revolved around transfers of title. He was an owner, not a renter. Maybe he'd see Ricky in a whole new light once he knew Ricky was his. Mercy was right. She had set herself up for the let downs by hoping for too much.

Then she pulverized the creole sauce in the garbage disposal and unset the table. She'd act surprised they were home so soon. *I guess I must have spaced out.* She sat in the sunroom, where she had a view of the driveway, and kept looking up from her Ladies Home Journal when she thought she'd heard Ricky's bike. She'd watched him navigate that incline many times without even standing on his pedals. She'd also watched him wipe his hands and shoes on the grass before coming into the house.

She saw Gifford's Lincoln lugging up the hill. Maybe it was better that Gifford arrived first she thought. She could listen to his horse racing news and get that out of the way before Ricky came home from his caddying. There was a passenger in the car and she begin regretting that she'd undone the dinner. Gifford usually warned her if he was bringing a guest home. She'd never turned him down, but it was nice when he asked. The car stopped in front of the garage and Ricky burst out. He must have gotten into an accident and his mangled bike was probably in the trunk. Ricky ran toward the house. Gifford yelled something at him, then slammed the car door. She waited for Ricky to come into the living room, but he came in the side door and she listened to his footsteps galloping upstairs. Gifford crossed the lawn, his brown leather zip briefcase under his arm, stomped his shoes on the mat, and flung open the door.

"Guess where I found him?"

"Is he hurt?"

Gifford hurtled his briefcase onto the couch. "The little bastard was at the track!"

"Don't talk that way, please!"

"Did you hear me? He was . . . at . . . the . . . racetrack! You said he was caddying . . . he's been scamming us."

They hadn't touched each other yet. There was usually at least a peck on the lips when Gifford came home. Lorraine enjoyed the linkage that could be accomplished by that first simple touch. "I'll talk to him."

"You talk to him all you want, but he's grounded. No more freewheeling. As long as he lives here, he's going to be accountable. I'm tired of this bullshit. He's just like his dad!"

"That's not fair, Gifford."

"As far as I'm concerned, they're both retards!"

Her insides flamed. "Damn you, Giff!" She'd never sworn at Gifford and she wanted to butt him against the Laura Ashley wallpaper with her head. He came across the room and wrapped his arms around her from behind, trying to nuzzle her neck, and she fought to escape him. "You've been wanting to say that, haven't you?" His thumb crossed her lips to silence her, and she bit it, grinding the cartilage against the bone. She hadn't bit anyone since fighting with her sisters in grade school.

"Quit it, Lorraine! Don't you think I'd rather have stayed and seen my race?"

Lorraine unclenched her teeth and started crying. She was angry at herself for crying in front of Gifford. It was so womanly and predictable.

Later that night, while she was reading in bed and still trying to decompress, the phone on her nightstand rang and Lorraine picked it up out of habit. It was Dean, calling from a phone booth, with street traffic in the background. His voice echoed and it seemed more bass than she remembered.

"Let's go away," he said, "you, me, and Ricky. We can stay in a little cottage on the Oregon coast with a porch and fly a kite on the beach."

Lorraine's head slumped against the headboard. "This isn't a good time to talk."

"He's gonna hurt Ricky. Tell him you're going with Mercy. Two days, that's all!"

She couldn't imagine how she could ever tell Dean the truth about Ricky, but until she did everything else she told him was going to be a lie. Still, she couldn't give him any encouragement. "Ricky needs the discipline," she said. She glanced over at Gifford, who was on his side of the bed reading his own magazine. She guessed that Gifford would know it was Dean even if she hadn't said his name. "Gifford and I are one on that."

Over the noise of tires against pavement and accelerating engines in the background, Lorraine thought she heard Dean crying. He was finally starting to wither, she thought. He'd always treated Ricky's condition like a case of overly fair skin. Once he tanned, Dean thought he'd be fine.

She hung up, and Gifford asked no questions. Usually he snuggled against the back of her legs and wrapped his arms around her like a flag before they went to sleep. She turned off her light and faced away from him. There was no flag wrapping.

On the off chance that Ricky might make a break for it and come back, Dean slept in the stable at the track that night with Orphan, using a couple of blankets. He curled up in the corner of the stall, but Orphan wouldn't settle down. She kept circling and pawing the ground, her restlessness a perfect reflection of his own. He thought it might be her foreleg, but they'd taken the wrap off, the swelling was gone, and her skin was cool to the touch. Dean brushed her down and rubbed her between the eyes. *It's not 'cause he doesn't love you, Orphan.*

When she continued to fuss, he put a bridle and the tattered Scotch plaid saddle blanket on her, cinched up the saddle, then peeked out to make sure nobody was watching. If anyone asked what was going on, he'd say the vet told him to walk her at night, to keep the blood circulating. They walked past Barn Five, then Four, Orphan's feet padding the ground like moccasins. Then they zigzagged over to Barn Two and past the cafe, which was closed, but there was a red glow in the window from the neon *Michelob* sign.

The swinging gate to the track was also closed and there was an ice-cold chain wrapped around the post that clanked when Dean uncoiled it. Somewhere under all that metal there was probably a padlock, but he had to try. Orphan bobbed her head, tapped her toes in the soft dirt, and neighed. "Shh, girl!" He gathered the extra chain into an increasingly heavier loop that he fed through the gate until he was down to the bare post. There *was* no padlock. Somebody must have lost it and covered it up with extra wraps of the chain. He swung the gate wide enough for horse and man and led Orphan onto a backstretch that was flooded with moonlight. He wanted to think of Lorraine curled up under the sheets alone, with her knees against her chest to stay warm. He wanted to figure out a way to pick the lock to her heart again, to insinuate himself back into her life in a way that would make her forget the bad times. Maybe he'd get that job at Boeing. But now she had a companion, someone on her side. How had Lorraine put it, they were *one* on Ricky? God, what a beautiful word *one* was. He ached to be a part of that idea again. Just to ride in the same car with her would be a rush, to look over and see the trace of a smile across that lean, honest face. They were probably talking about him now. Pillow talk. *That poor dumb bastard,* they'd say. A spasm passed through Dean, and Orphan jumped sideways.

"Sorry, girl."

He mostly just trotted her, to help her get a good night's sleep. When they came to the paddock area, Orphan automatically turned in with her head high, stretching out her neck, strutting to an imaginary audience and Dean let her lead the tour. He wished he'd been there for her races, but so far they'd always fallen during his new weekday swing shift at Bogle, which was still his lifeline to keep up his payments to Lorraine and pay for Orphan's room and board. Thanks to Jill, they'd entered her in several allowance races under the ownership of the *Lazy B.* No sense drawing unnecessary attention to Ricky's horse. So far Orphan had managed a win and a place, doing her part to pay for her own room and board at the track. He'd been able to view all of her races on Longacres filmed replays afterwards but what a kick it would have been to see Orphan come across the finish line ahead of a field of horses. And join her in the winner's circle. She was acting like a racer, and if you were a racer, why wouldn't you race at night? If you were a racer, why would you need an audience? Just pin back your ears and run. That's what Dean needed to do, just run. Lorraine didn't have to give him permission to be Ricky's father. The law couldn't take that away. There were Hostler atoms in there, dented maybe, but they were his.

When Dean came home from the next morning's workout, he told Jill about his plan to enter Orphan in the Gottstein Futurity. "I've been talking to Bud Holliday about it."

Jill slapped a packet of mail with a rubber band around it against the kitchen counter. "Jesus, Dean, you'll break her spirit! Don't put her in over her head! She'd be against the best two- year olds at the track."

"I've got to make a statement, Jill."

"Have you talked to Ricky?"

"Not yet."

"I thought Orphan was his, or was that just bullshit? You ruin that horse and you're gonna lose Ricky. If you're doing this because of Lorraine, it's even more bullshit." Jill had never even laid eyes on Lorraine and it was disarming to Dean when she talked about her by first name.

"The plan is to win big and then sell her!"

Jill clamped her eyes shut. "I don't even know your wife, but if she's half the mother you say she is I don't think she's going to take kindly to you bustin' Ricky's heart."

It would have been easier, Dean thought, if the women in his life spoke with the same voice. He went in and flipped channels until he found a baseball game. He didn't even like baseball, it was so slow and he didn't know the rules. There were supposed to be signals coming from the coaches to the batter, and from the catcher to the pitcher, but maybe it was all dummied up. Hard throws, blind swings. He still had a half hour before he had to be at the body shop so he switched to an *I Love Lucy* rerun. Now, *there* was a free spirit. Nothing phased Lucy, and like Dean, her husband Desi adored her. In fact, her screwups only endeared him to her.

He thought about walking over to the pantry, uncapping the Old Grand Dad and calling in sick to work. Jill was de-worming the cows and he knew he should have been out there helping her. He could feel himself on the edge again. One drink, and he probably would have slid back into the ooze and let somebody else figure it out. But Jill came back in, still agitated that he'd even think of breaking Ricky's heart by selling Orphan. "Be careful what you walk away from, Bub! It might not be there when you go back."

When Dean was young, he never understood how his mother could mop and wax the kitchen floor every Monday, wash clothes on Tuesday, iron Wednesday, empty and wipe the cupboards Thursday, and darn socks Friday, whether anything was dirty or needed fixing or not. She didn't care if anyone noticed. Weekends she baked and, in season, canned and pickled. When he once asked her why, she said, "I need something constant in my life." And that's also what Dean needed.

Orphan had learned to expect Dean again every morning by five thirty. She already had her neck out of the stall peering down the aisle in the direction of the parking lot as he rounded the corner in his cowboy hat. The first thing he'd do is pop open the gate to her stall and let her smell the bridle so she'd know she was going to get her run. Then he'd wrap his arms around her and give her a hug. Orphan had learned to lower her head and let Dean nuzzle her, temple to temple, then she'd go back to the gate and peer down the aisle for Ricky, but Ricky had been grounded.

In the meantime, Dean recruited Miguel, a kid from Hermosillo to serve as a groom and exercise rider for Orphan. Miguel was grooming other horses at the track but he very much welcomed the opportunity to ride the horses who actually raced. Even though he was doing it for free. In broken English, Miguel explained why he wore a Blessed Virgin medallion on his jacket, how the mother of Jesus watched over jockeys, which was what he dreamed of becoming. Not a bad job, Dean thought; maybe she watched over *wanna be* trainers too.

Bud Holliday would occasionally let Dean use one of his pony horses to accompany Miguel and Orphan to the track for workouts and, as often as he could, to see Ricky on her. Orphan loved the mornings and couldn't wait to start backtracking her way to the starting point for her run. Maybe it was the Spanish, but Miguel couldn't settle Orphan the way Ricky could. She wanted to turn and run every time another horse breezed past her on the inside of the track. Where Miguel had to rein her in, Ricky could just pat her on the side of the neck and whisper.

Jill started dropping in on Dean at the track, following him around, helping him with his Spanish. It was maddening how much she knew about horses, how at home she was at the track. The veteran trainers knew Jill and somehow sensed when she was on the grounds because they'd come by and shoot the breeze about old times, patting her on the rump as they parted. It didn't hurt Dean's stock though. People started to take him more seriously.

Taking breaks in the cafe, Dean kept his ears open. He'd always been a better listener than talker. All he had to do was grunt, nod and listen to the trainers. Some wanted their horses to set the pace, others preferred to stalk. Dean knew one thing: only Orphan knew how she wanted to run and it was his and Ricky's job to learn what that was. So he and Ricky set out to find a style that matched her personality, pushing her beyond what they saw everyone else doing, running her in company with different horses, holding her back and coming from behind some days, running head to head on others. They never let her run without control. They wanted her to take cues from her rider, to let the jockey buffer her from the frenzy of the race and remind her how she ran best. A horse race wasn't a mad dash, it was a clash of tactics.

The days that Dean spotted Gifford's Lincoln Town Car parked on the backside they'd hold Orphan back and not take her to the track until his car was gone. Dean also started paying attention to who was standing next to the fence. Some days he'd see a light on in the judge's station on top of the grandstands and wonder if Gifford was up there with his binoculars. He didn't want Gifford to even know he and Ricky had a horse at the track. If Gifford saw him, he'd put two and two together. *Slam bam, contempt of court.*

One morning, Dean had just finished bathing Orphan and hooked her to the hot walker when he spotted Jill coming towards him. She'd started fiddling with her hair, platinum one week and red the next. It wasn't fakery because she made no attempt to hide the fact she was messing around with it. She experimented with her hair the way Dean experimented with Orphan's workout regime. This week it was strawberry blonde with frizz on the sides. Jill walked more bow-legged when she was at the track, and there was a determination in her manner that always made her look half-peeved.

"Hey, Jill, I've been thinking some more about the Gottstein," he said. "Me being kind of messed up over Lorraine and all, I might not have been thinking straight."

"What's that got to do with your horse?" Jill never blinked when she talked about horses.

"I'm saying maybe I was wrong."

"Look, buster, you're just a medium! The horse tells you when they should race." She was looking straight at him, waiting for his answer. Dean would have welcomed a blink, so he could shift gears. He itched his groin, then the back of his neck. Wasn't she saying just the opposite last time?

Lorraine was dying to find out what Ricky had been doing at the track when Gifford caught him, but he wouldn't talk about it. He brooded in his room, playing punk rock on high volume, waiting until Gifford left the house to sneak into the kitchen for a sandwich. At least he wasn't going to fast himself to death. She offered to fix something hot, but he wouldn't even consider it. He was strictly mayonnaise, lunchmeat, and Diet Pepsi Cola, which Gifford had started ordering by the case because of Ricky.

Lorraine had long suspected that Ricky's absences had something to do with Dean's damnable horse, Ricky's *Black Beauty*, a kid's infatuation. She'd always pictured this horse in an undersized corral somewhere, a lonely, neglected animal, making up for what Dean wasn't doing to care for it. Never did she imagine her at a racetrack that was peopled with gamblers and get-rich-quick artists. A racetrack didn't nourish animals, she thought, it exhibited and abused them. They called it a sport, but Lorraine pictured it more like boxing, under the control of insiders who doped the horses and greased the palms of the jockeys. She thought it was exactly the opposite of the ethics she wanted to inculcate in Ricky.

She'd tolerated Gifford's interest in horses as a decent man's singular vice. Gifford didn't drink to excess, didn't smoke, didn't consort with other women. The horses and his occasional poker game with his salespeople were his *man things*. And, for him, anything he could pin an income and expense statement onto was a friend in waiting.

On the third day of his detention, Ricky spoke. Lorraine was in the kitchen, and he was slathering mayonnaise onto both halves of a sandwich. Under normal circumstances Lorraine would have cautioned him on his cholesterol.

"This is prison, Mom, 'cept I haven't done a crime," he said.

"You brought this on yourself, Ricky. If you'd asked, Gifford would have taken you to the races."

"You a'ways take his side," his mouth was full of sandwich, but she was used to deciphering his conversations through masticated food. "You used to take *my* side 'gainst Dad!"

"I'm taking your side now," she said. Ricky stopped chewing and rolled his eyes. "Gifford could give you a job right now if that's what you want, doing home detailing. You'd be working with grown-ups. And getting paid."

"Here's a deal, Mom. I'll stop buggin' you about marryin' him if you let me go to the track. Anytime I want!"

The Futurity

25

Dean asked around about the Gottstein Futurity and found out that it was named after Joe Gottstein, a local businessman with a passion for horses who built the Longacres racetrack in a hectic twenty-eight day period prior to the start of the 1933 inaugural season. They said the paint was still wet on some of the seats for opening day and Joe paid the cleaning bills for anyone who submitted them. Joe's father was a successful liquor distributor who gave his son a horse. He took his family to Paris in the spring where they watched thoroughbred racing at Longchamp and other fancy tracks. Joe so much wanted Longacres to succeed that he gave loans to horsemen and made down payments on their homes so they'd be able to field horses for the meet. He sold one of his downtown buildings so he'd have money to pay the purses.

As Dean filled out the entry form for the Futurity, he couldn't help but feel a kinship with Joe Gottstein. He wrote a check for the entry fee against an uncertain bank account and nominated Orphan Annalina. He figured either she wouldn't get into the race, in which case they wouldn't cash the check, or she would get in and she'd win something to cover it. The racing secretary posted the notice of the nominees outside his office that evening: eighteen colts and two fillies. The field would be pared down to the top twelve based upon the horses' performance in past races at the track.

"Shoot, Jill," Dean said, after looking at the horses nominated, "I'm not going to even get in!"

"Nicanora's got three wins," Jill said. "Two of them were stakes races. He'll be the prohibitive favorite. Something about those black horses."

As Orphan became more used to being with Dean again, their grooming sessions grew longer. He rubbed and scratched her withers, her loins, her hocks, wherever Orphan wanted it. And Orphan yielded to his touch, let him fawn and nuzzle her. Still, Dean couldn't read her wishes in the matter of the race. On that subject, she wasn't talking.

Dean succeeded in recruiting his favorite jockey, Pedro Garcia, to gallop Orphan in the mornings. Jockeys rode the workouts in the morning for free so they'd have the chance to ride the races in the afternoon for pay. And Pedro said he'd love to ride Orphan, "If she get in." Dean had stopped riding the pony escort for Orphan's workouts for fear that Gifford would see him. Instead, he put on a heavy coat and sunglasses and took a place along the fence, away from the other owners and trainers, to watch Pedro run her.

"Hold her back a little," Dean shouted, as they passed him on the way to the start of their run. *Save it for Sunday*, he thought.

Pedro reported back to Dean after his ride, "She feel pretty good, Mr. Dean."

And she looked good too. Despite the bumps and grinds, Dean's workout regime had tightened her flanks, given definition to her rump muscles. She wanted the bridle. The bridle meant the track. Orphan knew the way there on her own. Once they made the turn and her rider gave her some rein, Orphan quickly stretched out in long, graceful strides that resembled fly casting.

There were other Gottstein nominees working out in the morning that week. Some of them Dean recognized by the logos on the halters. One he could pick out naked: a black colt with a white stocking on its left foreleg and a white spot the size of a hardball on his forehead. This was Nicanora, the one who came out of the turn for home like a rock out of a slingshot, his mane fluttering, his neck extended, his tail parallel to the track. He was a man among boys.

"Hey, Pal, where you been?" Dean jerked around to see Gifford Pomeroy standing next to him, in a suit and overcoat with a fake fur collar. The hair went up on the back of Dean's neck. *How long has he known I'm at the track?* Gifford chuckled and extended his hand. *He's toying with me.*

"How *you* been?" Dean said, wondering where his bravado had gone? He should have used the cyclone fence as a cheese grater for Gifford's face. Why didn't he say something about his dragging Ricky away from the track? Why didn't he say something about Lorraine? What about the restraining order, was that just Gifford's to play with? "I gotta go," Dean said, and turned to leave.

Gifford was still talking but Dean couldn't make it out. He felt queasy and headed for the bathroom at the track cafe. The reality of being in the same race with Nicanora had messed up his plan. It *was* going to scar Orphan. Horses who'd never seen each other could establish a pecking order in the time it took to saddle up in the paddock and parade to the post. Nicanora would intimidate Orphan the way Gifford had just intimidated Dean. A good trainer wouldn't let that happen.

Something strange was going on in Dean's head. He'd lost his ability to block out the downside. The whole idea of this race was starting to haunt him. He was going to take an animal he loved and throw her into the ring with horses who were going to clean her clock. What was worse, he was going to lose Lorraine in the process. It was written all over Gifford's face. They *did* have their act together. They *were* cut from the same cloth. Lorraine didn't have to live any longer with a guy in dirty jeans and an empty wallet. She'd been the source of Dean's confidence, but without her he no longer had the confidence to win her back.

As Dean stumbled into the cafe, the smell of bacon and sausage put him over the edge and he went into the lavatory. The sink was spattered with grime, and he held the cold water faucet on with one hand while he lifted water to his face with the other. He smeared it across his forehead and under his chin until he could think clearly again. He knew what he had to do. He'd scratch Orphan from the Futurity and hand her over to a new owner unscathed. If nobody bought her, he'd give her back to the family who birthed her.

Lorraine turned down Gifford when he begged her to accompany him to the Gottstein.

"It's the last weekend of racing, sweets. You've never seen Nicanora. He'll turn your head. I promise."

"Go without me, I've got things to do. I haven't seen Mercy for ages."

It would have ended there if Gifford hadn't added another twist. "Let's take Ricky. If he likes horses so much, let's do the horses *with* him."

This was a first, a peace offering to Ricky. It deserved reinforcement. Still, she didn't want him to think she had no interest in his hobbies unless Ricky was part of them, or that she secretly disagreed with Ricky's being grounded because she didn't. Ricky needed side boards to keep him headed in the right direction. "That's nice of you, Gifford, but you don't have to babysit!"

He laughed. "Don't worry, I'll let *you* do that!" He gave her a kiss on the forehead. "It's settled then. We'll have lunch in the Turf Club. He might as well see the high end of the sport."

The more Lorraine thought about the three of them going to the races, the more pleased she was. It was the perfect antidote. Ricky had gotten into trouble for going to the track, so they'd celebrate the end of his detention by taking him back to the track, this time with permission. It would soften his feelings toward Gifford. Lorraine wasn't that keen on seeing a bunch of horses chasing each other around the track, but it was another opportunity to throw herself into the relationship. She couldn't just keep standing on the edges. Because Gifford was Ricky's father, there was really no choice.

She waited until Gifford was gone to ask Ricky about going to the track in case *he* threw a fit over it. She'd tried to shoulder the blame for the grounding, but Ricky knew better; it wouldn't have happened without Gifford. Lorraine would have talked it out, found a positive way to deal with it. His mom wasn't a believer in incarceration.

"I know how much you like horses," she said, imagining that Ricky's horse was probably being kept in some would-be corral on the outskirts of Renton.

"I'll go," he said, deadpan.

"That's all, 'I'll go?' I thought you'd be excited. *I've* never been to a race. You can tell me what's happening."

Ricky smiled, and put his hand on hers. It was his first smile in a week, their first touch in months. "I *really* want to go, Mom. Horses are incredible. They keep company with the gods."

His inadvertent paganism aside, she was delighted and kissed him on the cheek. She would have kissed him on the lips, but the therapist had urged her to start treating him like a young man instead of just her son, which wasn't an easy transition. She felt better the next two days, realizing how much the estrangement from Ricky had sapped her energy. At Gifford's suggestion, she went shopping for a new outfit to wear to the races.

The decision to withdraw Orphan had failed to lighten Dean's heart. Lorraine once told Dean that he could shed troubles the way a snake shed its skin. And maybe she was right, but that was before. As he drove past the Sprague's mailbox, Dean looked forward to telling Jill about his decision. Jill was a bit of a shedder herself. He couldn't remember her ever mentioning Didi again, the mare she'd lost giving birth. Not the next morning, not ever. She was peeling potatoes in the kitchen when he found her, heaping the skins onto a paper towel that was next to an unopened wine bottle still wrapped in its sack on the table.

"I've got something to tell you," Dean said.

She pointed the paring knife at him, "Me first!" Dean took a seat and watched Jill return to her potatoes as she peeled off the skins in wallpaper-thin scallops. "You know that night in the sauna." She stopped in the middle of her peel and looked straight at him. "I wanted you that night." Dean could feel his face getting warm, and he rubbed the insides of his shoes together. This wasn't something you talked about at the kitchen table. "I practically forced myself on you." Something stirred in him as he remembered what she looked like naked. "The thing about a farm is that everything dies. My first horse is buried in that pasture past the barn. I've got a couple of dogs under my garden. I'm always burying something, and I was afraid I was next. But you and Ricky changed that."

"Hey, you don't have to explain anything."

"You probably could have been anyone that night."

"Don't beat yourself up over it, Jill."

She had tears in her eyes, and it wasn't from the potatoes. "We didn't *do it*, Dean. I wanted to but we didn't."

"Was I . . . you know . . . lame?"

"It was Ricky, your son, that stopped me. I didn't want to cheat on him."

Dean went to the track that night, kicking himself for forgetting to tell her about his decision to take Orphan out of the Futurity. For old time's sake, he wedged himself between two bales and slept with Orphan, in her stall. He couldn't help thinking of Jill and regretting that he left her alone in the house, but he wasn't sure if her little confession was supposed to be an invitation to get lost or get laid. Then it started raining and Dean fell asleep thinking of Ricky. They'd had some pretty good times together with Orphan. Neither of them was very good at talking about their problems, but with Orphan as a shared stable mate they didn't have to.

Miguel was agitated when he came to Orphan's stall that morning. "Pedro's changed horses. He riding Nicanora!"

"He can't do that!"

"You got spun, boss!" That was one part about racing that Dean didn't like, the way people claimed each other's horses and jockeys abandoned their mounts for a better one. There wasn't enough loyalty. "Pedro say he have to have this one. So he can get job in California."

"He thinks Nicanora's gonna win."

"What does he know, boss?"

Dean had come to the track the night before intending to tell the racing secretary that he was withdrawing Orphan from the Futurity, but he wanted the withdrawal to be voluntary, with dignity. The idea of her being jilted for another horse bothered him. She didn't deserve to be insulted. He asked around, talked to the agents for other jockeys. There were eleven other horses in the race besides Orphan and the best jockeys had all been taken. Every time he passed Orphan's stall she stuck her head out to ask him if there was any news. He couldn't bear to tell her she'd been stood up. Neither could he bear to tell her he was pulling her from the race.

Dean retreated to his pickup in one of the stalls at the end of the barn, turned on the country music station, and meditated, something Lorraine would have done. She used to talk about the chakras in the body that were energy centers. She loved the sun chakra, she said, the third eye in the middle of the brow, and Dean put his fists against the top of the steering wheel, bent back his thumbs, and pressed the center of his forehead against them as hard as he could. The sun chakra was supposed to give you extra clear perception. Dean closed his eyes to feel the energy, but all he was getting was black and white photos from his mother's picture albums. And, somehow, Gifford Pomeroy was in all of them.

There was a knock on the window of his pickup. Jill was signaling him to roll it down, yelling over the noise of the radio. "You okay?"

"I don't know."

"Turn that damn thing down!"

He asked her to join him in the pickup, and tried to bring her up to date, walk her down the path that had gotten him to this juncture. Dean wasn't someone who could outline his options on index cards and rearrange them on the walls of his brain. Talking was his crucible. Until he could get his mouth in motion, he didn't always know what he was thinking. He explained to her over the candy wrappers and crushed pop cans on the seat between them how if Pedro had to have his win, then so did he, and whatever happened he didn't want to hurt Orphan.

"I wanted to surprise Ricky, make him think I was smart," Dean said. "Who was I fooling? Ricky's the one knows Orphan. I've got to talk to Ricky. And you gotta call Lorraine for me. In case Gifford answers."

"There's a phone in Bud Holliday's office," she said.

To be sure he had the right number, Dean looked up Gifford's home number again in the ragged phone book hanging by a chain from an eye screw on the back of the door. There were two business phone numbers behind Gifford Pomeroy's name besides what had to be the residence. No way Gifford was going to risk missing a deal. Dean pressed the directory flat against the door and wrote down what looked like the home number on the corner of a vet bill tacked to the bulletin board and handed it to Jill. "Just make it sound like you're doing a phone survey or something."

Jill held the phone while Dean dialed. He put his ear near the receiver and listened to the rings. Gifford answered and Jill asked for "Mr. Ricky Hostler, please," making it sound like something impersonal. She waited a second, then handed Dean the phone. He listened for voices. If Gifford came back on the line, he'd hang up. The music from *Les Miserables* was playing in the background, which meant Lorraine was there; Dean had watched a video version of this with her in French with English subtitles. She cried even in the parts Dean thought were harmless. Then Ricky picked up.

"Ricky, it's me. Don't say my name."

There was a pause, then a click. "It's okay," Ricky said. "They hung up the other phone. What's the matter? Is Orphan hurt?"

"No, she's fine. But that's what I'm calling about. I've entered her in the Futurity."

"The Godsteen."

"How did you know?"

"Jill told me. I said we gotta enter her. Two weeks ago."

"Yeah, but . . . do you know the company she's up against?"

"Kind of."

"Orphan's never been in a stakes race."

"We gotta run her, Dad!"

Dean was just about to launch into his speech about saving her racing spirit, but he realized that Ricky knew all of that. He'd been running races all his life that were over his head.

"There's one other problem. Pedro stiffed us. We don't have a jockey."

"That means I'm ridin' her."

"Whoa! This isn't like riding a bike, kid."

"I been ridin' her most every day, Dad! We know each other."

"You're not licensed!"

"I a'ready checked on that. A month ago. Sixteen and over in Washington you can be licensed."

"Yeah, but Ricky . . ."

"Dad, I a'ready talked to Mr. Holliday, the trainer you like. He said anytime I was ready, he'd *engage* me." Dean was silent. "It's a legal thing. He did, he engaged me. All he has to do now is sign a paper."

"But Ricky, the race is tomorrow! You can't . . ."

"Dad, Bud and I, we're friends. He help license me. Three weeks ago. The Board of Stewards, they okay'd me. I'm over the waitin' period. I'm a go!"

26

Mom and her real state guy don' even know what's goin' on. I had a can opener in my pocket when Mom got me in the kitchen. She asked if I was hungry. It wasn' even close to dinner. Usually she's worry'n 'bout wreck'n my appetite. Thas the problem. She's not even acting like herself anymore. I'm jus' takin' the stuff I'm gonna need. A spoon, a sharp knife, my sleepin' bag, and the can opener for tomato rice soup and spaghetti-o's. The opener's his. I don't want any of his stuff, but I gotta have somethin' to start out. Till I get my own dough. He'll call me a burglar, which I could care less about. He can buy another can opener with the money he'll save not sendin' me to that school in Orgun.

I got twenty-four hours to figure what kind of stink bomb to leave behind. Either gonna take a hammer and break the necks off his wine bottles and let 'em dribble into a pool on the floor, or somethin' worse. I thought of setting the house on fire, but that was jus' temporary insanitary. They'd chase me down for arsony. Besides, Mom has a bunch of stuff in his house. The paint idea is the most solid. There's gallons of it in the tool room. He wouldn' even know what hit 'em. His car'd jus' start chokin' on the paint I put in his tank. He'd be chasin' me till his car got the dry heaves. 'That bastard boy,' he'd say.

I'd be in Montana by then. I've a'ready got my route figured, places fancy cars can't go. I'm gonna follow the railroad. Go where the tracks go. Jus' ride Orphan in the Godsteen and keep on goin' right outta Longacres. We see a train comin' we'll just lay down in the bushes and let it pass. I'll have a new name figured out by the time I talk to anyone. I want people to think twice when I say my name.

Jill said there were Mustangs roamin' the prairies in Montana. Hundreds of 'em livin' off the grass of the land. I'd let Orphan pick our place. In some pasture so thick she could'n feel the ground when she lay'd down. I'd let her just roam. No ropes or fences. Maybe she'd meet a Mustang she liked and make a baby. I don't care. As long as she's happy. I'm gonna follow the bike trail 'til we come to the railroad tracks to Montana. Nobody's gonna stop us. I gotta take Orphan's medicines with me. And a bag of bran mash. Dad'll be glad not to have a horse to worry 'bout. Maybe with no horse, he can make up to Mom and get a better job. He'll understan' my leavin' is somethin' a man has to do when things get hot.

Mom's the one'll freak out. She doesn't understand that I gotta keep movin' frontwards. I can't live in a box. If she loved horses as much as houses, I'd steal one for her and we'd escape together. For now, the picture of her I took outta the frame on the real states man's bureau will have to do.

27

Race day it was raining, and the track looked like freshly poured cement, with long, troweled stretches of slippery goo. Dean walked along the fence on the way to the grandstands, trying to gauge Orphan's ability to get a grip in this muck, even with mud shoes. She'd worked out in the rain lots of times, but she'd never raced on a sloppy track and Dean wondered if this wasn't another sign he should scratch her. The Daily Racing Form had practically scratched her already. The lead article featured Nicanora, with a boastful account of his lineage, his connections, and the jockey change, which it called *Pedro's premonition*. None of the professional handicappers picked Orphan Annalina even for show. She was twenty to one in *Sweep's*. The marginal notes under *A Closer Look* said Orphan Annalina was in there "to fill out the gate."

Looking at the people filling the grandstands, Dean thought what a shame that this place didn't run year-round. What happened to the trainers, grooms and exercise riders when Longacres closed its season? It was like pulling the curtain on a whole culture. With many of the jockeys and grooms hitch hiking or bussing to find work and temporary housing at other tracks, in other states. Dean couldn't imagine them just working at gas stations and painting bedrooms.

Dean walked back toward the barns and peeked into the cafe to see if Jill was there yet but there was no sign of her. Being the last day of the meet, many of the horses had been trailered away, yet the kitchen was crowded with people escaping the rain. When he reached Orphan's stall, the farrier, a bearded man in dirty blue jeans and a leather apron, was sitting on a stool with an upside-down hoof in his lap. Dean stepped inside the stall and Orphan rotated her ears. The farrier reached under his armpit so as not to lose his grip on Orphan's hoof and shook Dean's hand. His muscular grip made Dean think of his great grandfather Otto.

"You think these mud shoes really work?" Dean asked.

"Everyone uses 'em. Gotta think it's more than superstition."

Dean massaged Orphan while he watched the man work. There were a lot of mysteries about a thoroughbred's anatomy, how you could drive nails into the hooves, how these spindly legs could carry the weight of a small car. Jill said it was fifty million years of breeding to get the horses we have now. Orphan's eyes were active and alive. She knew it was race day.

Then Dean saw the note tacked to the outside of the stall saying that Jill was at the racing secretary's office. One of the racing secretary's jobs was to dole out stable privileges at the track. Another was to write conditions for the races. Jill said you had to schmooze the secretary a little to get races that fit your horses. Dean had met the racing secretary when Jill took him there for his owner's license. Every licensed trainer had to pass a written and a practical exam. It was by virtue of Jill's license that they were able to have Orphan at the track. She was the *paper trainer*. Dean ran into Jill on his way to the office. There was a sheath of papers rolled up in her hand and an easy smile on her face.

"Well?"

"Piece of cake," she said, as she unrolled the papers in her hand and there it was on top with an official looking stamp, Ricky's jockey license.

Ricky's place in the *Pomeroy Realty* box was taken up by Mercy Kirk. That inspiration had come to Lorraine at breakfast while Gifford was still grumbling about Ricky refusing to go with them. Lorraine decided she couldn't do this one alone. She had to have someone next to her who wasn't a horse maven. If Mercy hadn't come, she would have brought a book, but Mercy was a whole library.

"Look at the lady in green," Mercy said, pointing to the group two boxes over. "She looks like a mint julep." Mercy wore the black cotton sheath that Lorraine wanted her to wear for their dinner at Ray's and that Mercy thought was too funereal. It hugged her like a body stocking. "The last time I was here," she said, "Buddy brought me, and we sat on the benches with the rabble. I wore short pants and sandals. Before I had varicose veins in my legs."

Lorraine was surprised how much time there was between races. Each race was like a high mass, with lots of procession and ritual. She'd assumed it would run more like a rodeo, with the horses coming out of the chutes one after another. If Mercy hadn't been there, she'd have needed two books. Nicanora's race was the ninth, next to last, and people stopped by constantly to shake Gifford's hand and wish him luck. More people knew Nicanora than knew Lorraine. When the stream of people coming to their box dwindled, Gifford left and went to their boxes, moving from one to another like he was running for office.

"You girls all right?" Gifford asked on his way by the *Pomeroy Realty* box, snapping his fingers for the roving waitress and ordering another Margarita for Mercy, a virgin Tom Collins for Lorraine, and a platter of shrimp with cocktail sauce.

Gifford had given Lorraine and Mercy each a $50 dollar bill to bet on the races. Mercy kept running hers under her nose. "You don't see these at the Ram."

Lorraine finally convinced her to spend it, and they collaborated on their bets for each race, taking turns picking the names of horses from the program. Whoever picked the horse, the other one decided whether to bet it win, place or show. Or put it on an exacta or trifecta. Mercy recognized the man in the window who cashed their first winning ticket on a warmup race, not a bad looking guy, Lorraine thought, and he certainly perked up at the sight of Mercy. They talked until someone in line behind them yelled "Move it!"

"Isn't that the beat?" Mercy said as they left the window. "Your husband owns the horses, and my friends just sell tickets on them!"

"Oh, come on, there's no small parts, just small people."

"Wrong," Mercy said, "I've seen small parts." They both laughed.

In the women's lavatory, they took stalls next to each other, and she heard Mercy flush before sitting down. She'd never done anything with Mercy and Gifford together out of fear they wouldn't like each other. And she'd told Gifford that Mercy was Dean's cousin.

"Okay," Mercy asked through the divider, "why am I here?"

"Oh, God," Lorraine's voice cracked as she spoke, "I'm banging my head against the wall again!"

"Crap!"

When they emerged from their stalls, there were women lined up in front of the sinks freshening their lipstick, straightening the tuck of their blouses, and putting dabs of perfume on their necks. Mercy redid her eye shadow while looking over someone's shoulder. On the way out she wrapped her arm around Lorraine and pulled their hips together.

"Ricky told me he'd stop fighting the marriage if we'd just let him go to the track," Lorraine said.

"Sounds like the price has come down."

Dean and Jill were the first ones in the paddock after the eighth race. The infield circle in the paddock had the numbers one through twelve painted on the curb, to match the horses' positions in the gate. Orphan had drawn the eight hole and that's where they stood, waiting for the horses to make their long walk from the barns. The rain had stopped, but it was still cloudy and threatening. They'd upgraded the condition of the track on the tote board from "sloppy" to "good."

The silks of the jockeys coming off the track from the eighth race were splattered like the mud flaps on a semi as they walked through the paddock and disappeared into the jocks room to get ready for the next race. Dean couldn't help but stare at these dwarves with racoon eyes who rode their Goliaths around the oval at forty miles an hour. Some of them wore two or three pairs of goggles; as one pair got dirty, they just pulled it down under their chin and used the clean one underneath.

"Here they come," Jill said.

The procession of horse heads for the Futurity bobbed over the crowd along the fence and turned into the paddock. Eleven colts and one filly. Each horse was led by its groom, in the same order they'd start in the gate. Jill said the paddock showed the personality of the horses and the track showed their heart. Some wore blinkers, some had colored leg wraps. They craned their necks and rotated their ears at the sight of so many people. In the morning workouts you could prepare a horse for everything but the crowd. Proximity to a mature thoroughbred still took Dean's breath away: more than a half ton of muscle and the grace of a ballet dancer. Number three was Nicanora, in black and white checkered wraps, high stepping, flirting with the crowd, his hind quarters like the pistons of an ocean liner. His groom, in a matching checkered shirt and shiny boots, was beaming as he passed them. Then Miguel turned the corner with Orphan and Dean's stomach flip-flopped. Orphan had never looked better. She fixed her eyes on Dean as she went by and didn't let go until Miguel jiggled the lead to make her look front again.

"Does a horse know if it's won the race?" Dean asked.

"A thoroughbred wants to please her connections," Jill said. "I think they know."

"I was hoping you'd say the opposite."

She laughed and slapped him on the back.

"You've done a good job with her, Jill."

"Me? You saw who she was looking at."

Orphan entered her stall and stood very professional while Miguel took the boots off and Dean threw the saddle across her back. Orphan neighed, and Dean wondered if she was nervous or this was part of her campaign to climb up the pecking order. Just as the horse identifier came by to check Orphan's markings, Miguel fed the girth strap under the belly and Dean cinched it through the buckle and slid his fingers underneath to make sure it was tight enough. Orphan's eyes were wild now, her feet tapping, and she was taking it all in.

Dean leaned in and whispered, "We love you, baby!" Then he kissed her on the neck and let go.

The crowd in the infield, consisting of horse owners, their friends and the friends of friends, had thickened and the groups for each horse had spread, merging like villages that had outgrown their boundaries. Then Dean's stomach flip-flopped again. "Lorraine's here, Jill! She's going to recognize Ricky."

Jill took Dean's forearm and squeezed. "Maybe she will and maybe she won't. But once those horses leave the paddock, she's got about twenty minutes to undo what we've spent twenty-four hours putting together. It's all legal, he's licensed." She pulled the racing program out of her back pocket and turned to the ninth race. "Pedro's still listed as Orphan's jockey," she said, "and over the din, the track announcer always sounds like he's in a barrel when he introduces the horses and their jocks to the folks in the stands."

"Now," Dean said, "I'm more worried Ricky's gonna get killed!"

"You surprise me, Dean. He's gonna be one with that horse!"

The jockeys were starting to come out of the dressing room, like circus performers, diminutive players in brightly colored silks that hung loose on their clothes hanger frames, with whips in their hands. They joined the clusters that had gathered on the grass next to their gate number to shake hands with the horse's owners and supporters, men and women in business suits and some with cowboy hats who towered over them.

The paddock judge yelled "Bring 'em out!" and the grooms led their horses, now fully saddled and equipped, from the stalls and into the parade line that circled the paddock, still without their riders. Orphan Annalina was skittering sideways, scattering people away from the edges of the grass. She wanted to get on with business. She was cocked and ready to fire. And Dean was trembling.

"Here comes, Ricky!"

"Don't tell him you're scared, Dean! A jockey doesn't need to carry that kind of crap onto the track."

Ricky, in his turquoise and pink silks, fussed with his cap and looked the other way as he passed Gifford's group. Ricky knew the score. He wasn't just running a horse race; he was a fugitive.

"How do I look, Dad?"

In truth, the silks looked like a Halloween costume on him, but Dean knew that Ricky was for real. The smile was gone, so was the kid. Despite his dad, Dean thought, Ricky had transformed himself into something hard and precious. Dean gave him a hug, crushing him to his chest, "You look great, son!"

"How shall I ride her?"

"You're asking me?"

"You're the trainer."

Dean had to take out a handkerchief and dab his eyes. He'd run this race in his head a hundred times and he wasn't sure he'd be able to put it into words, but it spilled out of him easily. "I'd stalk the leaders. Let her get comfortable a couple lanes away from the rail and save ground around the first turn. She's never raced two turns and you don't want to ask her till you're coming for home. Ride her like the sweet spot on a wave."

Ricky looked over at Jill.

"Ditto," she said.

Dean wanted to warn him of the traffic. Ricky had never captained a horse in this much of a crowd. "Just run your own race, Rick!"

"My mind slows down when I'm ridin' Orphan," Ricky said. "I'll float on her. She won't even know I'm there."

"Oh, she'll know you're there all right. That's who she's gonna be running for!"

The paddock judge called out his command. "Riders up!"

One of Dean's duties was to help his rider onto the mount by the jockey's leg. *Legging up*, they called it. There was something primitive about this practice, Dean thought, the one moment when horse, jockey and trainer were physically connected. Dean extended his cupped hands, but before he could feel Ricky's full weight he was up and looking back down. The bugle announced the entry of the horses onto the track for the running of the Gottstein Futurity. It was a royal affair, each jockey the prince of his own domain, carrying the colors of his people. The horses, sweat glistening on their muscular bodies, looked like gladiators who'd spent their lives toning themselves for this encounter.

"You comin' up to the stands?" Jill asked.

"Nah. This is something I have to do alone."

"It's out of our hands now, cowboy!"

They parted and Dean headed to the spot from where he usually watched Orphan run, next to the rail and just short of the finish line. The tote board showed eighteen minutes until the race, eighteen minutes for the crowd to place their bets, eighteen minutes for Gifford and Lorraine to figure out who was riding Orphan Annalina. Dean would have put everything he had on Orphan, but the minimum wager ticket was two dollars and Dean didn't have enough in his pocket to make a call from the pay phone. *Don't worry, Ricky, that doesn't mean I'm not with you.*

As Dean watched the horses slowly circle the track with their outriders, the hole in his stomach got bigger. It was like Sprague Lake in the Palouse; every time they'd passed it when he was a kid his dad would remind him they'd never found the bottom. Dean couldn't help but wonder if this race wasn't his biggest mistake yet, another colossal Hostler screwup. At one level, it was a way to get back at Gifford, to show him up. But it was much more than that, it was a way to empower his son, maybe a way to win back his wife. To what purpose it wasn't at all clear at the moment, because Lorraine hated competition. *Look at him out there, Lorraine. He ain't no stupid Hostler. The kid's a prince.*

As he stood shivering by the rail with his fingers locked into the cyclone fence, Dean was ready to admit that it might not have been the perfect scheme. If Lorraine ever found out what all he'd done, it would probably just sink him deeper with her. What he realized he really wanted at that moment, however, was something much simpler than Lorraine. He just wanted to see Ricky and Orphan come back safely to the barn. No hoofprints on Ricky's head.

The horses sauntered in a crooked line on the far side of the track as they headed to the starting gate, which was already in place across the track. Dean studied Orphan's forelegs, looking for the slight pronation the vet had pointed out to him months ago in the Sprague's barn. Ricky's knees were riding high, his back was rounded, and he had Orphan totally relaxed as they ambled toward the gate. As the horses reached the starting gate, Pedro Garcia sidled Nicanora next to Orphan, and it looked like he was saying something. Ricky nodded. Dean knew how much Ricky revered the jockeys he'd watched in the morning workouts, especially Pedro, and he wondered how he was able to block that out now. Where was the terror? Why wasn't he screaming to climb down?

Longacres was a one-mile track and the Futurity was always a mile and one sixteenth, so the starting gate that extended across the track was about two hundred and fifty yards from the finish line. They started loading the horses from opposite ends of the gate, which was a horrible looking contraption, a bulky green and white metal structure that looked like one of the drawbridges that spanned rivers all over Puget Sound.

Most of the horses entered the gate easily as the track men followed along behind and slapped the padded doors shut so the horses wouldn't change their minds and try to back out. Nicanora reared, his front hooves lifted off the ground, and Pedro looked nonchalant as someone took control of his horse and led him into his slot. It took three guys pushing on one horse's butt to get him into the gate. Ricky leaned over and whispered in Orphan's ear, and she walked right into the gate like her supper might be waiting for her.

Lorraine was already worried they wouldn't be able to get the gate out of the way in time for the horses who'd circled the track and were heading for the finish line. She reached over and patted Gifford on his sport coat, his shoulder unyielding and stiff. She'd never seen him at the track and she wasn't sure she liked the effect it had on him. He'd scolded his jockey in the paddock, and the jockey retaliated in unflinching Spanish. Lorraine thought one of them was going to take a swing at the other, and she was relieved when Bud Holliday, his trainer, finally legged his jockey onto the horse and broke it up.

Lorraine patted Gifford's arm, "Good luck, sweetheart!"

Gifford didn't notice her touch. His eyes were fixed like Ahab's on his horse. "God dammit, Nicky, don't crap out on me!"

The caller's voice resonated through the loudspeakers. *"They're all in the gate!"*

Dean stood at the rail, squeezed between a college kid in jogging sweats and a headband and a track addict with the Racing Form rolled up in his fist. Orphan's head was moving up and down in the gate and Dean tried to see if she had four feet on the ground. Then the bell sounded.

> *And they're off! Orphan Annalina stumbles coming out of the gate and City Light takes the lead moving quickly toward the rail . . . Secret Caper is shadowing him on the outside . . . with a half-length to favorite Nicanora, who's traveling well . . . then a length to Boca Luna, Midnight Prayer, and Viento three across . . . another length and a half to Vamanos by a head over Spanish Gypsy . . . then comes Sergeant Pepper as they head into the first turn, Sirocco, Solicitor General . . . and there's daylight to Orphan Annalina, who's trailing the field.*

The horses became strung out on the far side of the track, but Lorraine could still see their jockey's black and white checkered shirt near the front. Gifford had his binoculars trained on them and she knew better than to interrupt by asking how Nicanora was doing. She'd made that mistake with her father when he was listening to Puccini or Vivaldi.

Gifford kept mumbling the same mantra. "Come on, Nicky, come on!" Mercy jiggled up and down, her fingers digging into Lorraine's waist.

Orphan didn't seem herself, Dean thought, too much wasted up and down motion. She hadn't settled into her stride and seemed frustrated at being so far back. But Ricky was calm as cottage cheese. The horses disappeared from Dean's view as they passed behind the tote board on the other side of the track. It seemed like they were out of sight for the longest time as he listened for the caller to tell him where Orphan was, but the caller's attention was all with the leading horses. Maybe she'd stumbled again, or Ricky had pulled her up. When they emerged on the other side of the tote board, however,

Ricky had taken Orphan to the middle of the track and she was passing horses. Her stride had lengthened, her ears were pinned back and she'd made up ground on the leaders. This wasn't how Dean had wanted the race to develop. If she had to spend this much energy in the middle of the race, she'd have nothing left for the stretch run. But she just kept advancing despite lack of urging by Ricky.

Everyone stood up in front of Lorraine when the horses came out of the clubhouse turn and entered the homestretch. People were screaming horses' names, slapping their programs, and grabbing each other. Lorraine stood up and looked over at Gifford. He was cursing through clenched teeth. This wasn't just another real estate closing.

"Do what I said, Pedro! Do what I said!"

> *And they're turning for home with a new leader, it's Bo--ca Lu--na . . . still being pressed by Nicanora . . . but Orphan Annalina is making a run through the pack . . . now it's Nica -- nora and Orphan Anna -- lina in a ding dong duel for the lead with less than an eighth to go . . . Ni--ca--nor--a and Or -- phan Ann--a--lina head to head.*

Dean could feel the ground throb as the horses approached the finish line. Orphan was vying to pass Nicanora on the outside, Ricky hidden behind her neck, the top of his cap as low as his shoulders, his hands forward and light on the reins. Dean could make out the freckles in the band of white that ran down Orphan's nose, but he didn't like what he was seeing. Pedro's whip was hitting Orphan's head as often as it was hitting Nicanora. Ricky's back was parallel to Orphan's, his whip dangling passively from one hand, his other hand rhythmically slapping Orphan's shoulder as she inched her neck ahead of Nicanora. Dean was on his toes, his arms locked over the fence, biting his lower lip. As they neared the finish line, Nicanora veered out, bumping Orphan hard, and time froze as Orphan's butt went up in the air and she twisted and tumbled over in an explosion of mud speckled with flashes of turquoise and leather. Ricky vanished as the mass of flesh representing the trailing horses passed the finish line and blocked Dean's view.

Dean took off toward the gate to the track, jumping as he ran to see over the fence huggers. *"Dammit, dammit, dammit!"* A pack of charging horses was an avalanche that couldn't change direction. People from the benches surged to the fence to see what had happened. Dean wedged himself through the crowd, planted his hands on the top of the fence, and climbed over the backs of the people in his way. The jagged ends of the fence wire dug into his palms, then his crotch, as people tried to pull him down. He kicked and clawed his way over, falling onto the soft furrows of dirt nearest the fence that hadn't been touched by the horses. His hand was bleeding and Dean could feel the air on his thigh where his pants had ripped open.

There was only one horse still near the finish line, and it was Orphan Annalina, on the ground, struggling to get upright, and then hopping helplessly in a circle on three legs.

"Take the reins, Dad!"

Ricky handed him the reins and picked up Orphan's left foreleg trying to calm her. There was dirt all over his face, even his teeth were brown.

Orphan's eyes were on fire. She was confused. She wanted to race. Her mouth was foamy. Dean patted her on the neck as she continued to pivot on her right front leg.

A shiny pickup with its headlights on sped towards them from the backside of the track, towing the green wagon, that windowless box on wheels they used to carry away and sometimes put down injured horses out of sight of the crowd. The horse hearse. Close behind was the official car that trailed the field in every race. The state vet rode in that car with, as Dean imagined, his pentobarbital injection on the ready if he needed to euthanize a seriously injured horse. Two men in brimmed hats and jeans jumped out of the pickup and headed towards Orphan. The state vet stepped out of the white car with a black bag in his hand.

"Dad, don't let 'em!"

Dean yelled, "Back off!" and snapped his arm like a bullwhip at the vet and his helpers. "I mean it, get the hell away!"

More track men and grooms for the horses that had just finished the race crowded around. Jill appeared from out of somewhere and took the reins from Dean, who paced in a semicircle back and forth in front of Orphan, making sure nobody entered her space. One of the track men from the pickup and the vet tried to push past Dean, and he held them off with a stiff arm to their chests.

"I mean it! Back off! Nobody's putting this horse down!"

"We're just trying to help, sir," the vet said.

Dean could feel Orphan's hot breath on his neck, and he reached back with one arm to find her muzzle. "You're not touching her till you disarm. I mean it! Drop that goddamn bag!"

People stumbled over each other as they moved back. The vet dropped his black bag at Dean's feet, and Dean put his mud-caked boot on it. He felt no fear, neither was there any doubt, he'd never been more certain of anything in his life. He was at one with Ricky and Orphan. If anybody made a wrong move, he'd make sure *they* got the injection.

Lorraine still had her hand over her mouth as Gifford rushed her and Mercy out of the box, up the aisle, and into the elevator. Friends of Gifford's from work, people Lorraine vaguely recognized from the engagement party, crammed into the elevator with them, slapped Gifford on the back and hooted. Someone even kissed her on the cheek, but she couldn't respond. They'd just witnessed a car wreck, and the only other person in the elevator who seemed to know it was Mercy, who was dabbing her eyes and looking at Lorraine.

"I didn't expect this, honey!"

A man in a tuxedo greeted them at the entrance to the fenced-off circle of dirt where they took pictures of the winning horse. The Starter had not called the winner yet and the *Win* and *Place* slots on the tote board were blinking. There were more handshakes and pats, and she could feel Gifford's hand in the small of her back pushing her forward. Two girls in sequined dresses with goosebumps on their bare arms stood in the winner's circle holding a blanket of red roses between them, waiting to see which horse they would drape it over.

"Oh, God," Mercy said, "there's the horse!"

The people on the track were staring at Ricky, who was stooped under the horse, his back against the horse's belly, cradling that single leg like it was a newborn baby.

"There's Dean!" Mercy said.

Lorraine hadn't even noticed the man who was still her husband. Then the jockey looked up and she recognized him too. Gifford tried to grab Lorraine by the wrist as she scooted by the man in the tuxedo and stepped onto the track.

One of the track men yelled at her, "Where you going, Ma'am?"

It surprised Lorraine how fast she could push all of the books, therapist's advice, and common sense out of her head. None of that mattered as she ran across the furrows of dirt, sinking up to the straps of her high heels. Through the mudpack on his face, she could see Ricky's pain, and she moved in next to him and the horse, afraid to say anything.

Dean yelled for Doctor Babcock, the vet who had first met Orphan at Jill's place, when he saw him step onto the track in a yellow sport jacket and baseball cap. People stepped back as Doctor Babcock made his way over to Orphan. Dean's eyes flitted back and forth between the people still frozen next to the green trailer and his vet. "Say we can fix her, Doc! Say it!"

Doctor Babcock studied the horse from a distance. Then he walked over, let Orphan smell his hands, squatted, and ran his hands up and down her left foreleg. He stood up, patted Ricky on the butt, and came back to Dean. "Don't know for sure, but it looks and feels like a fracture. Above the fetlock. Pretty bad one."

"What's a fetlock?" Dean asked.

"The knee."

"Can she live?"

"Don't know yet, need an X-ray."

"Can we do that here? The X-ray. Like now?"

He pushed his hat up on his forehead. "We can do the X-ray once we get to the backside. But if she were mine, I'd send her to Pullman. Pronto!"

"Pullman?"

"Washington State University. The Vet Hospital. Hand's down, one of the best in the country. But there's no guarantee."

"That's all I need to know."

The other horses in the race were returning to the finish line to get their saddles taken off and be led back to the barn. Grooms started peeling away from the green trailer to take their horses and steer them around the standoff. Then Nicanora burst into view, spewing puffs of steam and whirling in circles. Orphan flattened her nostrils and let out a snort.

Dean yelled at Pedro, "Get that goddamned horse out of here, you bastard!"

Pedro pulled back hard on the reins and Nicanora reared again, pedaling his hooves in the air. People screamed. It looked like he was going to come down on Orphan's back, but Pedro leaned into his horse and steered him to the ground, away from Orphan. Two people grabbed Nicanora's bridle. Everyone was looking at Dean. It'd been so long, he thought, since anyone in this town knew he existed.

Dean raised his voice like a coach at halftime. "Look, folks, here's what we're going to do. Nobody's going to put poison in this horse's veins. We're going to fix her up, right, Doc?" Dean pointed toward the green wagon. "Open the door!"

The guys from the gate crew patted their wallets and rubbed the skin on their foreheads, as if making sure everything was still intact. One of them activated the hydraulic jack and there was a moan as the floor of the green wagon settled onto the track and they swung open one whole side of the wagon.

A racehorse with heart will run on a broken leg, charge through barbed wire, burst her lungs to please her jockey. All they had to do was get Orphan to hobble about ten feet on three legs into the wagon, which was windowless and dark. Jill jiggled the reins and clicked her tongue, but Orphan wouldn't budge.

"Give her some room!" Dean yelled, and people backed away from the trailer. Whatever happened, Dean didn't want Orphan to end up on the ground again. That was too much like death. She had to stay standing.

Dr. Babcock changed places with Ricky and took over the task of cradling her left foreleg. Jill handed the reins to Ricky, who gave Orphan some reassuring rubs on her neck. Orphan lowered her head and Ricky whispered something to her. The crowd hushed, letting Ricky teach them a lesson in trust. Then he urged Orphan toward the wagon in a herky-jerky limp, helped along by thrusting her head in the air. When she planted her good leg on the floor of the wagon, it squeaked and Orphan looked around. Maybe she was looking for the other horses, to see if anyone else was going to ride with her. Ricky jostled the reins and Orphan took another stutter step into the darkness, and then another. It was painful to watch her move.

Lorraine's gaze settled on Dean, who was standing there with his arms drooping at his sides. She knew that he represented every sloppy, irrational urge in the universe. He was the guy who thought a Saturday wax job on his pickup could make up for bad brakes and low gas mileage, the guy who hung himself over the side of the I-405 overpass with a rope and a can of cheap paint and wrote *PEACE* on the cement during the Vietnam War before anybody else cared, and the crooked letters ran until they dripped into the river. She tucked her tissue into the slit pocket of her Nordstrom jacket and headed for him.

"Shoot me, if you want," Dean whispered.

"I should."

"You're wrecking your good shoes," he said.

"You could of killed him."

Dean pointed Lorraine toward the back of the wagon. "Go to him. Please."

She walked over to Ricky and pulled his muddy face against the breast of her new jacket. They were beside the horse and she reached behind Ricky to make contact with Orphan's neck which was still hot and sweaty. She couldn't remember ever touching a horse. One of the gate crew told Ricky he needed to be checked for injuries by a doctor in the jockey's room, but Ricky waved him off and stepped into the trailer with Orphan. With Ricky's urging, Lorraine took a seat in the cab of the truck and she looked back at Gifford as the wagon pulled away. He was standing there, his camel slacks dirty at the cuffs, looking confused. He'd offered her everything he had to give. And, in so many ways, it was just what she had wanted. Mercy was behind him, blowing her kisses.

Word of Orphan Annalina's fall reached the backside before the green wagon did. Grooms, exercise riders, and trainers ran out to escort the wagon to the vets' barn, jabbering in English and Spanish. There was also a groom Dean didn't recognize, who was cradling Marmalade against his chest.

"All these people," Lorraine said. She seemed to be out on her feet.

They opened the door to the green van and shooed everyone out of the way except Ricky. Dean watched the procession of vets and track workers tromp into the wagon, bend over, look at the leg and go out again. Someone brought in a bucket of ice water to immerse Orphan's ankle and she kicked it over. One of the vets took in a padded support that looked like the shin pads for a baseball catcher and tried to secure it around Orphan's left foreleg while Ricky kept his head against Orphan's neck. The first vet failed to secure the splint and Doctor Babcock took over, securing it on the first try. "A Kimzey splint," he said, "just something to secure her for the trip to Pullman. Where she's gotta go. Now or not at all!"

Jill, meantime, had jumped onto the phone in a cubbyhole of an office near the van, and Dean could hear her cussing with transporters, trying to find a trailer for the trip to Pullman. Lorraine was standing outside the office in her heels, watching Jill make her calls, looking very much out of place, not so much because of how she was dressed but because of how crippled she seemed. The horse trailer that finally showed up had a nose like a Boeing jet, with aluminum sheathing, side windows, two stalls separated by dividers and a bin in the front for hay.

The kid with the attention deficit hadn't lost focus for a moment since the fall. He was still holding Orphan with a tight grip on the lead rope. Ricky's breath merged with Orphan's breath. Dean knew it was Ricky's eyes that Orphan was using to calculate the depth of her troubles and Ricky was trying his hardest to be optimistic. Lorraine poked her head inside the trailer to ask Ricky if he wanted a change of clothes, and he said no. Miguel gave him a leather jacket anyway, which he put on over his muddy silks.

"You go!" Jill said to Dean. "I'll get hold of someone at the hospital while you're in transit."

Dean looked at Lorraine, who was gawking at Jill, and he realized he hadn't even introduced them. "Can you give Lorraine a ride home?" he said to Jill.

Lorraine spun to face Dean. "Oh, no, you don't! I'm going too!"

Ricky insisted on staying in the trailer with Orphan and Lorraine took the seat in the cab between the driver and Dean. The air was pungent with the taste of cigarette ashes. On the drive to Pullman, Red, the driver, talked nonstop at Dean about cars he'd owned, wrecks he'd been in, and college football. When Dean stopped responding, he aimed his conversation at Lorraine.

"They don't usually try to fix 'em, you know. Unless you're gonna breed 'em." She could feel Dean looking at her, maybe wondering where she stood on the subject of rescuing injured horses, but he turned away when she looked back at him. "Ruffian was a breeding horse," Red continued. "One of the greatest female racers of all time. She broke down in a match race with Foolish Pleasure. Nineteen seventy-five. Battle of the sexes, they called it. No offense, Ma'am." She looked at Dean to see if he was going to say something, but he was staring into the windshield. She'd never seen him so subdued. He was somewhere else. "Broke her leg pretty bad, just like yours," the driver said. "Only reason they tried to save her was because of all the nuns and ladies singing hymns for her. Four of the best vets in the world worked on her. Chips and pieces of bone were floating around in her leg like a fishbowl. She woke up from surgery in a tizzy. People tried to hold her down and she threw 'em off like rag dolls. They finally had to put her out of her misery."

"Do we have to talk about this?" Lorraine said.

"Sorry, Miss. Hey, listen, horses are my life. I love horses. It's just that sometimes, well, sometimes it's just better to put 'em down."

Lorraine knew the ride should have been a time to reacquaint herself with Dean, maybe talk about the journey he'd taken with Ricky, ask him how exactly it had happened that their son had ended up on the back of a race horse. She knew it wasn't the time to tell him the truth about Ricky's lineage. One catastrophe at a time. She heard a thud from the back, then the truck tilted from the sway of the trailer, and her heart sank as she imagined the horse keeling over. Dean must have had the same feeling because their eyes met.

The Horse Hospital

28

The Orphan Annalina entourage reached the Washington State University campus in Pullman about ten that night. "Well, thar' she blows," Red said. "A regular barnyard college! Hell, they might even let me in someday."

Red backed the van up to a concrete loading dock behind the hospital. When the bumper of the horse trailer scraped against the concrete, it set Dean's teeth on edge, and he jumped out of the cab to meet the man in a blue gown who had appeared on the loading dock with a clipboard.

"Do you have mortality insurance?" the man asked.

"What do you mean, mortality?"

"If the horse doesn't make it."

Of course, he had no mortality insurance. *But why are we talking about death? This is a hospital.* Dean went back over to the cab and signaled Lorraine to roll down her window. "They want to know how we're going to pay for this."

She turned around and looked at the horse trailer they'd just towed across the state. "We can hardly stop now. Tell them we're self-insured." A flare akin to putting a match to magnesium went off inside Dean.

He walked back over and gave the man his answer, which seemed to satisfy him. Dean knew how it was. Sometimes you just needed something to fill in the blanks on the form.

Everything in the large animal wing of the hospital was the size of Texas: high ceilings and galvanized steel sliding doors with lumber coverings, something you'd expect to see in an airplane hangar. Dean thought Orphan's ears perked up as they passed a stack of hay bales in one of the recovery stalls. There were horses in some of the stalls, with medical charts on clipboards hanging from the gates. Everything was remarkably clean and bright and lacking, Dean thought, the reassuring scent of manure. Dean had never seen Orphan so immobile and corpse-like. But no matter which way the gurney turned, Ricky managed to keep a hand on some part of her.

The veterinary team, dressed in drawstring pants and shower caps, stripped off family members at the entrance to the surgery room and wheeled Orphan into a cavernous space with bright ceiling lights. There were steel loops attached to the walls and a winch hung from the ceiling like an upside-down bat.

As an attendant led Orphan's entourage away from the surgery room, Dean imagined hearing a long whinny that ended in a nicker, the same call she'd made from the podium at the auction. Dean had always assumed that he'd rescued Orphan, that she was another mule deer in the draw who wouldn't have survived without his intervention. Now he couldn't help but wonder whether he'd sacrificed her. They sat in a small waiting room with *Western Horseman, Horse & Rider* and *Blood Horse* magazines strewn on the coffee table and Dean thought again of what the horse transport driver had said about Ruffian. Had they reached the point where snuffing out Orphan was the humane thing? *Who am I doing this for, anyway?* What would his great grandfather Otto, the blacksmith, have done? He wished Jill were there. She'd know what to do.

Ricky stood next to Dean's chair in the oversized white hospital smock he'd finally accepted in lieu of his dirty jockey silks. His face was purposeful. *Ricky Angel* purposeful. "What's Orphan think'n," he said.

Lorraine watched Ricky, who was watching the hallway that led to the operating room, guarding it with his eyes like an expectant father. Periodically, he'd get up, walk part way down the hall, then return to the chair next to the reading light that nobody was reading by. Dean and Ricky spoke in whispers as if what was going on Lorraine couldn't be privy to. Something had happened to Ricky since Dean moved out and, as much as she might have wanted to credit it to Dean's absence, she realized that it probably had more to do with his presence.

She tried to think how she would have handled this at Ricky's age, when she was the skinny little girl with white legs who her father thought had a future in medicine. What a joke that was. She'd never kept anything alive in her life. Her guppies had ended up floating on their sides in the fishbowl, and for weeks she had to look into the toilet before going to the bathroom to make sure they hadn't swum back up. When her mom gave each of the girls an avocado pit and showed them how to suspend it in a drinking glass with toothpicks, Lorraine's was the only one that didn't sprout roots.

The Judge always thought Dean had taken advantage of her, but the evening Dean drove her up the Cedar River in his Chevy with the leopard skin seat covers and pearly steering knob, she had intentions too. She'd already put this guy up on the bulletin board of her imagination. He may not have been a genius, but he was courteous and when he talked to her his eyes locked onto hers like the rest of the world didn't matter. Lorraine was the one who'd suggested they spread the checkered tablecloth across his hood, which was still warm from the motor. She didn't want her first time with Dean to be in the backseat of a car looking up at an overhead light and upholstery fuzz. She wanted sky, tree branches, a little bit of heaven. Dean had asked, even after her pants were down, if this was the right thing. He'd never seemed so cerebral and prudent, and it made her want him even more.

Ricky's voice woke Lorraine in the middle of the night. A man in running shoes and a blue gown was standing in the waiting room with Dean and Ricky, and she joined the circle of men, still in her stocking feet.

"You must be the mother," the doctor said.

Lorraine started shivering and grabbed onto Ricky. Surprisingly, he was warm and solid. "She might not make it, Mom!"

"He didn't say that," Dean said.

The doctor looked at Dean and Ricky as he spoke, as if *she* wouldn't understand. "There was a condylar fracture of the cannon bone. We had to put screws in, three of them. To hold things together. A fracture like this was once considered the sure death of a horse. I'm just saying . . . she may need a second surgery, and I'm not sure she can handle it. She's got to be comfortable in putting weight on it.

Otherwise she might founder. If you're religious, this would be a good time to say a prayer. We're just doctors."

Although the surgeons had suggested that Orphan's entourage find nearby lodging and come back in the morning, Ricky refused to leave the hospital. So they slept on the chairs and couches in the waiting room. It was five-thirty a.m. according to the black and white school clock on the wall when Dean returned to the waiting room with another Diet Coke. The hospital had given them the run of the staff coffee room which had instant Maxwell House, Lipton tea, and an assortment of soda pop. The shelves of the refrigerator were littered with brown bags just like the refer in the lunchroom at the body shop. Dean had opened several bags, but the half-sandwiches, carrot sticks and Jello didn't look that appetizing.

The taste of the hours that followed was a familiar one for Lorraine. There was a phlegm in the back of her throat she couldn't spit out, yet couldn't swallow, fear marbled with vacillation. Maybe the fate of the horse would dictate her next step. With her coat pulled up over her head, Lorraine was a lump in the chair across from Dean.

Neither Dean nor Ricky slept much all night. Instead Dean kept playing the race over and over in his head. They had to whisper so as not to wake up Lorraine.

"What really happened out there, Ricky?"

"It doesn't matter, Dad."

"What do you mean it doesn't matter? We're going to find out what happened. Then we're going to sue your mom's fiancé!"

Ricky had a sock on his right foot, and his left foot was bare, in solidarity with Orphan. He was cupping his exposed toes to keep them warm. "Come off it, Dad! Then we'd all be livin' off his money."

Dean shut up. He didn't have a comeback and turned away, looking at the tent Lorraine had pitched over herself, wondering if she was really sleeping. He was afraid to ask her what her coming with him and Ricky to the vet hospital had meant, just as he was afraid to tell her what he felt, because he knew words were cheap, especially his. And, besides, he wasn't so cocksure of his intentions anymore. They'd gone foggy when Ricky and Orphan went down. He studied each fold of her coat, followed the zigzags from the ankles to the knees, back to the hips, over to the arms and head. He hadn't forgotten her shape. A shock of black hair was poking out of the collar, rising and falling with the rhythm of what had to be sleep.

He went to the restroom, ran cold water into the sink, plugged the drain with paper towels and submerged his head. Water filled his nostrils and leaked into his ear drums. He opened his eyes and it was blurry until he blinked a few times and then he could see the holes in the sink strainer magnified by the water. He opened his mouth just to see what would happen and water rushed in, but he had no sense of drowning. His throat closed on its own. That's probably why he was still alive, he thought. Survival wasn't a plan; it was a reflex.

Waking up from a cat nap, Dean found an exit door and went outside. There was a pink light on the horizon and spindly vertical clouds with knobs like the legs of his mom's antique butterfly table, the only decent piece of furniture they'd ever owned. Even though Dean had a light sensitivity, he'd learned to hate the night even more. Darkness fed his paranoia. The grounds in front of the hospital were landscaped, with alternating rows of red and white geraniums. There were no moving cars, only a jogger who was making his way up the hill past the hospital. Dean knelt down and picked three red geraniums and one white one from different rows so they wouldn't be missed. There were dewdrops on the petals that Dean tried not to disturb as he dug one-handed through a garbage can near the front door of the hospital until he found a pop bottle. Then he went back to the restroom, filled the bottle, slid in the flowers, and set the bouquet on the coffee table in front of Lorraine. Old times.

The smell of geraniums must have stimulated the dream Lorraine remembered when she woke up. She was next to a flower cart in the courtyard of St. Peter's Basilica in Rome. Judge Culhane had arranged a private audience for the family with the Pope, but Lorraine didn't want to see the Pope. She argued with her father on the cobblestones while a group of nuns watched in horror. "You're insulting the Holy Father," he said.

"There's just as much of God in the flowers," she said.

A doctor from the next shift entered the waiting room, his gauze mask bunched under his chin, his pot belly a hump under his droopy gown. She didn't want to hear his report, but he was waiting for her to join the discussion. Her limbs were heavy and getting herself to him was like walking through blankets. Maybe that's what had woken her, their voices.

"As we said, it was a displaced fracture," he said. "We were able to get some screws in it and close her back up. We've wrapped her pretty good. To keep the wound dry. The key now is how she comes out of it.

"Will she be able to walk?" Ricky asked.

Dean put his hand on top of Ricky's shoulder. "Let's not get ahead of ourselves, pal."

"I don' care if she runs. I jus' want her normal."

Lorraine wandered outside and followed Troy Lane until she came to the Compton Union Building somewhere in the middle of the campus. Once inside, she followed her nose to *The Lair*, a fast food cafeteria that was serving a "Breakfast Special" with hash browns, eggs, and bacon, not unlike what she used to serve at the Ram, except they were mostly dishing the meals onto Styrofoam plates for takeout. She reported the news of her discovery back to the men in the waiting room, but Ricky refused to leave until Dean found a pen and scratched out a note for the doctors across an advertisement from the newspaper, saying where they'd gone, and draped it over a chair facing the surgery hallway.

"You need more sleep, Ricky. Look at his eyes, Lorraine."

"I'm not tired."

"Remember, you still have school this week," Lorraine said.

Ricky shot his mom a terrified look.

Dean was called to the hospital administrator's office and Lorraine and Ricky went to the cafeteria without him. Ricky played with his food, pushing the hash browns into a wall that circled the outside of his plate and then making ditches in the Styrofoam with a prong of his fork to outline the food left in the middle. Yoke congealed in a triangular pool where he'd taken a wedge out of his fried egg. Neither of them said anything. It was the first time since the race that Lorraine had been alone with Ricky and she realized that she'd been counting on Dean to deal with his distress. This was the son she used to soap down and bath in the plastic dishpan, the one whose sleeves she taped shut one time so he wouldn't scratch open his scabs, the boy she took the blame for not tutoring when he came home with warnings from his teachers. She'd always assumed that the more of him she could possess, the less Ricky would have to deal with alone. But something had changed.

"I'm not goin' to that school, Mom!"

"Let's talk about it later, okay?"

Ricky went back to rearranging the food on his plate, and Lorraine went back to rearranging the characters wandering around her brain. She knew the old Lorraine Hostler, the one who'd left Dean so she could have a shot at raising her son in a responsible environment; she wasn't sure she knew the Lorraine who was camped out in a horse hospital trying to reestablish contact with her son.

"It was all my fault," Ricky blurted out. "I let Orphan get too close."

Lorraine reached across the table and put her hand on his arm. "Don't say that!"

"You don' know racing, Mom!"

"Well, I know something about accidents, and that was an accident."

"I didn' keep her clear."

Lorraine wanted to take this pain away from him too, but she lacked even the vocabulary to carry her part of the conversation. "Everyone makes mistakes," she said. "Look at your dad and me."

When Dean came back to the cafeteria, his hair was sticking up in thatches like someone had been pulling on it and there was a quizzical look on his face. Something had happened to the horse, Lorraine thought.

Ricky laid his fork across the top of his food. "What's a matter, Dad?"

Dean dropped into his chair, put his elbows on the table and pushed his palms against his forehead. "Guess what? They disqualified Nicanora and confirmed Orphan as the winner!"

Ricky straightened his spine for the first time since they'd arrived at the hospital. "Wow! The Godsteen! I didn' know we even made it o'er the finish line!"

"It was a dead heat but Nicanora was disqualified for letting his whip hit Orphan in the face and for letting his horse veer out. But that's not what I came to tell you."

"There's more?"

Dean covered his face and mumbled into his hands. "They said the operation and recovery will take as much as we paid for her. We don't pay . . . they keep her."

"No way," Ricky said. "How much do we get for first place?"

"Whoa, boy, that money's to pay your mom back for the Nashua!"

Lorraine wanted to protest, but she wasn't sure exactly why. Maybe it was because that would take away the one thing she was sure of, the moral high ground. She didn't need the Nashua. She hated the Nashua. If she wanted a house, she had Gifford. She pushed her chair back and fled the cafeteria, cutting across the grounds back towards the hospital. She went in a different door, ending up in the wing for small animals. A janitor pointed her back to the equine center. Her coat was still draped inside out over the back of the chair she'd slept in, and she grabbed it, wanting to get out of there before Dean and Ricky returned. She asked the attendant at the reception desk to call her a taxi for the Greyhound station.

She waited in front of the hospital and felt relieved when she saw the dome light of a cab coming up the hill about a block away. The lime green sedan was entering the driveway when Dean appeared in a dead run, panting. "What're you doing?"

"This is trespassing!"

"That's crazy!"

"Crazy was coming over here. I had no business." She reached for the door handle before the driver could come around to help her, and Dean put his hand over hers to stop her.

"Don't go back to Gifford! Even if you won't have me, don't go back to *him*!"

She couldn't hold it any longer. She'd grown up with the sacrament of penance, where she could whisper her sins in the dark, say her Hail Marys and wipe the slate clean. She'd stopped going to church regularly when she found out she was pregnant with Ricky. She had to let it out, let it out and run. She spoke to his hand, which was on top of hers. "Dean, that man you don't want me to have is Ricky's biological father . . . a doctor confirmed it."

"No! He's not!"

"Before you, I was with him. It was an accident . . ."

"Quit it, Lorraine!" She tried to slide her hand out from under his and he trapped it hard against the windowsill of the taxi.

"I should have told you. I didn't know until long after we married. I thought he was ours. I wanted him to be ours. I couldn't bear to tell you. Your blood type doesn't match Ricky's and Gifford's does." She finally looked up at him. His hand had gone limp and he was crying. She didn't think he would believe her, but he did. The harpoon had gone clear through.

"Does Ricky know?"

"Just you. I haven't told Gifford." She put her hand flat against his chest. "I misjudged you, Dean. I didn't think you even knew Ricky. But I was too near sighted. He needed a jolt and you gave it to him with the horse." She looked into the empty backseat of the taxi. "I gotta go. Before he gets here."

"Do we have to tell Ricky?"

"I don't know."

The cabbie asked if there was any luggage and Lorraine shook him off.

"Stay, Lorraine! Please."

"If I'm here, I'll crowd you out, same as I've always done." She pushed her way into the backseat and waved at the driver to go.

29

Dean watched Orphan's recovery from the outside, through one of the windows in the door. The worry was that she'd reject her left foreleg, try to free it. Dean had talked them into letting Ricky go in for her recovery. No one knew Orphan better; Ricky could find meaning in the moisture of her breath.

Dean kept trying to make sense of what Lorraine had dumped on him. He'd never considered himself Ricky's father the way she was his mother. He'd left most of Ricky's upbringing to her out of a sincere belief that she was better at it. Now, just when something real was happening between him and Ricky, she said he was not even his real father. And damn sure if she'd known her baby wasn't his, he wouldn't have been her husband. Ever. That's what he hated about history. When you were there, when you could have done something about it, you didn't even know you were making it.

Dean pressed his forehead against the windowpane. Orphan was on her side on the floor of the recovery room, with a bulky white wrap on her slender foreleg. They'd put a halter on her with two leads, as if they thought she was going to wake up and fly. Dean saw her tongue move, then her eyelids blinked. She lifted her head off the floor and put it back down, too groggy to hold it up. Her mouth must have been dry because she kept stretching her lips and baring her teeth. She moved the good front leg, then the one with the sleeve, and Dean studied her face to see if she'd noticed. She lifted her neck off the floor and stared at Ricky in his smock. The front half of Orphan was North America, and South America still hadn't moved. Dean had watched his Labrador come out of surgery after he'd eaten a rock that lodged in his intestines. The body parts farthest from the brain were the last to wake up. The vet in the recovery room was kneading

Orphan's injured leg trying to get the circulation going. Orphan gave a sudden kick with her back legs and Ricky and the doctor moved out of the way. Her head was up and she surveyed the pads on the walls, looking for the gate. She made an attempt to get up on her feet, then settled back down again. Finally, she got up, seesawed front to back, wobbled, and pushed herself up. Ricky sat on the heels of his shoes and stared at her like she'd just pushed the boulder away from the entrance to the tomb.

Seeing her standing there, Dean started crying. Not just wetness around the eyes, but a sheet flow down his cheeks. It felt like the center of gravity had fallen on top of their family. There was something horrible about the loss of possibility. That's what he didn't want to happen to Orphan. Or Ricky.

Dean bought Ricky a sleeping bag so he could stay next to her stall at night -- hospital rules didn't allow anybody to sleep *in* the stalls. There was always someone available from the hospital staff, including a 24-hour colic team.

They found a cheap motel within walking distance of the campus. Although there was a 21-inch color television set in his room, Dean went days without even turning it on. He'd also abstained from alcohol since arriving in Pullman. When he managed to drag Ricky away from Orphan for a meal at the Student Union, he couldn't imagine telling him what Lorraine had said, not while Orphan was still in jeopardy.

One evening someone knocked hard on their door at the motel. There was no phone in their room and Dean had to go to the office to take the call. The office was also the dining room for the proprietors. They must have had sauerkraut and sausage that night because the air was heavy with it. The handset was off the cradle, resting on the wooden table. As Dean picked it up, he noticed a mustard fingerprint on the earpiece.

The caller said she was the night attendant at the equine hospital. "You're wanted at the hospital, Mr. Hostler. There's been a new development with your horse."

"What, what's wrong? Is Ricky there?"

She was maddeningly calm and tight-lipped. "I'm not the one to discuss this with. Are you able to come over?"

Dean didn't mean to slam the phone onto the receiver, and both the old man and his wife looked up from their TV program to give him a dirty look. As he ran across the campus, all he could think of was at least it wasn't Ricky in trouble this time, but that was a lie too. Orphan had looked good, he thought, when he saw her that afternoon. She was eating and her vital signs were all within ranges of normal. When he got to Orphan's stall, there was a group of medics around her again. The more doctors, the worse for the horse, Dean thought. Ricky poked his way through when Dean caught his eye.

"They said she might wreck her right leg," Ricky blurted.

"What're you talking about, it's her *left* leg that's broken?"

"That's the trouble. She's not puttin' enough weight on the bad one, and it could wreck the good one."

They'd put Orphan into a sling and she looked like a puppet on strings, begging Dean or Ricky with her eyes to step in and stop this nonsense. Dean couldn't help but think someone was overreacting. The instruments here were calibrated too fine. What wouldn't be noticed somewhere else came across their screens as a medical calamity. Dean tapped the nearest person in the crowd who looked like a vet, a man with bushy eyebrows and a receding hairline.

"This is our horse. Can you please tell me what's going on?"

"Dr. Canfield is the chief on this one, but I can tell you what I know," the man said. "In the rounds tonight, we found an inflammation of the left front hoof. Your horse is at risk of foundering." Dean shook his head. "She's favoring her right foreleg, taking her weight off the injured leg. It's a common problem with leg injuries. The result is she may be damaging the tissues that connect to the bone in her right hoof." Dean was getting it, but the medic must not have been convinced because he dumbed it down. "It's like putting a cap on the toothpaste tube and squeezing it. The paste has to come out somewhere. That's what she's doing with her weight." Dean was unable to respond.

"I told you, Dad. She's shafted."

Their stay at the WSU Veterinary Hospital had just been extended.

The next day, Dean received a call on his walkie-talkie while he was making his rounds as a temporary security guard for the hospital. Someone was in the lobby for him. He was in the small animal wing at the time, gawking at someone's chocolate Labrador who had come out of surgery for removal of a tumor in his head and was still under sedation. He took a shortcut, taking the interior stairs two at a time.

At first Dean didn't recognize the man in jeans and a blazer pacing the reception area. He'd never seen him anywhere except the track. It was Pedro Garcia, the jockey who rode Nicanora in the Futurity.

"Hello, Mr. Dean." He had on a tie that bunched tight against the throat of his collar and his rich black hair had been slicked down with pomade that gave off a pleasant green apple fragrance.

"Pedro, you surprise me!"

"I come to see Ricky. How is the horse?"

"She's standing. At least part of the time."

Pedro tried to smile, but there was something eating at him, something that turned his smile to a pucker. "That's good, that's good."

Dean knew where Ricky would be, and asked Pedro to follow him through the equine wing. Pedro had trouble passing by the rooms that were occupied, and Dean had to slow down as Pedro let his eyes scan the horses like he was looking for a lost cousin. He'd ridden horses on the track all his life, but he'd never seen one in a hospital. "First time," he said.

Ricky was flat on his back in the stall. Orphan was nibbling on his belt buckle. Ricky was situated to Orphan's right, forcing her to bear weight on the broken left leg. That was his new mission, to make Orphan balance her weight on both front legs.

"Hey champ, we have a visitor," Dean said, almost whispering, but Ricky jumped up, startling Orphan.

"Pedro. *Buenos Dias!*"

"*Muchas gracias. Habla español?*"

"Like a klutz."

"Your Spanish *muy inteligente.* Orphan, she looking good?"

"Ricky," Dean said, "come out so you can talk to Pedro!"

"No, no Mr. Dean. I go inside."

When Ricky opened the gate, Pedro headed straight for Orphan, with his hands extended and low. Orphan eyeballed him, rocked her head up and down, then smelled his hands and pushed her muzzle inside his blazer. Dean sidled over to the gate to watch them. He'd never noticed how close Ricky and Pedro were in height and build. When Pedro leaned his head into Orphan's neck, he had to stretch his arm to reach over her mane. Then he stepped to the front of Orphan and spread his thumbs across the bridge of her nose. "The marks are mine," he said. "I made bad ride, Ricky."

"What're you talkin' about?"

"My whip. I should have switch hands. My boss say win the race or no come back. *'Bótala,'* he say. 'Trash 'em.'"

"Wait a minute," Dean said. "You're saying Mr. Pomeroy told you to trash our horse?"

"Anyone who threaten," he said. "That's why I veer out."

"I told you, Ricky!"

"I come here to say sorry. *Apenado*! I never mean to hurt anyone, Mr. Ricky." Pedro's mouth was close to Orphan's nostrils, and she was inhaling his words. "The money, is not for me. I send to family in Guadalajara. Six kids and mucho cousins."

"God damnit, Pedro!" Dean yelled. "You almost killed Ricky *and* his horse."

"I never do before, sir. I am good rider, but I need the money." Pedro turned to Ricky again. His voice quavered and his English became less clear as he veered into Spanish. "You be good jockey, Señor Rick. Love the horse. *Con amor e respecto*. Don' follow me. I am . . . *ignominia*."

Dean expected Pedro to extend his hand, to ask for Ricky's forgiveness, but Pedro was choked up and turned away as if he didn't want Ricky to see that either. Dean undid the gate latch, stepped out of Orphan's stall, and stopped in the middle of the wide hallway with his back turned. He rubbed his hands over his face to gather himself.

Ricky followed Pedro out of the stall like he was one of Pedro's children. Dean's inclination was to give Pedro a piece of his mind, and he thought that's exactly what Ricky would do. He'd paid for that right. Instead, Ricky walked over and pulled Pedro's head against his shoulder. Pedro just stood there letting Ricky handle him, then he reached his arms around Ricky's waist and the two of them hugged.

The Saturday after Pedro's visit, Gifford Pomeroy showed up at the entry way to the Vet Hospital wearing a blocked hat pinched in the crown very much like the one he wore the day Dean met him in front of the Renton Post Office. Dean was sure that Lorraine had told him by now that Ricky was his. He was here to claim him.

"What're *you* doing here?" Dean said.

Gifford took off his hat and smoothed his hair to erase the creases. "I wanted to make amends, Dean." *A parade of apologies*, Dean thought, *I don't think so*. "I wanted to make sure Ricky and the horse were okay."

"Not yet," Dean said.

"I never meant it to go that far, Dean." He must have known that Pedro had already paid them a visit, but Dean was surprised that he didn't blame Pedro for the whole thing.

"You mean injuring our horse or taking my wife?"

"Dean . . . I wouldn't have started up with Lorraine unless I knew you were getting divorced."

"That's not what I was talking about."

Gifford was turning his hat in his hands, sliding the brim between his thumb and forefinger. "Jesus, Dean, I'm coming to you with an olive branch. I've been a schmuck." Coming from Gifford, this tack didn't play as well as it did for Pedro.

"My brain's a little simpler than yours, Giff. Not as many places to hide things."

Gifford looked like he was going to say something sarcastic, but he turned to Ricky, who'd meantime showed up. "How's the horse doing, kid?"

Ricky was dead calm. "Still day to day."

Gifford looked around, as if making sure they were alone. "Look, I have a proposition to make. I checked with the hospital and they told me the tab you've run up." He looked down at his hat. Dean's dad had always told him that anyone who talks to their hands is lying through their teeth. "I think with the right sire Orphan could make a pretty damn good broodmare. I'm willing to pay all the hospital bills and give you three times what you paid for her. Both of you can visit her anytime you want. How about it?"

Dean looked at Ricky, but Ricky was leaving this one to his father, waiting to see if he'd learned anything.

"You're saying you want to buy her?" Dean asked.

"I can set her up with a private vet, first class care. Breed her to a champion."

Dean's fingers were trembling, his head bobbing in its socket. This wasn't about him and Lorraine anymore; this was about Dean Hostler. He knew what he wanted to say. He had to be every bit the businessman that Gifford was. He'd learned to count and he wasn't going to get it wrong this time.

"Let's see, Giff. You almost killed my kid. You seriously injured his horse, who will never race again . . ."

Gifford held his hand up, "Whoa, Dean!"

Ricky is smiling as Dean continues. "Don't whoa me, sir, till we're finished! Because we're going to file a complaint against you with the track steward, asking them to permanently take away your owner's license."

"Come on, Dean, it was a horse race!"

"Then we file the lawsuit against you in King County. First, to prohibit you from racing anywhere in this state, hopefully beyond. Second, asking for the loss of Orphan's future earnings and payment of her feed and first-class vet expenses. For life!"

"You're out of your league, Dean! This isn't a game for sissies! Shit happens!"

"Don't get vulgar on me here, Giff!"

"I think you're just pissed that your wife's dumping you!"

"Let's not go there, Giff! I can't imagine this whole thing improving your chances to steal my son's mother."

"I'll have my attorney get hold of you! This week!"

"Giff, please, you don't have to piss your pants! This horse isn't for sale. And neither is my son."

30

Dad and I talked some more 'bout me bein' the son of the real state man after they moved Orphan to the outside stalls at the hospital. He was try'n to sound like he was okay with it, but the way the words were stick'n in his throat I knew it had pretty much wrecked his life. He said he could sooner live without Mom than without me, but I'm not sure that's true either.

Mom said the real state man and Dad were two sides of the valley. One in the sun and one in the shade. An' no way I was gonna live in the shade. Mom might a been Joan of Arc but she didn' want to burn again either, so she went back to Mercy's, at least for the time bein'. I knew I was gonna miss her like crazy, but at least she'd finally seen the horse. With me on her.

After Orphan got outta the hospital, we took her with us back to Jill's place. Dad said that was only temporary, till he got back on his feet. Orphan still had to take her pills and couldn' be let loose in the pasture yet. Dad and I had the part of the house with the sauna.

Goin' down on Orphan like that seem'd to knock some sense in me. And it sure as heck knocked the old *ADD* for a loop. Just when I was kinda fall'n in love with it.

But I also got to think'n 'bout my dad. I mean the dad that raised me and got me Orphan. My real dad. If I gotta little bit of the ol' ADD, I think I got it from him. He's the one who does all the crazy stuff. Like buy me a horse when he can' even afford a decent car. Me an' Dad make each other laugh. We make sparks. You gotta read some more ADD books, Mom! Go for wha's in the package 'stead of the label. You can do better'n the real state man. Go on a date again with my real Dad and trade stories with 'im..

I also know somethin' 'bout the law now. You can be a jockey if yore sixteen and you can be 'mancipated when yore eighteen! So I don' care what the blood drops say. Life's not a science project. I wanna live with the man who's like me, who laughs at my jokes, an' who really cares what's happ'n to me. I told Mom all that when I came back with Orphan from the hospital at Wazoo an' we met at the rifle range. I told her there's not much sense mov'n to tha' new house the real state man is build'n. Yore Cinderella, I told her, so the shoe's gotta fit.

An' I told her I didn' really care whose sperm started me. I didn' know whose sperm started Orphan. None of that could change anythin' that happen'd. Orphan was really mine now and the vets said I couldn' race her, but I could sure as heck ride her. She was mine for life and we were gonna have some ventures. I told Dad Orphan had a'ready pract'ly fixed my dope a mine problems. An' he said if you can describe somethin' in words it takes away the power.

He also tol' me that horses been watchin' the human comedy since the beginnin' of time. They seen it all. Without horses, there wouldn' be America.

ACKNOWLEDGEMENTS

Thank you to my grandparents, Edwin Keegan, Sr. who ran the *5th and Altamont* grocery store on Spokane's east side with my Grandma Hazel. Grandpa could finish his pickups and deliveries in the morning and still make the races at Playfair in the afternoon, betting his $2 on the best grey horse at the track, while Grandma ran the store. Their life's dream was to someday go to the Kentucky Derby, which they finally did, except that when they finished their sack lunch on Derby Day, the ham was so salty that Grandpa had to stand in line for his repeated drinks from the water fountain and miss some of the races.

Dad and I also shared an affection for horses and with Mom's consent we bought a quarter interest in our first thoroughbred, Faithfully, from Doris Harwood, the trainer, and her husband Jeff. And, once the appetite was whetted, Dad and I proceeded to buy and race more thoroughbreds on our own, all without injury or harm - Zipizape, Country Clover, Betsy's Valentine and Betsy's Gold. Thank you, Doris and Jeff, for your generosity in helping me write this story.

Thank you to the Huether family, who moved to a farm in Rosalia, Washington after Herman's brother Leo and one of his boys were tragically killed at the railroad crossing closest to home one snowy winter day. The Huethers had a beautiful work horse named Dolly who provided us with many hours on her back as we roamed the hills and gullies in the Palouse pretending she was mine.

Thanks also to my fellow students at the Iowa Writer's Workshop who read and critiqued the beginning versions of this story.

And thank you again to Kenny and Marleen Alhadeff who are such huge supporters of live theatre not just at the Seattle Rep but on the best stages in America and around the world. Come from Away, my friends.

And, of course, thank you, Nancy Jo, my wife, my brothers Mike, Pat and Mark, our children Carla and David, and Bruce Wexler for your patience in helping me imagine the stories that rattle around in my head.

Praise for John Keegan's Other Novels

CLEARWATER SUMMER
Selected as a New York Public Library "Best Book"

"A strong sense of place, solid characterization, and an excellent plot all work together to create this novel's considerable power. Packing the punch of Stephen King's novella, *The Body* [*Stand by Me*, the movie], a classic of small-town life disrupted by violent death." Library Journal

"Keegan's powerful *Clearwater Summer* conjures recollections of another little book, *To Kill a Mockingbird.*" The Milwaukee Journal

PIPER
"As Piper manages the first tough months following her mother's death, she is forced to examine some of her naïve assumptions – about her parents, about the nature of friendship and betrayal, about her own sexual identity and most of all, about love." Publisher's Weekly

"Keegan is an exuberant and playful storyteller, full of wit and unique eccentricity, which he shares generously with his characters. This is a delightful novel, very funny, sincere, and memorable." Bellingham Herald

A GOOD DIVORCE
"The author resists turning his sociologically burdened characters into stereotypes, and explores how family members, even kids, grope for ideological rationales to make sense of the inchoate dynamics of daily life. This emotionally rich and socially aware novel touchingly evokes a time when the personal became awkwardly political." Publisher's Weekly

"Keegan is a smart and sensitive writer as careful with his choice of words as he is with his character's emotions. And the story is compelling and sweet covering a variety of subjects from a father's love to a child's fear and a woman's sexuality." Anton Mueller, Grove/Atlantic

ADHD Postscript

The American Psychiatric Association has determined that the attention deficit/hyperactivity disorder (ADHD), which was formerly referred to more simply as an attention deficit disorder (ADD), is one of the most common disorders affecting children as well as many adults (an estimated 8.4% of children and 2.5% of adults). ADHS is diagnosed as one of three types: inattentive type, hyperactive/ impulsive type or combined type.

Knowing that there are many famous people with this disorder, e.g. Albert Einstein, Bill Gates, John F. Kennedy, Michael Jordan, I became enamored with the idea of attempting to portray a teenage kid in my story, Ricky Hostler, whose school teachers and later others opined that he was touched with both the downsides and the upsides of a combined type of ADHD (in the late 1980s when this story happens, people still commonly referred to Ricky's condition as "ADD").

In this story I chose to treat Ricky's condition not as a deficiency but more as a potential asset. Only you the reader will know whether I succeeded in that quest.

CPSIA information can be obtained
at www.ICGtesting.com
Printed in the USA
BVHW081925100921
616545BV00001B/103